RAGING SEA

A NOVEL OF THE STONE CIRCLES

Terri Brisbin

A SIGNET ECLIPSE BOOK

SIGNET ECLIPSE
Published by New American Library,
an imprint of Penguin Random House LLC
375 Hudson Street, New York, New York 10014

This book is an original publication of New American Library.

First Printing, October 2015

Copyright © Theresa S. Brisbin, 2015
Penguin Random House supports copyright. Copyright fuels creativity, encourages diverse voices, promotes free speech, and creates a vibrant culture. Thank you for buying an authorized edition of this book and for complying with copyright laws by not reproducing, scanning, or distributing any part of it in any form without permission. You are supporting writers and allowing Penguin Random House to continue to publish books for every reader.

Signet Eclipse and the Signet Eclipse colophon are trademarks of Penguin Random House LLC.

For more information about Penguin Random House, visit penguin.com

ISBN 978-0-451-46910-6

Printed in the United States of America
10 9 8 7 6 5 4 3 2 1

Penguin
Random
House

This one is for my readers—those who have been fans since the beginning and those who have just found me. It's amazing to me that I've been writing for twenty years (since 1995!) and I would not be doing it if there were not readers who enjoy it! A special thanks to all the readers who contact me about my stories—I love hearing from you. So, thanks to you, readers!

THE LEGEND

Centuries ago

The six gathered inside the stone circle and around the seventh, awaiting her acceptance of their sentence. Her next actions would determine the fates of humanity and of this world. Taranis hoped Chaela would choose to step back from the abyss of evil. Her words tore his spirit apart.

"You are fools!" she screamed. "I can destroy you all."

Knowing now that there was no other way, Taranis looked at each of the others. Only by combining their powers against her would they be able to save this human world and yet, the thought of taking this action against her made his blood freeze. His feelings changed as she unleashed her destruction on the humans who gathered there on the open fields around the henge.

Changing into the form she favored, Chaela rose into the sky on black-and-red wings. Flames spewed from her mouth, burning people, plants, and even the earth in their wake. The screams echoed in the air as the smoke evaporated, leaving ashes everywhere. With no other alternative, Taranis nodded to the five gods and they began the ritual of silencing one of their own.

She laughed at the destruction she'd wrought and inhaled a deep breath, one that foretold a killing strike. Drawing in their own breath, the chant began between them, swirling in the air and encircling them, her and the stones beneath them. Only a moment passed before the power began to control her.

As a weaver wraps the threads over and under, through and around, they wove the thoughts of the spell that would take away her power until they could imprison her. Building a cocoon around her, the ritual blocked her words and her powers and surrounded her so completely that even her thoughts were contained within it.

Taranis knew the moment she realized what they were doing. And, once more, they offered her a truce.

"Chaela," Belenus, the god of life and order, called out to her. "Cease this and you will be allowed to live."

"Fools!" she roared back when her voice would serve her mind. "I cannot be destroyed!" Struggling against the bonds that held her, she could not do more than scream out in frustration. An elemental power such as hers was created by the universe and could not be extinguished.

"You can be defeated, Chaela. You will be imprisoned in the endless pit and never return. Your name will be forbidden and forgotten," Sucellus, the god of war, warned.

They could feel her disbelief and resistance. She

would never give up this mad quest for complete domination of humanity and of them. Steeling himself, Taranis waited for Cernunnos to begin.

The earth buckled and rose at his brother's command, exposing the endless pit within the circle as they chanted the sounds of power. Taranis guided the winds to wrap around her, securing her in his grasp even as their spell did. The current swept her over the yawning chasm and held her there. Now, the final step, a terrible one, would seal her out of this human world. The human male who carried Chaela's blood and power stepped into the circle and joined them in the ritual, adding his voice to theirs. Her screams pierced the spell.

She knew.

She feared.

Taranis pushed her down into the blackness, forcing her deep into the chamber that existed within and outside this world. The words they sang created it and would seal it. And the sacrifice of Chaela's only blooded son would keep her there forever.

The human walked to the pit and threw himself off the edge, soaring over the abyss. Sucellus created a spear of iron and threw it at the man, impaling him on it, piercing his heart and spilling his blood into the pit.

The other gods honored the sacrifice, freely made, with their words, completing the ritual that sealed Chaela away. After the destruction and horror of the day, a blessed silence and peace filled the area as the ground and chamber closed and disappeared. The stones returned to their usual size and positions and everything was right with the world.

Taranis's brothers and sisters gathered around him, all weary from the struggle of exiling one of their own. They'd barely accomplished it against her formidable powers and only with the blood sacrifice had they triumphed. Now, the world and humanity were safe and would remain so.

Forever.

They would leave here, knowing that humanity could continue without them, but they imbued their own human bloodlines with their powers to keep watch... always. A race of men and women who could use the powers to keep this evil at bay. Warriors of Destiny, not war.

But, with their course of action this day, they would never be needed to do that.

Never.

PROLOGUE

Broch of Gurness
Northern Coast of the Orkney Mainland
Late winter, AD 1286

Einar Brandrson paced around the chamber at the base of the broch, chanting the prayers he knew better than he knew the names of his kin. His bones ached and the cold air sliced into his skin, but he would persevere because he must.

The words echoed around him as he called on the gods of old to grant him a few more months of life. And to grant him the knowledge he needed to aid his grandson.

Since it was in their service, his prayers became demands as he circled seven times around the chamber and then seven times in the other direction. He listened closely for signs of an answer. Or a word of wisdom or confirmation.

None came.

They never did.

The old gods could be capricious and silent when they wished to be. Though some said they'd left eons ago, Einar believed that not. They were still there— waiting in the earth and trees and wind and water for their followers to rise again.

He knew it in his heart and soul. As he knew he would not live long enough to see it. Or to help.

Sighing, he gave up praying and searched for the charcoal stick he'd brought in his sack. If he would not be here to guide his grandson, he must leave something for him. Mayhap Soren would remember the songs he'd taught him and understand the significance when the time came.

He scratched some of the most important symbols into the stones of the walls, each one in the correct position around the tower. A beast. The sun. A war hammer. A tree. A lightning bolt. Waves. Flames. Using the charcoal, he colored the scratches in until they almost looked alive.

Praying in the old language, he blessed each symbol with the name of the god it represented—Epona, Belenus, Sucellus, Cernunnos, Taranis and Nantosuelta. The last one, the flames, he did not bless for it was that of Chaela the Damned.

It would take many days to sanctify the markings, days that he probably did not have left to him. It mattered not. All that mattered was that he must continue until his last breath so that mankind had a chance against the vile destructor who now tried to push her way out of her prison.

Einar returned every morn to the broch to repeat the sacred words and blessings. And he watched from the top of the tower, searching the skies for portents of things to come. Yet every day his strength lessened and he felt his life coming to an end. And he damned his own stubbornness, too, for he had not passed on the knowledge to his kin as he was supposed to. There had been no signs for so long that he'd grown complacent. Now, his failure could doom humanity.

If only there was more time, for he could feel that Soren's blood would rise soon and he would need guidance.

If only the gods would listen.

If only the gods would answer.

He learned over the next days and weeks that the gods had heard him—and ignored his pleas after all.

RAGING SEA

While those of the blood advance
and the lost lose their way,
Water and Storm protect the Hidden.
The Hidden reveals its secrets
only to those who struggle with their faith.

CHAPTER 1

Broch of Gurness
Northern Coast of the Orkney Mainland
Early spring, AD 1286

Soren Thorson covered his eyes and searched the beach near the ancient broch for someone almost as old—his grandfather. He'd made certain his father's father was not in the round stone tower itself before heading toward the sea's shore. Glancing east and west along the sands, Soren could not find him.

In his eighth decade and longer-lived than all of his friends and family, Einar Brandrson would not relent and die. He clung to life with the tenacity and will that continued to surprise Soren and the rest of his kin. The old man watched the horizons, day after day, waiting for something. Soren guessed he would die once that thing for which he waited arrived.

A movement near the water caught his eye and Soren walked in that direction. There, kneeling at the sea's edge, his grandfather rocked back and forth while dipping his hand in the water. It had to be frigid and yet Einar never took his hand out. Soren's calls were ignored; no surprise for the man's hearing had been deteriorating for years. He reached the waterline and touched his grandfather's shoulder.

"Grandfather, you must come away now," he said as he guided his grandfather back and up to his feet. Or tried to. The old man resisted Soren with a strength that also surprised him. "Come."

The rocking to and fro continued and now Soren could hear that old Einar also chanted or sang some melody. Bending closer, he recognized the sounds, for he'd heard them from the time he was a boy and was taken in by his grandfather on the death of his parents. Though he did not understand them, he could repeat them and did so now, whispering them as he tried to lift his grandfather away from the water. Continuing to struggle against Soren's efforts, old Einar did climb to his feet.

"Come, Grandfather," he said, sliding his arm under the old man's and stepping back from the edge. "Aunt Ingeborg will think you lost once more."

His aunt had claimed just that when asking Soren to find him. Old Einar roamed the coast, day after day, starting at dawn and ending only when someone dragged him back across the miles to Ingeborg's cottage. The broch was a favorite destination and Soren found him here more times than not, usually at the top of the tower, staring out across the rolling lands of the island or across the strait to Eynhallow or Rousay. Always watching.

"You are a good boy, Soren," Einar said, turning to

face him. "You have listened to my words and never mocked me." His grandfather's voice was sure and clear and his gaze now focused on him, something it had not done in years. "It is time. It is coming."

"Aye, Grandfather, the night is coming and 'tis time to get you home," Soren replied. "I brought the cart. It is just over the hill," he said, nodding in the direction of the dirt path.

"Some say that the Old Ones left our lands eons ago but they are never forgotten. I have remained faithful, but I am the last of my line and too old to fight as I should."

"Nay, Grandfather, we have no battles to fight. The earl's claim to Orkney is clear and he is high in the king's esteem."

He'd seen the man get overwrought before, but this felt and sounded different from those times. His grandfather was coherent and clear-eyed. Soren continued to urge him away from the water.

"Do not ignore my words, Soren. You have the blood of the gods in your veins. You have a place destined in the coming war," his grandfather whispered. "There is so much you need to know. We must speak on these matters."

"And we will speak," Soren agreed. "But we can do it before the fire in the comforts of your daughter's cottage. Come, Grandfather."

The man's mouth opened and then he shook his head as the strength leeched from his body. Soren caught him up, wrapping his arm around the frail figure and helping him along the sand to the path and the waiting cart. The sun descended in the west and the winds began to whip around them in the growing cold as they traveled along the road.

Blood of the gods? Soren chuckled at that. Which gods would that be? Many had been worshipped here in Orkney, from the Picts to the Norse, and now the One True God of the Christians held sway. Not a particularly religious man, Soren had done whatever duties were expected but never truly thought on matters of faith.

His family was of Norse descent as were most who claimed lands on Orkney. Though the Christian god had supplanted the old Norse gods centuries ago, there were many signs and places all over this and the other islands marked with the Norse symbols and runes for them. Even his father had borne the name of one of the most known—Thor, Odin's son, the god of thunder who bore the mighty battle hammer *Mjölnir*. A god who was linked to both farmers and sailors—the two main ways men made a living here in Orkney.

Soren had no time to contemplate those spiritual matters, for his concerns were more about the timing of preparing the land for planting. And about when the soil would thaw and warm. And whether there would be enough sun to cultivate their fields before the winter's winds and cold blew once more across the islands.

His grandfather now huddled on the bench next to him, shivering as the coming night's chill grew. Soren glanced west to gauge if they would get to Ingeborg's and its promised warmth before darkness fell. He'd not brought a blanket with him, so he tugged the old man closer to share his body's heat for the rest of the journey.

If only he could control the winds or the weather!

His grandfather's mumbling began anew—he was whispering those words again. The ones he'd sung at the water's edge. Soren could not help himself; he fell into the pattern of sounds and cadence and sang the words under his breath.

If he could do that, he would turn the winds warm, like midsummer's winds that blew across his fields and helped his crops. If he could, Soren would make them gentle and soothing rather than bitter and stinging.

If only . . .

Old Einar lifted his head and smiled. "Blessed by the gods, Grandson. I told you."

Soren was about to argue when he noticed that the icy, strong winds had ceased. Glancing about, he thought they might have passed into the protection of a thick copse of trees or some other shelter that blocked the winds, but they had not. They rode along the open path, away from the sea. Then the winds turned warm, warm as he'd wished them to be, and his grandfather laughed.

"Make them cease, Soren," he urged. It was daft to think he could make a difference. Mad even. Old Einar nudged him, pushing against his arm. "You made them warm. Now stop them."

As much as Soren wanted to laugh off his grandfather's words, something deep inside of him loosened and a desire to attempt it urged him on to . . . try it. Even knowing he did not, indeed could not, control something as powerful and uncontrollable as the winds, he pulled the reins and brought the horse and cart to a stop.

"Grandfather," he began. "You must know . . ."

"I know more than you imagine," Einar whispered. Then he nodded and began the chanting again, low and even.

Now Soren's blood stirred, in a way he'd never felt before. Some force raced through him and, for a moment, he believed he could stop the winds. And, for another scant moment, they did. Soren lifted his face and felt nothing. He tilted his head in a different direction . . . still nothing.

"Summon them now, Soren. Bring them forth," the old man said. His voice, more forceful and steady than Soren ever remembered, echoed around them. Soren thought he heard another speaking, too, but only his grandfather was there.

Foolishly, he began to follow his grandfather's order and imagined the winds rising and encircling them. He closed his eyes and asked them to warm again.

And they did.

The winds swirled around them in a cocoon of warmth, gently at first and then faster when he but thought the command.

Wider, he thought.

The winds loosened their hold on him and his grandfather and swirled in a larger circle, enclosing the cart and the horse. The animal tugged against the bit, whinnying its dismay and fear.

"*Away*," Soren said.

Within seconds, the winds blew wider and wider, softer and softer, until they were gone and only silence filled the area. Shocked, Soren turned slowly and found his grandfather's knowing gaze on him.

"How?" he asked him. "How is such a thing done?"

Before his grandfather could say a word, Soren's arm stung. Ignoring a possible injury in the face of understanding this weird and strange occurrence, he waited on the old man's words. A wave of fire shot through his forearm then, forcing Soren to gasp. Pulling the edge of his tunic's sleeve up, he saw a strange mark on his arm. Something rose under the skin and moved about before disappearing.

"You carry the blood of Taranis within you, Soren. Worshipped long before the Norse gods arrived here. The god of winds and storm and lightning and thunder. You command it all to do your bidding," his grandfather said, smiling and nodding. "The power is awakening now. The bloodlines are rising. The battle is coming. It is now your destiny. Do not fail in this as I have, Grandson, for the fate of all humanity is at stake."

Soren took in a breath, preparing to argue but his grandfather collapsed against him then. When he could not rouse him, Soren shook the reins and urged the horse to move. By the time they arrived at his aunt's cottage, the old man seemed even more fragile than before. Soren carried him inside and put him in his bed. Even deeply asleep or unconscious, Einar mumbled those familiar words.

He sat with his grandfather, listening until no more sounds came. And all the time, Soren's blood heated and raced and the skin on his arm stung. Questions filled his mind and the only person who could answer them lay asleep. Soren accepted a bowl of stew from his aunt and remained at Einar's bedside through the night, waiting for him to awaken.

The next morning, the sun pierced through the small chamber and found Soren still there. He'd fallen asleep in a chair at some time during the dark of night. He rubbed his eyes, pushed his hair out of his face and peered at Einar. His grandfather had not moved since Soren had placed him here, not even when Soren tried to speak to him.

"Grandfather," he said softly, reaching out to touch his hand. "Are you well?"

His hand was icy and had lost any suppleness. Soren's heart clutched as he leaned closer and listened for the sounds of breathing. Placing his hand gently on Einar's chest, he felt no rise or fall. No movement at all.

His grandfather was dead.

Scuffling feet behind him grew closer now and Soren turned to face his aunt. The only other one of Einar's kin alive, she'd seen to his care even after the death of his son, her husband.

"He is gone?" Ingeborg asked.

"Aye," Soren said, standing and moving aside so she could sit by the man she treated as her own father. "I did not think he would go so quickly. He seemed . . ."

"Indestructible?"

"Immortal, truly."

She leaned closer and touched Einar's cheek, whispering something under her breath. Then she moved her thumb across his forehead and touched his closed eyes and mouth before bowing her head three times. The mumbled words were similar to what he'd heard from Einar and those he'd repeated. A child's rhyme? Had Einar passed it down through his children?

"No man can live forever," she said, as she faced

him. Tears tracked down her cheeks and Soren drew her into his arms. After a few moments, she leaned back and wiped the tears away. "And he lived a good and faithful life, Soren."

"He seemed stronger on the ride back here last night," he said. "I found him at the broch, near the water, swaying and mumbling. But, he spoke clearly on our way here."

Clearly, but certainly not sanely. Now, in the bright sun of morning, believing he could influence the winds seemed like a farce. Had he simply given in to soothe his grandfather's agitation and mad claims? When Old Einar grew anxious and wandered, Soren would do or say whatever he must to ease the man home and back to calm. As had other kith and kin. When the man ranted and raved without making sense, but was concerned over some matter or another, they tried to smooth his way through it.

"The dizzy spells and confusion lasted longer and longer these past few months," Ingeborg answered. Patting him on his shoulder, she smiled. "You were a good grandson to help me see to him. You treated him with respect and kindness. Your father would've been proud."

"And now?" Soren asked. "What will you do?"

"My sister's kin said there is a place for me there, with one of her nieces. After we see to Einar's burial, I will make preparations to go there."

"Do you need help?"

"Nay. The women from the village will help me prepare him. He wished to be buried next to his wife, so that is where he will lie."

"A Mass?" he asked, somehow knowing the answer would be no.

"I did not agree with his beliefs," his aunt said quietly. "But I think there is no call to summon a priest."

Those who lived closer to the main city on Orkney worshipped more often and lived and worked under the scrutiny of the Church. But those who lived on the edges of the isle or on the smaller ones did not suffer such a close watch unless attention was brought to their heretical beliefs. Soren shuddered then and turned back to his aunt.

"Call on me if you have need of anything. I will help with the burial," Soren said. His aunt nodded.

He leaned over and took Einar's hand, rubbing the weather- and age-roughened skin and trying to accept the man's death. More father than grandfather to him, this was the man who'd taught him so much. How to run a farm. How to fish and sail. How to be loyal to kith and kin, though clearly Soren had not learned that lesson well enough.

His last link to his father now severed, Soren's heart filled with grief as the reality struck him. No more stories. No more songs. No more tales of the history of the islands. And the worst was that Soren would never again hear his grandfather teach his lessons of life.

His death was not unexpected—Einar had lived many more years than most did. Soren should have been ready for this, but losing kin was never easy, no matter their age or infirmity.

"He knew." Soren had forgotten his aunt remained with them until she spoke. "He knew his end was near.

He left something for you for when"—she paused, her voice thick with emotion—"for when he passed."

Soren followed her into the other chamber in the cottage and waited as she searched through a trunk for whatever his grandfather had left him. She lifted a small packet of parchment from within and held it out to him. A spark surprised him as he took it from his aunt. Her expression told him nothing. Did she know what was inside? Did she know what Einar left for him? As though he'd asked aloud, she smiled and shook her head.

"That is between you and Einar. He made me promise." Even with tears filling her eyes, her mouth still carried the hint of a smile. "Men's work, I suspect."

"I will return later," he said. "I will see to my farm and come back to do whatever you need of me."

"Soren?" His aunt met his gaze and Soren knew what was coming. "Will you send word to Ran? She held him in high esteem."

As Einar had held the young woman high in his regard.

"I know not where she is, Ingeborg." Thinking that would end the painful subject of Ran Sveinsdottir, he turned to the door once more. But his aunt did not know how to let that dog lie quietly and poked him again.

"As though I would believe that, Soren. Well, the matter is yours, but I think she should hear it from you." Ingeborg wiped her hands down the front of her apron, telling him clearly what she thought.

His heart heavy with sorrow, he made his way to the door and pulled it open. Clouds raced across the sky over his head and swirled, covering the bright sun and changing from day to near-dark. The smell of rain filled the air and bolts of lightning lit the sky ablaze. The thunder that followed each flash made the ground beneath him shake. 'Twas as though the elements saluted the passing of the old man.

He tucked the precious parchment inside his tunic and readied his horse to return to his home some miles away. The skittish animal pulled from him and tugged with every bolt of lightning. Soren would never make it home in this storm. He'd find himself facedown in the dirt or worse if the horse fought him. Glancing up as another bolt flashed, he thought on Einar's word last night.

Laughing at the sheer folly of it, Soren whispered in his thoughts to the winds.

Take the rains away, he thought. *Go south and do not bother us now.*

Stop the lightning and thunder.

A second later the rain and lightning ceased. The clouds still circled above him and Soren could almost feel them waiting on him for his next command. Realizing what he was thinking, Soren shook his head and chuckled. He knew how strange and changing the storms could be on Orkney. Pushed by the sea winds, rain could come and go in an instant. As these surely had. How could he think otherwise?

He mounted then and the horse obeyed his commands, heading for his farm in the interior of the island. Within the shelter of the hills, his lands prospered and never more than when his grandfather had guided him.

Now, Einar was gone.

Mayhap the parchment he carried would tell him more? Until he examined it, he would not know and, by the time he arrived back at his cottage, he had no answers to the questions that had already plagued him and many more questions to add to his growing list.

After the burial, he would see to matters and questions brought up by Einar's behavior and his passing.

At least, he did not have to try to find Ran to tell her about his grandfather. She'd left the island two years before and had not returned since their parting. The only thing he could do was to send word through her father—and that was something he simply could not do.

Northwest coast of Scotland

It seemed as if the fates and now the weather conspired against them.

Marcus stood outside his tent, his face lifted to the sky, offering another prayer that the gods would side with them and allow their passage. The prayer had not changed, nor had the weather, over the last five days. He turned, watching as Aislinn approached in the rain.

The young woman, like a daughter to him, had shown her mettle during their recent test against the evil goddess's followers. Now, she seemed more at ease with the role she would play in the coming confrontations.

"Could I have misinterpreted the prophecy, Marcus?"

Marcus nearly laughed at her words, but he held his amusement in check, for they exposed her vulnerability.

The words of the old gods directed them north, away from the Scottish lands to those of the Norse. He'd recognized the truth in them as she spoke them to those who now gathered to fight for humanity.

"Nay, Aislinn," he said, drawing her into the shelter of the edge of the tent. "I heard the gods' words in what you said. And we know that Lord Hugh heads north, too."

Her gaze darkened and he reached out to her, trying to offer what comfort he could, for terrible, dark days awaited all of them ahead. Embracing her and wishing he could save her from the pain and loss to come, he nodded at the group of warriors who trained in spite of the torrential rains and lashing winds.

"See, our new allies prepare themselves to meet the challenges ahead. With the warblood and the fireblood at our side, we will defeat the evil one . . . again."

The first battle had been theirs, but not without the steep price of lives lost. But they'd found the truest of allies, two who had inherited their powers directly from the gods. And William Warblood's sworn men to fight at their sides.

"And the two we seek now in Orkney? Will they join us?" Aislinn asked as a shiver shook through her.

"The powers that rise in their blood make them Warriors of Destiny," he said. "That cannot change. But only they can decide on which side they fight." Marcus released her and stepped back. "It is our responsibility to find and teach and guide these new ones, just as we did with William and Brienne."

The two whose names he had just spoken touched his mind then with their thoughts, curious about the reason. Once they had successfully sealed the first circle, the gods had gifted them with a bond that connected their thoughts with those of Marcus and Aislinn. A bond that had also cost them dearly but one that would be a huge advantage in the coming battles. Marcus and Aislinn faced those two and Marcus waved them off.

"Our prayers seem unaccepted," Aislinn whispered, as she pulled her cloak tighter around her slim form. "It has been days."

"Ah, but if we are trapped here, so is Lord Hugh," he said. "And it gives us more time to train the men."

Aislinn nodded and watched that training in silence at his side. She left when Brienne summoned her, leaving Marcus to contemplate their next voyage and their next confrontation.

Though they were victorious the first time, he did not underestimate their enemies or their determination to free the goddess from her otherworldly prison.

The sun burst through the thick clouds then, illuminating the area around them. The warriors training and fighting let out a cheer at the sight and warmth of it, but it did not warm Marcus's blood or raise his spirits.

Darkness was spreading. Chaos threatened all that they held dear. Destruction of the world in which they lived was the goddess's promise. And no amount of sunshine could remove those fears from his heart.

He only hoped his prayers would be heard and that the Warriors of Destiny would finally prevail against the evil one who could destroy all of humanity.

CHAPTER 2

North Sea, off Mainland of Orkney
Spring, AD 1286

Ran closed her eyes and lifted her face into the sea winds. The boat sailed across the dark surface of the firth between Scotland and the islands that made up Orkney to the north. She did not hold on to the ropes or the side of the boat for she could keep her balance no matter how rough the waves became.

Though winter was losing its grip and days would soon grow warmer and longer, Ran Sveinsdottir knew better than to underestimate the calm-surfaced seas. Since the time she could walk, she had sailed at her father's side. In good weather and bad. In all seasons and seas. The ominous weather seemed to stay to their south and the dark, threatening clouds hugged the northern edge of Scotland and did not move.

She leaned against the side of the boat, not their largest, and peered out at the lands just rising from the sea ahead of them. Ran squinted into the distance and allowed herself to savor the view of . . . home. Two years. Two long and lonely years had passed since she last walked on the island of her birth.

Ran moved a couple of paces forward and shielded her eyes from the unusually bright sun. The boat lifted and dropped as it crossed the waves, bringing her ever closer. Her breath caught then, as memories of her departure flooded her mind. She pushed them away, refusing to allow them to intrude on this return. She had a new life now. She had plans for a future. Her father's influence and wealth had created opportunities she would not have had if she'd remained on Orkney with . . .

Ran shook off the maudlin feelings and turned when someone said her name. Finding no one close or even watching her now, she shrugged it off and peered at the islands that grew larger and larger with every mile crossed.

Ran.

She'd heard it quite clearly then and turned once more to seek out the source of the voice.

Ran.

This time it seemed to come from the sea itself. Was someone in the water below her? She leaned over the railing of the boat and searched the water there. Nothing. No one.

Ran.

This time she was paying attention and her name whispered forth from beneath the surface of the sea there before her. Shaking her head in disbelief, she was caught unaware when a swell hit the boat, sending it tilting to one side and tossing her over the railing. Grabbing for something, anything, to stop her descent into the water, she grasped at air. Preparing herself to hit the icy water, she instead found herself in a pocket of warm water.

Holding her breath, she prayed that someone had seen her fall for there'd been no time to call out in alarm. With the many layers of heavy woolen skirts and cloak she wore, she would have little time before sinking into the depths below. Ran could swim, but the weight of her garments would pull her under and deep. And quickly. Tugging on the ties of her cloak, trying not to panic . . .

I can swim, she told herself over and over, as the water covered her, pulling her down. Then it began.

All around her, voices whispered her name. The sound of it floated and surrounded her in the sea. The water moved, too, shifting and encircling her, almost caressing her. Its warmth eased her fears and she stopped fighting the downward pull, staring at the sparkling, shimmering flashes that enclosed her in a silent embrace. The murmuring sounds began then, as though voices spoke there in the sea.

Ran.

Daughter of the sea.

Waterblood.

Power.

Command us.

Each word resonated with joy and welcome and want. And with each sound came a touch, a caress of hands that could not be possible, for the sea had not hands. Had she lost consciousness? Was she dreaming or dying and imagining this in her last moments of life? Turning and glancing up to the sunlight above her, she knew she must get to the surface.

Up, she thought. *Up now.*

At only the thought, the touches turned to pushes, swirling and moving her through the water toward the brightness above her. An instant later, she shot out of the sea as though thrown up into the air. Ran prepared for the gasping she knew would follow, as her body fought to reclaim its breath.

As one of the sailors caught sight of her and called her name aloud, she realized something unbelievable had just happened to her—she had never stopped breathing. Ran had not even tried to hold her breath under the water. She was practiced at it and could remain under it for a few minutes, but this time, the instinct had never begun.

Then another shocking occurrence—when she had fallen back into the water, she did not swim but did not sink. Instead of the water sucking her down, it seemed to hold her up there, waiting for rescue. Warm, impossibly warm, though it felt almost solid beneath her body. She grabbed the rope and tugged the large loop over her head and down under her arms.

"I thought we'd lost you, Ran," Bjorn said, as he pulled her over the side and helped her to her feet. "I've never seen a boat pitch that far without capsizing completely. It seemed to pause for a moment, neither leaning nor righting itself. Strange that."

"Nor I," she said, tugging the laces and freeing her sodden cloak. "A sudden wind?" Ran glanced at the man who'd sailed for more years than she'd lived. The winds could be unpredictable any time on the sea, but during this transition from winter to spring, even more so.

"Nay, calm." Bjorn waved to one of the other men. "Get blankets."

She should be shivering. She should be shuddering from the temperature of the seas at this time of year and yet, the water that her clothing and hair held remained warm. Just as it had beneath the surface. Ran allowed Askell to wrap a thick woolen shawl around her shoulders.

"You should go and change out of those garments. I do not wish to explain your sickening or worse to your father, Ran," Bjorn ordered in a soft voice. From the expression in his gaze, this had scared him.

It scared her.

More though, it confused her. She rarely lost her balance when sailing. And Ran did not suffer when moving onto land after being on a boat or ship—each step was sure and steady. So, falling into the water as she had puzzled her.

No matter what or how, she did not wish her father to be concerned and question her suitability for the tasks that lay ahead of her. Their bargain had been bitterly fought and she would not give it up now.

"A rogue swell," she whispered before facing Bjorn. "A rogue swell caught the boat. I am well," she said. "There is nothing to tell my father." Bjorn's weathered face told her nothing. "All of us have ended up in the water. 'Tis the way of it amongst those who spend their lives on the sea."

Ran met his gray gaze and waited for his decision. Her father sought an excuse to forbid her from sailing on his ships, and this would be enough. He wanted her married and settled, whether in Orkney or one of the many ports where his business interests lay. She wanted the freedom of the sea.

"You look no worse for it, lass," he finally said, glancing away. "But if anything else . . ."

She reached out and hugged Bjorn, kissing his leathery cheek before he could say more. "We are nearly home. All will be well, I swear it," she said.

"Go now," he stepped back and nodded. "You are soaked through to the skin. Change your garments."

Knowing how much it took the man to agree not to reveal this to her father, she nodded and left him there without another word. As she went below deck, Ran glanced back to find Bjorn staring at her. Had he heard the voices? Had he seen the way she'd been thrown back into the air? Or had he noticed the warmth in her wet clothing?

She would not ask him for it was pure folly to think that there could be voices in the water. Or to think that she breathed under its surface. Or think the water somehow saved her. Ran was not prone to visions or hearing things that were not there, so she could not explain it all. Better to let it lie rather than bring up matters she could not answer.

As she undressed and dried off, Ran noticed the new mark on her arm. Had she hit it as she'd fallen over the railing? Or mayhap as Bjorn and the others pulled her up? It was red like a bruise but, as she examined it, it changed. It moved. It almost looked as though there was something moving under her skin. And then the burning began, sending little bursts of pain through her skin.

Tearing off a strip from her still-wet shift, Ran wrapped it around her forearm, covering this injury. The coolness of the bandage soothed it as she'd hoped it would. One little bruise or scrape was nothing compared to what could have happened to her, so she continued dressing and returned to the deck above to watch the rest of the journey.

Though Bjorn and the others never took their watchful gazes off her, the final part of the journey was uneventful. Within hours they turned northward and made their way into the center of the islands and her father's home in Orphir. His fleet of ships moored in nearby Kirkwall harbor during the high sailing season but he kept only a few this far north over the winters. The rest would be moved soon, since Orkney was the center of the world in which Svein Ragnarson ruled with his widespread shipping business.

A shipping empire that she would be part of. That she would inherit. One that she would control.

For that, she could bear returning home and chance seeing the man who had driven her away two years ago. The possibility of seeing Soren Thorson again and the pain she would suffer were costs she would willingly pay for the rewards she would gain.

They arrived in Orphir to find that her father had not yet returned from northern Scotland. 'Twas not unusual, especially considering the storms she'd seen to the south. The last message from him said he would be here within a sennight of her arrival. So she would have time to visit with other kin and even the few people she called friends before she left Orkney for good.

Her father's servants were as efficient as ever and she found herself settled into her old chambers quickly. Aired and with fresh linens on the bed, the room welcomed her home. A hot meal was promised for later and a tray of bread and cheese sat before her within minutes. Waiting on her father's return would not be such a bad thing while she was being cared for like this.

She did not sleep while at sea, so she decided to rest a day before going into Kirkwall, to the market and to see to tasks she needed to complete before her father arrived. Tasks her brother would have seen to if he'd returned with her. But Erik had been a victim of Soren's betrayal as much as she'd been and he'd vowed to never return to their home.

As she drifted off to sleep, it was not dreams of that man that filled the hours until dawn, but the sounds of the water swirling around her. Especially the voices in the water. Impossible voices speaking impossible words.

Ran.

Daughter of the sea.

Waterblood.

Power.

Command us.

Only at dawn when she walked out of her chamber to the edge of the water did she realize that the sounds were not in her dreams. The same voices whispered to her from the water there, like the sirens of legend, luring her to enter their world.

Northeast Coast of Scotland

Lord Hugh de Gifford strode toward the tent erected there for his use. Surrounded by lackeys and followers, he considered his next move. His plans, the goddess's plans, had stumbled in the first battle with those of the fire and war bloodlines, but he was engaged in a war.

One battle, though it would have been sweetly satisfying, did not matter. There were four gateways. Four possible places for Chaela to reenter the human world and take control.

And destroy her enemies.

He would savor that scene. As he would savor watching those who had stood against him grovel at his feet, begging for mercy. A mercy that did not exist. If the daughter of his flesh thought she would be spared, if any of them did, they were mistaken. Waiting here for passage north had given him time to plan their executions.

Once the goddess was freed, his own powers would soar and he could easily destroy the other fireblood. And he would. But for now, he had to wait for these damn storms to pass. If he did not know better, he would suspect that the stormblood was controlling them. He did know better though, for he could and would feel each bloodline as it arose and no more had . . . yet. Or was he so far from his source of power that his own was lessening?

"My lord?" Hugh whirled around to face Eudes, his commander, who'd managed to come upon him without warning. "I have found enough boats to carry us north."

Time was critical now and he must get to Orkney and find the stone circle there. It was a more difficult task, considering the number of islands and places it could be. And he must discover the identities of the two warriors who would determine the outcome of this battle and possibly the entire war. It was the easier of the two tasks, but finding them would not guarantee success. He clenched his fists, trying not to strike out at the man before him. Hugh needed him for now.

"When do we leave, Eudes? When?"

"Once the weather clears, my lord. The man said they've never seen a storm like this before."

Hugh glanced up at the sky, watching the storm clouds spinning, dumping torrents of rain down on them. As he searched to the west, there was no break in those clouds and the sun was completely blocked. It would not be this day, he knew.

"As soon as there is any break in this weather, send that message north to the earl."

"Aye, my lord." Eudes did not move away so there must be something else.

"What is it, Eudes?"

"Should I continue to train the men?"

Hugh's answer to the impertinent question was a gauntleted hand across his half brother's face, a blow heavy enough to send the hulk of a man to his knees and to tear open his cheek. "Do not question my orders again."

The first battle had not been won or lost by the soldiers on the field but by those of the bloodlines with the powers of the ancient gods. Very few who'd witnessed the event understood what they'd seen. Even Eudes, who had seen many strange and inconceivable things while serving Hugh, was no more prepared for what would come than the others.

Hugh crossed his arms over his chest and waited for Eudes to rise. This time Eudes was smart enough not to meet his gaze or to say anything at all. Eudes backed away with bowed head, not daring to touch the new wound while in Hugh's sight.

If Eudes questioned Hugh, Hugh's authority would

be undermined and his control would waver. Hugh could not allow that. A show of power was called for and he smiled as he contemplated how best to do it. His blood raced and heat built within him as he thought on how and whom to offer up to his goddess to continue in her favor.

His cock rose as his flesh roused at the very idea of burning someone for Chaela. Their encounters always had that result—pleasure of the painful and fleshly kind. How better to worship her than with a sacrifice of the same kind? And in view of all, so that no one would dare question him or his power without remembering the cost of such an offense.

"Eudes!" he called out. The man stopped and returned immediately.

"I require a virgin. Search out the farms we passed," Hugh ordered. "And a large flat stone to be placed"—he looked over the area where his troops occupied—"there." He pointed to the center of the encampment. Eudes lost all color in his face and Hugh smiled again. The man understood what would happen. "Now, Eudes."

His commander nodded and bowed and walked swiftly away to carry out his orders. Small groups went riding off down the roads to the south and west in search of the necessary virgin while others looked for the stone. Though this whole area was filled with large collections of ordinary stones and boulders, they'd passed a hillside covered in an arrangement of stones some miles south that had shimmered with power.

The obedience he'd expected resulted in the arrival of everything he needed and his blood rose in eagerness to shed the virgin's blood on the stone altar before burning her in honor of his goddess. The disappointment of the last few days was dimmed by the anticipation and excitement he always experienced before and after such an act.

How would it feel when he sacrificed the rest of the Warriors of Destiny? If a simple human sacrifice gained him this much vitality, how much more would be given to him then? He chortled and went to gather what he needed before striding to the center of his soldiers.

Hugh ordered everyone to gather and watch as he proceeded to first sanctify the stone chosen with his own blood before placing the screaming woman there. With the eyes of hundreds on him, he carried out the ceremony slowly, savoring every scream of terror and pain and every drop of blood spilt. He relished every moment of her agony when his seed exploded into her as he became the fire that burned her to ash beneath him. Not even the incessant rain that fell could quench his flames.

Though the rain and storms continued for three more days and into a fourth, not a question was raised about his plans. And there was never even a moment's hesitation in following his every order.

Power displayed was power proved. Though the delay in sailing did not make him happy, Hugh de Gifford was very pleased with the results of his display of power.

CHAPTER 3

Three days after his grandfather was buried, Soren knew he could not ignore the parchment any longer. There had been little time to examine it before, so Soren had put it out of his thoughts and had seen to the tasks needed to ready his lands for spring planting. Those who worked the fields with and for him were in preparations, and soon the fields would be plowed and sown and ready, God willing, to be fertile in the short growing season here.

Now, though, curiosity lured him to look. His heart wanted to know what was so important to the old man that he took pains to put it in writing on an expensive piece of parchment. Einar had served the old earl in his younger years and had learned to read and write in both the Scots common language and the more formal Norse used by the earl and king. Latin was required for anyone involved with the court or the Church. Einar had insisted that his son and grandson be educated in those skills as well.

Soren sought out some privacy in a copse of trees

near his barn and opened the packet. Unfolding it, he found two larger pieces of parchment and a smaller one. None of them were actually letters, but rather he found one had a map, one had some symbols and the last, the smallest one, had some words scrawled across it. Foreign words he could not understand. Mayhap the language of the Gaels?

Studying the map, he could identify several places noted on it. His grandfather's favorite place—the broch—sat in the center of the map, surrounded by other markings. Several of the ancient stone circles and standing stones and tombs were there, as well as some of the cities on the island, like Orphir and Birsay. There were some places outlined in square or round shapes—the land that sat between the lakes of Stenness and Harray, the tidal island off Birsay and a beach on the north-central coast of the island. Kirkwall, now the main city and location of the earl's palace and the cathedral of St. Magnus, was strangely omitted.

Putting the map aside, Soren studied the other large parchment, which was covered in symbols. One, the war hammer, was familiar to him as Thor's hammer. Many sailors and farmers carried or wore that symbol, for Thor was known to be friendly to those who worked the lands or sailed the seas. Others were easy to identify like the shape of flames, or the shape of a horse, or the sun or the tree or the moon or a flash of lightning.

Lines connected some of the symbols but he knew not why. The fire and the hammer. The lightning and the water. The tree and the sun. The moon and the horse. Soren ran his finger over them and shivered at what he felt there. This was not just a parchment; this was a talisman, filled with some power he could feel but could not explain.

The symbols were arranged in a circle, too, outlined in shapes that resembled the stones near Stenness and Brodgar's Ring. And in the center of that sketch, a black circle, completely filled in. A word he could not read was next to it and underlined several times. Another word, written then struck through several times, was under the black spot. When he touched that circle, screams filled his ears and visions of fire burst before his eyes.

Soren drew back, not certain what had happened. The sounds and sights stopped when he no longer touched the parchment. The sick, queasy feeling that settled in his gut made him want to burn the thing. Only that it was the last contact with his grandfather stopped him from doing so. Standing, he held the paper in the sun's light to see it more clearly. Other shadowy figures were revealed then, along the edges of the drawing, but he could not identify them.

Placing the disturbing drawing down, he looked once more at the piece filled with words. More like words than symbols, he realized, but the language did not look familiar at all. Soren had seen Latin and English and Scots and many others and yet this did not seem similar to those.

Einar would not have left them for him unless they were important and unless they could be understood or translated. So, if he could not translate these words or symbols, who could?

The only man he knew who might be able to help lived in Kirkwall. A childhood friend, Ander Erlandson worked for the bishop now. Though Ander was a priest, Soren thought he could trust the man.

Soren would not be able to travel to Kirkwall right away though he would as soon as was possible. Until then, he would protect these pages and say nothing about them to anyone. After speaking with Ander, he would go to the broch and try to find any sign that would help him understand whatever this information was that Einar wanted him to have.

If only his grandfather yet lived . . .

Ander looked from the parchment he held to Soren and back again, squinting and peering closely at the strange words. Soren could see both the amazement and curiosity in his friend's gaze as the priest scrutinized the sheet again. Soren left the other two—the map and the diagram—tucked safely inside his tunic. Until he had some idea of what these were, there was no reason to share too much with others. Even friends.

"I have never seen the like, Soren," Ander said, lowering the parchment to the table between them. "Where did you come upon such a document?" Ander moved a candle closer and bent over to look once more.

Soren chose not to answer and waited on Ander's examination to continue. When his friend happened on something curious or different, he would quickly become lost in it. Minutes passed as Ander turned the parchment this way and that, holding it up to the candlelight and away from it. Then he'd hold it up against the glare of the midday sun coming through the window in the corner of the chamber. Soren stood and walked to the window, away from the table so his pacing would not interrupt his friend.

Peering out of the round tower of the bishop's palace, he could see the cathedral of St. Magnus rising over the other buildings of the city. Ander's position was important enough that he worked in the lower chamber of the bishop's private residence.

"May I keep this a few days, Soren?" He turned as Ander approached, parchment in hand and a furrow in his heavy brow. "I want to compare it to something I saw in one of the bishop's books."

"You have no idea of what it says then?" Soren asked, fighting the urge to tear the paper from Ander's hand.

"And no idea of what language it is either," Ander admitted. "I am baffled by it," he laughed as he shrugged. "And I do not like to be baffled." No, Ander did not. It was one of the reasons that the bishop took him into service—Ander was relentless when meeting an obstacle. Ander looked at Soren and waited for an answer.

Could he part with it? Einar had trusted it to him. But Soren trusted Ander and he needed his help, so Soren nodded. "How long?"

"Two days, three at the most. I have an assignment to complete before I can give my attention to it."

"Three at the most," Soren repeated, more to convince himself than to confirm his friend's words.

Ander nodded and smiled, like a predator who scents another prey. "And if I give it back to you in two or three days' time, you might even trust me with the others."

"The others?" Soren asked.

"You keep touching something over your chest.

More of the same, mayhap, or something different?"
Ander asked, holding out his hand.

Soren stepped back and shook his head.

"Ah, so there is more."

"Nothing really," Soren assured. "Only something
personal from my grandfather." He met Ander's green
and knowing gaze, hoping the lie worked.

"Very well," Ander said, backing away and placing
the parchment on the table once more. "I will protect
this one and you can make up your mind later on the
others."

"I thank you for your help, Ander," Soren said. He
walked to the door and pulled it open. "I will come
back at week's end." About to leave, he finally remembered the name his grandfather had mentioned. "Have
you heard the name Taranis before?"

"Aye," Ander said. And nothing else.

"And . . . ?"

"I remember not where or when, but I will seek that
out, too," Ander said, lying as Soren had. The man's
left eye began a slight but noticeable twitch. Soren
laughed then.

"Lying is a sin, *Father* Ander," he reminded.

"A weakness about which I pray daily," his friend
said, ushering him out of the chamber. "I will see you
at week's end."

Soren nodded and walked down the steps to the
main corridor. Almost to the door leading to the outside, Ander's voice called out to him and Soren paused
and turned back.

"I forgot to tell you. Ran has returned."

He'd always told himself that he would not react to

this inevitable news. The woman had been born and raised here in Orkney. Her father's shipping business was centered here. She had other kith and kin here—she would return here someday.

Ran had returned.

His life had barely returned to a normal one and now she was back. It would be torn asunder, even if he managed to avoid her, just by knowing she breathed the same air he did. Soren found he could not breathe, so he nodded and wordlessly left, seeking something he knew he would never find now—peace of mind.

He stumbled down the busy streets, not caring where he went or what he did. He mind reeled at the thought that she was on the island. Her father's business was here in the city. There would be too much to explain and too much he could not explain if they met. Deciding to leave now and go to the broch, Soren realized he'd wandered far from where he'd left his horse.

Turning back, Soren walked through the marketplace where he found himself, greeting the merchants and nodding to the vendors selling their wares. Kirkwall was a blending place, filled with people from all parts of the north and beyond. Norse, Scots, French, English all used Kirkwall and Orkney for replenishing supplies, stocking ships for travel and trading goods.

But something this day, now, was different.

As he walked the streets, Soren noticed a change in the air around him. In the colors of the fabrics offered in the weavers' tents. In the faces of the villagers. The brightness and hues had been leached from the world in which he lived.

The realization stopped him between paces.

He glanced around to see if something had thickened above him and had blocked the sun. The clear, blue cloudless skies answered him. What was happening?

And then she walked out from one of the alleys.

Ran Sveinsdottir.

The woman he'd loved. The woman he'd betrayed.

Soren stepped back into the shadows, to regain control over himself and to watch her. Tall and svelte, she moved with the same easy grace on land that she did on her father's ships. Her blond curls were tamed into several smaller plaits framing her face and one larger unruly braid. 'Twas a hopeless attempt to control the uncontrollable, but the longer woven tresses lay down her back and swung in time with every step she took. His body recognized hers. His mouth remembered the taste of hers and his hands itched to glide over those curves and touch every inch of her.

He shuddered and released the breath he did not know he'd been holding, continuing to watch her make her way through the crowded street. Without considering the folly of it and without thought he followed her, drinking in the sight of her, of her every smile and glance and movement. She bestowed that smile on many as she greeted the merchants and tradesmen along the street. Ran was the one woman he'd loved and the one he could never have. It had been two years since he last saw her and yet—

His vision flickered then and he realized that she was surrounded by color and light. They were missing in everyone else around them and were vibrant and almost alive in her. Turquoise—the color of the seas—surrounded her body, glowing and glimmering. He blinked several times, trying to clear his vision, for what he saw was simply not possible.

When that made no difference, Soren even dragged the sleeve of his tunic across his eyes, but it did not change. Her blond hair was bright and golden, her skin glowed and her eyes shimmered. Unsure of what was happening, he hissed in pain as his forearm began to burn.

Lifting his hand, he tugged his sleeve back and watched as the skin there grew red and an outline of a bolt of lightning became visible. It changed as he watched, growing brighter and clearer in shape. And it burned as it did. Covering it with his other hand, he glanced around to see if anyone else noticed.

Those seeking goods or food did not spare him a second glance. Those selling their wares did not either. Everyone else walked around him, ignorant or uncaring about this significant change in their world. As he looked around the area, Soren realized that Ran had the same bewildered expression on her face that his must have been wearing. She clutched at her arm, touching the same place on her forearm that yet burned on his.

He'd taken three steps out of the shadows and onto the street toward her when he finally pulled himself back and stopped. As much as he wanted to understand what was going on, he knew she would not welcome his approach. Or his questions.

Two years. Two years and much more than time separated them.

Since he knew her father would remain in Orkney while his ships and boats were prepared for the sailing months ahead, Soren doubted she was going anywhere too soon. If this strangeness somehow involved her, he knew where he could find her.

He would always know where to find her. Now though, he turned and walked away. He would seek out his grandfather's tower and try to put her from his mind. As he rode out of Kirkwall, north along the sea, he understood the truth that stood between them—he would never be able to completely rid himself of Ran Sveinsdottir.

Though he stood in the shadows between the merchants selling their wool and other fabrics, she would recognize him anywhere. Taller than her brother and her father, Soren towered over most men she knew. The years of working the fields and ships had built muscle and strength in his body, and she could not help but notice that he looked even larger now. Her traitorous body responded to the memories now filling her mind of their times together. The feel of his skin on hers. His strong hands moving over her and bringing her to pleasure. Relentlessly. As he did everything.

Could it be the mere sight of him that was causing this eerie feeling within her? The strange buzzing that filled her ears? The way her vision dimmed and flared?

Before she could do anything foolish, something in the world around her tilted and changed. Ran grabbed for the table in front of her as she lost her balance. Then, in an instant, her vision flickered again and the colors of the world disappeared. Everyone looked like a pale, drab version of themselves.

Except Soren.

He had changed now, not only looking stronger and

healthier, but also an eerie silver-gray glow outlined his body. As she watched this happening to him, her arm began to burn. Clapping her hand over it, she lifted her gaze and met his in that moment.

In that second, everything and everyone around them disappeared, leaving only the two of them. Time slowed and she gazed at the man to whom she'd given her heart, body and soul. Their life together had been laid ahead of them, shining like jewels and holding the promise of happiness. Those hopes had crumbled in an instant when he betrayed her faith in him.

Now, though, all that passed by in the blink of an eye, and she found herself staring at Soren as her arm burned fiercely. And, realizing that his action mirrored her own, she waited for his acknowledgment. Instead, he did again as he'd done before—he turned and walked away.

The bright, shimmering color of molten silver continued to swirl around him as he made his way along the street and away from her. Her heart, the one she'd sworn would never be hurt again, pounded in her chest, reminding her of the weakness of her will when it came to Soren Thorson.

Her arm felt as though it was on fire, so she tugged her sleeve up to look. As on the boat when she'd been rescued from the water, her skin burned and reddened with heat, changing as she watched. A shape formed and smoothed, only to form again. Two wavy lines etched into her then, undulating and moving as the waves or current did through water. For a moment, she believed them real. Then the burning began anew and the markings grew deeper and longer across her forearm.

What was going on? First the strange change to her vision and hearing. Then the alterations to the world's coloring—and Soren's. And lastly, this marking on her skin and, from his reaction, on his, too.

With more questions than answers, she wished there was someone she could ask. Someone who could counsel her and help her discover the truth of this.

And she wished with all her heart that it was someone other than the man who had betrayed his every vow and his own words.

As Soren turned and walked off toward the edge of town, Ran knew one thing—she had lied to herself about her feelings for Soren. And the only way she would save her soul and her sanity was to keep away from him.

So, that was what she would do.

Stay away from Soren Thorson.

'Twas only as she reached her father's house in the city after finishing some of her errands that she realized there was another from whom she could seek advice. A man wiser than her father who had more patience with her willfulness and questions, whom Svein Ragnarson would never allow her to consult.

Einar Brandrson, Soren's grandfather.

It would not take long for her to ride to his cottage near the northern edge of the island and seek his counsel over these strange occurrences. Surely he would know about these things.

CHAPTER 4

Ran realized her error as she left her father's small house in Kirkwall and took the north road out of the city. Old Einar's interest and time was being spent, not at his cottage, but at the stone tower that sat near the beach at Gurness. His letters, sent over the past two years, carefully avoided any mention of what had happened between her and Soren but were filled with stories of the tower and the discoveries he'd made there.

Although the broch had been deserted and unused, the old man had been digging around the base of it and found bits of old pottery and other evidence that people had lived in it long ago. Those bits encouraged him to continue exploring it and so he had, until the last letter some months ago, which had spoken of fearful events. Since she knew she would be returning to Orkney, she had not replied and had expected to see him in person and ask about the strange claims he made.

Once out of the city, Ran felt the tension leave her. On the sea, she was never alone. In her father's houses or in the storage barns and buildings, she was always surrounded by others. But, here, now, she reveled in the solitude as she followed the path along the sea.

Unfortunately, thoughts of her peculiar encounter with Soren and the changes she now noticed in the world around her filled her thoughts during the ride. Even now, the colors that should fill the sky and land around her were muted and understated. Everything appeared as though it was the gloaming when the light of the sun dimmed and everything was seen through a gauzy overlay.

Except Soren. He had appeared bright and vibrant, so much so that he almost sparkled. And the steel-gray color that outlined his shape did glimmer. How could that be? How could any of it be?

She reached the part of the road that followed along the edge of the sea for a short distance before turning inland slightly. And the voices began.

Ran. Daughter of the sea.

Come to us.

Join us.

Waterblood, use us!

Ran tugged on the reins, making the horse stop, and she looked around to see who had called to her. The voices sounded like the whisperings she'd heard before, but these were bolder, more humanlike. And yet, no one was there. No one on the road. No one in a boat on the sea. No one.

She looked out over the sea and noticed that the waves seemed to form slowly and remain in shape, almost as though they were watching her as she rode by.

As she continued on toward the broch, the words also continued. The same words repeated over and over, sometimes louder and sometimes softer. And Ran found she was not unaffected by the pleas. Something deep within her wanted to answer their call. Wanted to feel the warm caresses and welcome she'd felt when she'd fallen in the sea on her journey here.

Would it be the same?

Would they keep her safe again? Would they touch and whisper to her? Would they allow her to leave?

Ran shook her head, pulling herself out of the reverie in which she'd sunk. Voices in the water? Daft! Safe in the sea? What folly! She shook the reins and the horse began moving again. With each step away those voices cried out louder to her. Her horse began to sidestep and falter, whether because it could hear the voices too or because she was tightening her hold on the reins.

"Stop!" she cried out as the voices threatened to overwhelm her. "Be quiet!"

And there was silence around her in the next moment. The waves went back to their normal ebb and flow from sea to shore. Ran glanced around and everything looked as it should.

Was the upheaval of seeing Soren without warning causing her to be overset with emotions? 'Twas often claimed that women could not handle strong emotions and became hysterical. She did not feel out of control. She did not feel daft. She just could not explain these strange occurrences around her. Ran prayed that Einar was at the tower and could help her. The old man knew so much. Surely he could help her.

The rest of the journey passed quickly and soon the tower came into view. She hastened to get there, anxious to see Einar. Spying another horse tied outside, she smiled. He *was* here. As she walked up the path, she glanced around to see if he was outside or on the beach. Not finding him, she climbed the wooden steps, pulled open the door and entered the tower.

He'd spoken of a lower chamber in his letters, but she saw none. The wooden slats beneath her feet seemed solid. Across the chamber were the stairs to the top. Leaning over and looking up, she could see no one moving about. And only silence met her when she listened.

"Einar? Are you here?" she asked aloud as she climbed to the first landing. "Einar?" Footsteps scuffed along the floor above her, so she clutched the length of her gowns to hasten her pace and reached the next landing and the second story chamber there. "Einar."

"Nay."

Her body recognized that voice before she even saw the one who spoke. He stepped out of the shadows and into the square of light from the open window carved into the stone wall.

"Soren," she said on a breath. It took a huge effort to focus on her mission and to ignore the whirlwind of questions and accusations and reactions that filled her. And to force the next words out. "Where is Einar?" She lifted her head and glanced toward the top of the tower. "Is he above?"

"Ran," he said quietly, almost intimately.

Fearing a traitorous act, she avoided looking at him. Looking at him would remind her of everything she'd wanted, everything they'd had and done . . . and lost.

"Ran," he said. This time his voice forced her to meet his gaze. A terrible sadness lay there within his blue eyes. "He is gone."

Tears filled her eyes and burned in her throat at his words. She did not need to ask what he meant, for she knew. Einar Brandrson was dead. Grief for the loss of her friend shattered her heart. Soren had not looked away and, even though she wished she did not think of him kindly, she realized his loss was so much greater.

"I am so sorry for your loss," she whispered. Wiping her sleeve across her eyes, she cleared her throat. "When did he pass?"

"A week ago." Soren began to approach her. Ran wrapped her arms around herself and he stopped. "He was old. He went quietly in his sleep," Soren explained.

"I cannot imagine Einar doing anything quietly," she said. "I'd always imagined him as a fierce Viking of old, being taken in battle and carried to Valhalla by a Valkyrie." When she looked at Soren, she saw that he'd glanced away. And she saw the sorrow, and something that resembled guilt, in his gaze. "How does Ingeborg fare?"

"She has accepted his passing well enough. 'Twas not unexpected to her. His age and his growing infirmity . . ."

He walked away then, over to the window, and stared out at the sea. The silvery outline that surrounded his body reminded her of her reasons for coming to find Einar. Fruitless, hopeless reasons now.

"You thought him here?" he asked quietly. "Why not go to his cottage?"

"He spoke often of this broch in his letters," she answered. Soren turned and faced her, his face and expression now unreadable.

"He wrote to you?"

"Aye. He is, was, my friend."

"What did he say of this place?" Soren asked, his eyes blazed now. "What know you of this tower?" He stepped closer.

The memory of what had torn them apart flooded into her thoughts, reminding her that she could not trust him. He'd never answered her questions. He'd never defended himself. He'd simply turned and walked out of her life. Which was exactly what she wanted to do now. If Einar had not told him of his discoveries here, then mayhap it spoke of his lack of trust in his grandson and he did not wish Soren to know. She shrugged.

"Only that he liked to visit here and watch the sea."

His gaze narrowed and never moved from her face, as though waiting for more. She had nothing more to say to someone she could not risk trusting ever again. She needed to get away. Away now.

"My father is expecting me," she said, walking to the steps.

"Your father has not returned to the islands from Caithness," he said.

"How do you know that?" she asked. Why did he know her father's movements?

"I heard from the merchants in town." Now it was his turn to lie. Again. His lower lip twitched from the corner to the middle when he spoke an untruth.

If she was looking at his mouth, it truly was past time to leave. It mattered not how he knew about her father's travels. It mattered not, she repeated to herself several times. She owed him no explanation of any kind on any matter at all. None.

"Again, I am sorry for your loss," Ran said, walking past him to the steps.

He let her pass in silence and she made her way down and out of the tower. She would return to it when Soren was not there, to honor Einar's passing in her own way. She would also visit his daughter-by-marriage, Ingeborg, to offer her sympathies. The woman must be heartbroken, in spite of what Soren might believe.

Soren must be heartbroken.

Ran almost stumbled at the thought of how deep his grief must be. Einar was more father than grandfather to Soren, his only kin left alive as far as she knew. Part of her wanted to run back inside and console him and tell him of the letters and Einar's discoveries.

But two years of her own grief and anguish served her well in that moment of weakness. Ran righted herself and walked to where she'd tied the horse. Loosening the reins and gathering them in her hand, she prepared to mount.

And instead sank to her knees as the loss of her dear friend became real to her.

Einar had been kind to her so many times and in so many ways. She'd always known him in the way that kith and kin do—her brother had been Soren's closest friend and their families spent much time together. He was well respected amongst those living here on Orkney, and even her father sought his counsel on matters of business and farming.

When she and Soren had fallen apart, Einar kept in contact with her. Before she left and even while she lived elsewhere these last two years, he informed her about life on Orkney without her having to seek out the information. He told her of the important changes in Kirkwall and amongst her friends. And other than one line—*a great wrong has been done to you*—he never mentioned Soren or referred to the humiliating occurrence between them.

And now he was gone. Tears poured down her cheeks as she sobbed at the thought of never seeing the old man again. Of never hearing his wisdom or humor. Of losing another piece of her life. She released the reins and cried out her sorrow.

Hands clutched her shoulders. Strong hands guided her to her feet and then arms enclosed her and held her close. She knew the feel of them and the scent of the man who held her to his chest and whispered soft words. For a moment she allowed the embrace. Then, a shock stunned her. Stunned him, from the expression in his eyes.

The glow around him grew brighter and, from the way he stared at her, he saw something as well. The way her blood heated was familiar to her—he'd always affected her that way. Their passion had never been soft and gentle. Their joinings had always been hot and deep and shattering.

But this heat was different somehow.

Those watery voices returned and grew louder and louder as the very sea shouted her name from its depths. She turned and watched the waves grow violent as they seemed to throw themselves into the sky and dissolve only to rise again. Above them, the clouds swirled, dark and light, in small circles then larger ones, ebbing and flowing like the waves in turbulent eddies.

Her arm began to burn and it brought her to her senses. Ran pulled herself free of his embrace and the sea returned to its usual color and the sky cleared.

"I did not mean to . . ." Soren reached out to touch her again and then dropped his hands at his sides. "Your pardon, Ran. I should not have touched you."

Ran shook her head and nodded and shrugged, completely overwhelmed now by the emotions seething within her. And from seeing him. And touching him. And smelling his scent. Had he not witnessed or heard what she had? Did he not see the changes in the world that she did? Earlier, he'd touched his arm as she did. And now?

If he did see or feel anything as she did, he spoke not of it nor acknowledged it at all. Backing away, she grabbed for the reins of her horse and managed to pull herself up onto its back. Soren watched her without saying a word, until she was ready to move around him. Why she'd ever thought she could manage seeing him, she knew not.

"I have no right to ask and you have no reason to agree, but it would mean much to me to see the letters he wrote to you, Ran. These last months . . . he has, he had been confused. I but wish to understand what he was going through. Think on it, I pray you."

Ran felt the truth and the pain in his words and nodded. "I will do that," she agreed. He stepped out of her path and she touched her heels to the horse's sides, urging it to go.

She pushed all thoughts and questions out of her mind and rode as fast as she could back to Kirkwall. Allowing him to see the letters meant contacting and seeing him again. She'd lost control this time and she'd blame it on being surprised by his presence and the news about Einar. There was simply no explanation for the rest of what she'd seen though.

Seeing him in Kirkwall across the marketplace had shaken her; this encounter scared her, for it demonstrated that not only would she always be in his thrall but that other strange things were happening to and around her. Things she could neither explain nor understand.

If only Einar yet lived . . .

Ran decided to worry on that later. For now, she must carry out the responsibilities and prove to her father that she was worthy of his faith in her. Soren Thorson and whatever was happening here on Orkney was a complication she did not need.

CHAPTER 5

Soren watched her ride away. His hands clenched and his body ached with the need to take her and hold her and have her. She was his. When she had been his, his life had been right. His life had been full. Just now, for the moment when they'd touched, he had become something else, filled with some heart-pounding power caused by her closeness. He even heard the clouds above calling his name and coming to him.

And Ran became something more. As the sea-colored glow shimmered around her, she stared at the waves and they threw themselves into the air in sheets of water against the turbulent sky. With her gaze on them, they seemed to dance and come to her.

She'd stepped back out of his embrace and everything ceased, as though the colors and the sounds and the visions had never happened. Was she somehow connected to the strange abilities his grandfather claimed Soren had? Thinking on it further, Soren wondered if that was why his grandfather kept in touch with her over these last two years.

Damning himself a fool, he cursed aloud—several times—as he paced around the perimeter of the stone building. He'd finally reclaimed his life after the debacle that was Ran Sveinsdottir. The terrible results and repercussions of the devil's bargain he'd made could not have been foreseen or planned. Yet, he had lived through it all and regained control over his life only to see his life shattered once more.

Was it a coincidence that both times it somehow involved Ran? And his grandfather as well? Soren kicked the dirt in front of him and gazed down the road, watching the dust rise as her horse rode away.

It mattered little that Einar was dead now, not in the whole order of things. The agreement struck with Svein Ragnarson remained in place and too many would be harmed if he revealed it to her or to anyone else. Many would pay for his weakness.

And Ran was indeed his weakness.

Caught unaware when she entered the tower, he could not be blamed for his shock and his reaction. When she called out Einar's name, no one could have been more surprised than Soren. The revelation that she'd kept in touch with Grandfather alone was astonishing but that there were letters was completely unexpected.

When Ran finally rode over the rise of the next hill and out of sight, Soren walked back inside the broch and looked around. If Einar had mentioned this place enough that Ran sought him here, it was significant, more so than he first thought. Climbing the steps to the top, he gazed out and watched her cross the distance toward the city. Every part of him wanted to chase her down and say everything he'd never had the chance to. To make her understand the truth of it all. That she was his and always would be.

But that could never be.

He could also not admit to her that, as his aunt suspected, he'd kept aware of her location over the last two years. He had. He'd told himself he did it because he did not trust Svein Ragnarson to treat her well enough. To hold to the bargain as promised. No matter the strange turn of events or that she had returned at all.

Glancing around the chamber now, Soren turned his attention back to the puzzle left behind by Einar. He took the parchment out and placed it on the stone floor, adjusting it so that the points on it matched the positions of the places around the tower.

Eynhallow and Rousay lay across the water to the east and north, with Wyre and Egilsay to the south and east. His grandfather had visited those islands and more while working for the bishop and he'd marked many standing stones and circles on his map. Some places that Soren did not recognize were also outlined. Several circles joined and the overlapping area spanned the beach on the western coast. A dozen or so squares covered the stretch of land between the lakes Harray and Stenness. Concentric circles outlined and covered the tidal isle of Birsay, where the bishops of Orkney had previously lived.

Soren had traveled all over this island and knew nothing existed in those places now, save the ruins on the Brough of Birsay. That isle had been inhabited by many peoples in its history, from the ancient Picts to the pagan Vikings and the Christian Norse. But it lay empty now, so this drawing made no sense. If the weather held and the work on his farm was done, he would travel there to see for certain.

His arm stung and he lifted it closer to examine the skin there. Tugging his sleeve up and out of the way, he revealed the ever-growing patch of skin inside his forearm. The mark, a bolt of lightning, grew more defined and deeper, pulsing and moving as though real.

He'd seen this somewhere before. This exact shape and size. The same image was right before him—in Einar's other drawing. Soren opened that carefully, kneeling down and spreading it out on the floor next to the map.

There it was. A lightning bolt that matched the one that was now visible on his arm. Comparing it to the sketched one, the resemblance was uncanny, as though the same person had created both of the images. As remarkable as that was, it was as nothing when Soren followed the line connecting some of the symbols to others and found the lightning bolt paired with the image of waves.

Waves like the ones he'd seen when Ran stared at the sea. The color outlining the black image was the same as the one he'd seen around Ran—the same turquoise hue that was the color of the sea surrounding Orkney.

He fell back then, landing hard on the floor and skittering across until the wall at his back stopped him. She'd grabbed her arm as he had when he saw her in the marketplace. The same spot. The same arm. Did she have a mark as he did?

Soren pushed his hair back and took in a breath, trying to sort through the pieces of what he knew. There were connections hinted at in the drawings and the map, but he resisted thinking on them. To accept them would mean believing in some outrageous things. Things his grandfather had suggested that were simply too fanciful or ridiculous. Or mad. Or heretical.

He shuddered at that. If declared heretic, his lands and life and soul would be forfeit. That was the fate his bargain would have prevented from happening to his grandfather and now he stepped close to that fate.

Glancing at the drawings, Soren knew he was already too far into this matter to turn away. The mark of lightning on his arm burned then, taunting and teasing him. Alone, away from prying eyes, he could try what his grandfather had suggested the night he died. Though it seemed real to him that night, mayhap a simple test now, in daylight, would reveal his foolishness and send him on a path away from this one?

He stood and climbed the final set of steps that led to the roof of the tower. The winds buffeted him, tearing and pulling at his cloak and hair as he walked to the edge. His name echoed around him in the winds. Or mayhap the winds swirling around him sounded like voices?

Soren.
Stormblood.
Son of the wind.
Son of the storm.
Command the lightning.
Command us!

Soren turned around and around, seeking the source of the words. They came from above and around him, in the winds and in the clouds that gathered there. White and gray, the nebulous mists pulled at him. He could feel that they wanted him to speak to them. Forming and dissolving, almost playfully, over and over, surrounding and hiding the tower on which he stood.

Command us! The voices rang out as one, echoing within the fog they'd formed. And then a myriad of whispers grew around him, louder and louder, until he could hear nothing else. Soren turned round and round, searching for the source, for he simply could not believe what he was hearing. There had to be a source of it all.

He found none. No one was nearby. No person spoke at all.

The sounds were in the winds and clouds. Hell, the sounds *were* the winds and clouds. As he tried to discern what was truly happening, his grandfather's words came to mind.

Do not ignore my words, Soren. You have the blood of the gods in your veins. You have a place destined in the coming war.

Soren felt the truth in his blood as heat rushed through his body and his hands began to shake. Sparks arced from his fingers and he held them out away from his sides. The fiery flashes became stronger and brighter as a fire flaming to life when lit. The mist answered with a shower of sparks around him.

His whole body burned now and the flashes of light became something else—stronger, fierce, dangerous. Soren aimed his hands at the wall of the tower and concentrated his focus there. A bolt coalesced from all the smaller flashes and shot across the distance to the wall, exploding against the stones.

The wall crumbled beneath the onslaught of power.

His power?

Son of the storm!

He called the lightning!

Soren Stormblood!

The voices grew louder and more excited and his blood reacted. Soren felt the power there, growing and pulsing. He listened to the words and believed. Soren thought about the storms, the gales off the North Sea, and the winds began to swirl and dive between the tower and the strait separating the two islands. A thick black bank of clouds built there and rain pelted the land and sea.

His hand itched then, tingling and shaking once more, and he knew the lightning readied to strike. With a flick of his wrist, he tossed it at the storm. The bolt heaved through the clouds, expanding and multiplying until dozens of them shot through the air into the water. The surface exploded into waves of water, spreading out in all directions in an instant.

Soren stood, watching in shock as the very real possibility that he could control the clouds and winds and lightning sank in. He laughed aloud, for it was truly a mad idea and yet . . . He pushed with his hand and the storm clouds were shoved over onto Rousay, away from the Mainland. And there they remained as he watched them test the limit he'd placed on them.

He could command the storm?

He could command the storm!

Soren watched his hands as they glittered with power. He could feel it seething in his blood, coursing through his body. And, though he'd destroyed the wall, he could sense that there was much, much more power hiding within. But what else could he do? How could he test these new abilities?

What did storms do? Or clouds? Or winds?

They blew. They rained. They soared.

Before he could even put the thought in his mind, the winds picked him and lifted him above the tower. As it spun around and under him, Soren looked down to see the ground below him—far below! Higher and higher, he flew until he could see across the island and across the sea. Too shocked to contemplate the method or meaning of this, he stared south and could see across the other Orcadian islands down to the Scottish coast.

He blinked, unable to take it all in. It was still there below him when he opened his eyes. If he could see all of this, could anyone see him? What would they see?

The clouds swirled around him now in answer, masking him from anyone beneath him. To anyone looking up, he would be seen only as a cloud moving quickly in the air. Indeed, he could see everything clearly. Or he thought he could until he held his hands out before him and he could not see them. He moved them and realized he was looking through them as though they were like the costly glass in church or palace windows.

Shaken by the sight, he turned to look around. The tower was directly beneath him and he wanted to return to it. The winds and the clouds took him there. When his feet touched the stone floor of the tower, he fell to his knees. The clouds, mist and winds dissipated after whispering his name and rustling through his hair, almost as a gesture of farewell.

Alone, Soren pushed to his feet and glanced around. How could the world be so usual when his entire existence had just changed in an instant? What else had his grandfather not told him? He raced down the steps to the chamber where he'd left the map and parchment. The only thing he could do was seek out the places marked so prominently and search for those other symbols. Mayhap old Einar had left signs in other places?

Ander might be more helpful than Soren had first thought. Soren's knowledge of God or gods was limited, but Ander was highly educated and knowledgeable about many things, including history. He'd reacted at the name *Taranis* yet he had withheld it, just as Soren had withheld the other parchments from Ander. Soren would give his friend a few days and then approach him.

Ander's singular failing was his curiosity. It had gotten him, them, in trouble many times in their youth and continued to plague him now. Once curious, Ander was like the best hound in seeking out an answer or bit of knowledge or some obscure detail. Soren did not doubt that within a day, two at most, the priest would know what the words were and all about Taranis. By the way his grandfather spoke his name, Taranis must be some ancient, forgotten god.

A fresh, searing pain in his arm made him swear aloud. Pulling up his sleeve, he found the indistinct mark was nothing of the kind. Now, a rippling lightning bolt sat there, pulsing with power, reminding him apparently that no god, ancient or otherwise, liked to be forgotten. Or mocked.

Soren folded the parchments with care, tucking one inside the other, and left the tower. As he rode away, his mind filled with questions and plans. He would ask his mother's cousin to take over his daily duties on the farm so Soren would have time to follow this collection of clues left for him.

Whether a fool's errand or a true quest, he knew not. But Soren hoped, when all was revealed, that his grandfather's words had some meaning. Einar deserved at least Soren's best attempt to find out and would do so to honor the man to whom he owed so much.

CHAPTER 6

Ran was concerned.

It was well past a week and her father had still not returned to Kirkwall. There'd been no reports of storms or mishaps from other boats and sailors who arrived from points east, west, south and north. If he got caught up in some matter, he would send a messenger ahead.

And yet none had arrived from him.

Shaken by her encounters with Soren and devastated by the loss of her friend Einar, she'd spent two days alone at the house in Orphir unable to regain the emotional control and balance it had taken her two years to attain. She also mourned for the old man who'd seemed to care for her more than her own father did.

Ran needed to speak to Ingeborg, for she had cared for Einar for years and could tell her of his last days. If she had departed for Orkney only a few days earlier, she could have seen him . . . could have asked him . . . She shook her head in grief and frustration. But for a few days.

Ran had read and read again all of his letters from the last two years. Filled with his ironic humor and funny way of looking at the world around him, they had been her only connection to the place and people she'd tried to leave behind. It was as though he had known that she did not wish to break all of her ties. He kept her informed in a way that no one else could or did. And with but a few words, he supported her when her heart was broken and prevented her spirit from the same fate.

Yet, Ran was not here when Einar needed her. That failure cut through her as surely as a knife would, but there was no way to make amends.

Unless she helped his grandson.

Soren.

Ran moved along the corridor and out into the yard, walking to the edge of the water and onto the pier. The winds whipped around her and pulled her hair free from her braid. Gathering it in her hand, she stared at the bay.

She'd known she might see Soren and she had. She'd suspected she would speak to him and that she'd done as well. But to seek him out and share something personal, something meant only for her to see, was a different matter.

As she considered her choices, the water began swirling under the place where she stood. Rather than startling her, the slow movements soothed her and she found that watching them made her thoughts clearer. Sitting on the wooden pier, she leaned over and dipped her hand in.

The water changed, warming at her touch. She

thought how nice it would be if all the water in the bay would warm like this. It would be a pleasure to swim or bathe in. Even though the water would warm over the summer months, it never lost its chill.

Closing her eyes, she heard the voices again. They whispered and soothed, the sounds undulating as the water did around her hand. Ran slid down as she had many times as a child and let her hand dip lower into the current. When she opened her eyes, her hand was gone.

Shocked, she pulled back out of the water. Her hand was there. It was fine. But for that moment, she had not been able to see it. Mayhap she had fallen to sleep? Or was lost in her thoughts? Or had she seen something that was not there?

Ran.

Waterblood.

Come with us.

Something deep within her answered, drawing her back to touch the surface. The water moved over her hand, caressing it and tugging at her. They called her to come in and she wanted to.

She wanted to.

Dare she? Dare she enter the water on her own?

Standing, she decided to follow the call and see what would happen. She was not mad so she walked off the pier, going to the edge of the water where it was shallow. Glancing around and seeing no one, she unlaced her gown and pulled it over her head. Ran removed her shoes and stockings as well, leaving only her shift.

At the water's edge, she paused for but a moment, not long enough to change her decision, and entered.

One small step and a second one. The voices shouted now, their tone jubilant and excited, her name rang out.

Ran Waterblood!

Ours! Ours!

The water swirled around her, moving up from the surface to cover her. Like a thing alive, it enclosed her and pulled her in deeper. She drew in a breath, and after several more halting steps, Ran leapt the rest of the way.

As the first time, she felt welcomed and treasured by the water. How could that be? She could not survive here, not without breathing air.

And yet, here she was, under the surface, surrounded, still breathing . . . something. The voices became like chattering children, fast and high and excited, saying her name. Laughter and joy all around. She smiled and turned to see thousands of shimmering lights there with her.

Who are you? she asked in her thoughts.

We are the power that lives in the seas. We are you, Waterblood. You are ours!

How is this possible?

You are the waterblood, they whispered back. *You have our power in you. Command us! Tell us!*

Ran let go of her fear and laughed then. *Take me. Show me the sea.*

Once more the excited whispers increased. Then the water took hold of her and pulled her away. Turning and moving, Ran tried to see what lay on the bottom of the sea or other creatures like fish. Several large fish moved away as she was pulled through the water. Glancing toward the light, she knew which direction was up but she looked down again.

Never had she seen such a sight. Large rocks lay strewn along the bottom, covered in moss and other growths. Plants with long leaves that floated toward the surface, sea grass and seaweed grew amongst the rocks. The water took her to the bottom, many yards beneath the surface and she touched the plants. Ran put her feet on the sand and looked around in wonderment and awe.

A noise caught her attention and she glanced toward the surface. A large vessel passed overhead and Ran noticed the way it sat in the water and moved through it. How far from shore was she to see such a large ship? The sea lifted her and soon she found herself just beneath the edge of the water. Ran pushed her head into the air and watched the ship sailing west and out of the bay.

She was several miles from her father's house in Orphir!

Ran knew how to swim and had swum good distances from shore, but never had she traveled this far or this fast. When she looked down into the water, she could not see her body. Frightened, the voices eased her worries.

You are with us, Ran Waterblood. You are safe.

She lifted her hand from the water and it appeared as flesh and blood. When she let it drop, it became part of the sea. The euphoria and wonder racing through her prevented her fear. Ran let go once more and became part of the sea.

This was miraculous. And awesome. Completely strange and inexplicable. As she spent an hour or so in the sea, traveling far from Orkney and back again, she had no idea of what this incredible change meant or how it had happened.

We have always been part of you, Waterblood, the sea answered. *Now you are one with us.*

I must go home now, Ran thought.

She was propelled through the sea then, faster and faster until they reached the bay around which lay several of the southernmost islands of Orkney, including the Mainland. Lifting her head from the water, she watched as they brought her back to the very spot from which she'd leapt, and placed her softly on the sand. Ran rolled from her belly and sat up, looking back in amazement.

The water of the bay before her burst with waves that rose and crashed into one another, creating a huge spray of water filled the squeals and chatter of the voices. The sounds echoed softer and softer until she sat there in silence. Though she should be shivering from exposure to the cold air, the water in her shift and on her skin and hair remained warm.

Standing, she gathered her clothes and shoes, planning to return to her chambers by the back way so she would remain unseen. But her mind was filled with the significant questions left unanswered by the sea.

Why me? To what purpose is this happening?

Without a moment's hesitation, the voices answered her. But it was not a collection of voices, but one, a woman's voice.

You are and have always been waterblood, carrying the power of the seas and rivers within you, Ran. Your purpose is to save humanity from the great evil who is coming.

Shocked by both the words and meaning, she shook

her head in confusion. She was simply a woman, one woman, not some type of shield maiden or heroine from the old sagas still told here on the islands. A great evil? They were under the control and protection of the Norse king and his earl. They were safe.

The great evil sends her minions even now, Ran Waterblood. Prepare to meet your destiny.

Ran shivered then, in deep shudders that racked her body as something within her raced into every bone and muscle through her blood and into her heart. The water was within her, as was the power about which the voices, and voice, had spoken. But what her destiny was or who this great evil was, she knew not.

She yearned for Einar more than ever in that moment. She needed someone to confide in about these wondrous but frightening changes and events. Her father had not returned yet, though she knew Svein Ragnarson had no patience for things that did not involve shipping goods, sailing or making a profit.

Matters of faith or other facets of life meant little to him. Even his children were important to him only for what they could bring to his collection of power and wealth. His long-dead wife had been acquired as an asset to his business interests. Part of his disinterest in his children had played to Ran's benefit, for once she was too old for a nursemaid and had reached the end of her education, Ran had been left on her own much of the time.

Ran could do as she wanted. See whom she wished to see. Fall in love without rules.

That thought forced her feet to move. Ran made her way to the back door of the house and opened it quietly. Her bare feet made no sounds as she walked to her chamber. Her father's house was staffed by only a small number of servants until he returned. So she did not worry overmuch about being discovered as she was.

"Another encounter with the sea, Ran?"

Ran turned and faced Dalla, the woman who kept house here and oversaw the other servants. She also was her father's bedmate when he was here.

"Dalla, I did not see you as I passed." Ran continued walking, hoping the woman would let the matter lie. Had Bjorn spoken to her in spite of his agreement not to speak about what had happened? If Dalla knew something, her father would know it within minutes of his arrival. "Pardon my rudeness."

"Is the water not too cold to swim in it now, Ran? You could catch your death and become ill."

How did the woman manage to convey both concern and hope for a bad end in one utterance? Dalla had that talent. Ran stood up straighter and offered her best glare to the woman who was no more than a servant and a whore.

"I do not answer to you, Dalla. Do not mistake your place."

"Ah, but you will answer to your father. Will you not?" Dalla walked closer and returned her glare with a haughty one. "'Tis you who should not mistake my place here, Svein's *dóttir*. You will be married off soon and leave forever while I will remain in your father's favor in a way you will never be."

Ran slapped the woman's face for such an insult, watching as the servant was shocked by the action. No one put Dalla in her place, not even Ran's father, so the woman carried on as though she were mistress of this house. She was not and never would be, for her father would never honor Dalla with marriage.

Yet, the insult and the reminder of the other part of her bargain with her father stung. Without another word to or glance at Dalla, Ran made her way to her chamber and slammed the door shut. Now reminded of the rest of the bargain—a marriage of her father's choosing in exchange for two years of control of the shipping business in Orkney and a large share of the profits made— Ran, threw herself on the rope-strung bed and screamed into the pillows.

She'd wanted some control over her life, unusual as that would be, and her father wanted to use her to make an alliance, so the agreement gave them both something they wanted. In two years she would still be of marriageable age and in the prime of her childbearing years, too. But she would have money of her own and her children would inherit her share of Svein's business interests. It was practical. It was beneficial. At the time she'd agreed, a marriage of convenience and business was the only kind she would consider, especially so close to Soren's betrayal.

Now though, this new happening, this strange change, forced her to consider what to do. Did she pursue the cause of her new ability? Or ignore it and discover the reason for it when it revealed itself to her? An ability to control the seas would be an advantage of immeasurable opportunity for her father. If she could use her power to move ships as fast as she'd traveled, there would be immense profit.

Somehow she knew that this power was about something much, much larger than profit. The voice said her destiny was to save humankind from some great evil. And she knew to the depth of her soul that it was true. The voice also said something evil was coming and that she must prepare. How could she do that? What was her part? Rolling to her back and staring at the ceiling above her, she realized that whatever was happening involved both Einar and Soren.

Einar's seemingly innocent and unconnected words now made sense to her. With his brief message of consolation he had also included words about a larger future and her place in something bigger than Orkney. She'd thought he meant a marriage to a man from across the sea in Scotland or in Norway or elsewhere, part of her father's plan for an alliance that crossed boundaries. Now she thought Einar's words were connected to this power.

And Soren . . .

His arrival in the marketplace was a surprise. His departure should not have been. But in those few moments before he'd walked away, he'd grabbed his arm in the same place she had held hers—the place where that peculiar mark now lay. If they shared the same mark, did he have the same power as she? Or was his different?

Ran sat up and pushed her damp hair from her face. She held her arm up and examined the mark. It no longer burned or stung, but now it appeared alive. The two lines resembling waves undulated under her skin, the marks moving like the sea did.

The only way to find out if Soren bore the same mark

and how he was involved would be to see him again. On the morrow, she would visit Ingeborg and leave word for Soren that he could examine the letters his grandfather had sent to her. Then, when he came to get them, she would try to find out whether he bore the mark. And what Einar had told him. For she could not believe for a moment that his grandfather would not have shared such knowledge with Soren if he'd known it.

Ran spent the rest of the day and evening in her chambers reading and reading again the missives from Einar. Now, his words seemed to carry a message she'd not seen before this change had taken place. Now, she looked at the words and phrases in a completely different way and wondered at their meaning.

As she collected the letters into the box where she kept them, Ran was convinced of one thing—Einar Brandrson had known much more than anyone else about all of this.

CHAPTER 7

Ingeborg greeted her warmly and invited her inside. It had been two years and yet she could detect no hint or trace of anger or disappointment in the way Soren's aunt spoke to her. In little time, they sat close to the fire, sipping some hot tea. Ingeborg knew much about herbs and plants and made several different varieties. This one was her favorite, and Ran was pleased that Ingeborg remembered.

"So you saw Soren and he told you of Einar's passing?" Ingeborg asked.

"Aye. I went looking for Einar to thank him for his letters these past two years, and found Soren at the broch." Ran could not stop rubbing her hand across the lid of the box in which the letters sat. "He said Einar passed quietly?"

"Ran, I know you were special to him. He spoke of writing to you after . . ." Ran shook her head, tears filling her eyes. "Soren spoke true—Einar passed in his sleep. He was buried next to his wife." Ingeborg nodded to the box. "Are those his letters?"

"Aye. Soren asked to see them. He said Einar had been confused the last few months and he wanted to see if the letters could help him understand why."

"Einar was disturbed, surely, but never confused," Ingeborg said with conviction. "I've thought on it much since he passed. At first, when he lived, I did think him confused, but not now. He was disturbed over some matter."

"Disturbed?"

"He was convinced he had failed in some duty and that his end was coming without having the opportunity to carry out some task. It brought to mind a holy vow made and broken."

"But to whom would he make such a heartfelt promise? His wife before she died? Their son?" Ran watched Ingeborg's face as she shook her head. "Then who?"

"That I know not. Mayhap Soren does? Einar left a packet for him."

Ran did not speak then, thinking on seeing Soren again, at the broch. Mayhap Soren did know more? In the silence, she took a deep breath for courage and asked the question she wanted most to know.

"How does she fare?"

Ran could not speak the name of the woman Soren had seduced and ruined, then had to marry. Not yet. Not ever. Ingeborg's face lost all its color and she dropped the cup she held. Tea splashed on her skirt and the floor, but Ingeborg only stared at Ran.

"You do not know? Your father did not tell you?" Ingeborg asked. Ran found it difficult to breathe, knowing that whatever Ingeborg said was going to be terrible. She shook her head and put her cup down.

"Tell me what, Ingeborg?" At her request, Ingeborg slid from the stool and knelt in front of her. Taking Ran's hands in her own, she met Ran's gaze and whispered the news.

"Aslaug is dead. She died just after you left, falling from the cliff near her father's house."

Ran gasped and shook her head at this. Dead? Her brother Erik had loved Aslaug for years and planned to marry her. When his best friend, Soren, betrayed all of them and seduced Aslaug, all their neatly made plans for the future fell apart. In one act of betrayal, Soren had torn apart three lives and his own. When her condition was made known, her father disowned her, forcing Soren to marry her or lose all honor.

"She was carrying . . ." Ran could not finish the words.

"Aye. Both gone in a moment."

Ran's throat was thick with burning tears as she thought on the ending of the young woman's life. And that of the babe she carried. No matter what she might have blamed Aslaug for, Ran had never wanted her death or that of an innocent life either.

"Soren?" she asked, using only his name.

"He was not there. 'Twas said that Aslaug went to beg her father's forgiveness and he denied it. They found her body the next day when Soren went looking for her. He was . . ."

The opening door stopped her words.

Soren stepped inside and looked at Ingeborg and then Ran. When no one spoke, the uncomfortable tension told him that he was the subject under discussion.

From the pale look on his aunt's face and the shock on Ran's, he knew exactly what had been said.

Aslaug.

Aslaug's death. And her babe. There was nothing he could say. Not then and not now.

He noticed Ran clutching a wooden box and nodded at her.

"Are those Einar's letters?" he asked.

She blinked several times and seemed to realize she was holding the box. Ran looked at it and then at him and nodded her head. Ingeborg released her hands and sat back on her heels.

"Aye. I think you should see them," Ran said, holding out the box to him. Did she know that her hands shook? Or that she would not meet his gaze?

"My thanks," Soren said, taking it from her. "I will return them as quickly as possible." He understood she was giving him a precious gift, made even more so because she did not and could not trust him.

The color that shimmered around her pulsed brighter when she did look at him. There he saw disappointment and anger and hurt, but mostly he read sorrow in her gaze. When he began to say something, she shook her head and walked past him. Soren reached out and touched her arm to make her stop.

"Ran, wait. I would speak with you before you go," he said.

She pulled free and walked out. He nodded to his aunt and followed her. Ran was almost to her horse when he caught up to her. He wanted to tell her what had happened but could not. When she stopped and turned to face him, the sorrow was ebbing away from her eyes, but the aura around her did not lessen.

"Why did you not tell me? Why did I have to learn this from your aunt?" she asked in a furious whisper. "Even Einar kept it from me."

"Tell you when, Ran?" he answered, crossing his arms over his chest. "When you'd just learned of Einar's death and were distraught over it? Or should I have come to your father's house to tell you and risk seeing him or Erik?"

"Erik will never return here. He is betrothed to the daughter of one of my father's . . ." Ran stopped then. Erik was another uncomfortable topic between them. Her brother, his best friend. All in the past.

"Just so," he said.

Ran crossed her arms, mirroring his stance, and lifted her chin. She was about to ask an impossible question. He recognized it in the way she stood and held her head. And the way she worried her lower lip. He tried to prepare himself for anything.

"Did she fall or did she . . . jump?"

Nothing could have prepared him for that. Ran was smart. She was one for details. She'd listened the way Ingeborg must have said it and heard what had not been said. And only a very few people knew or had guessed at the truth.

"She was buried in hallowed ground, Ran," he replied with the only words he would allow himself to utter.

He would not lie to her again. He might not be able to tell her the truth, but he would not lie. Aslaug's death was another mark against his soul but he would not damn hers for eternity by exposing her own sin.

"I am sorry for her death. I would never have wanted that, Soren," Ran said, her arms dropping to her sides. "I did not want that."

He nodded and stepped out of her way, changing their discussion to something less damaging. "I will see this is returned to you."

She mounted without help, as she always did, and gathered the reins in her hands. Urging the horse to turn, she paused.

"Once you read those, I have questions for you. Will you meet me at the broch the day after next?"

Ran knew there was more to this than a man and his death. Did she see the same things Soren did? Did she bear the same mark? Was something pulsing through her blood as it did in his even now? He nodded.

"At midday?"

"At midday," she agreed, and then she turned the horse and rode away.

Soren should not have agreed, for it broke the bargain he had with her father. But he suspected that in the coming days, he would break most parts of the damned thing.

"She needed to be told, Soren." Ingeborg walked up next to him as Ran rode off toward the south.

"Aye." Soren turned to his aunt. "When I learned that my grandfather had been writing her, I thought that he would have revealed it to her."

"Well, now you will see what he told her and when,"

she said. "Will you tell me, Soren? Tell me the truth about what bothered him so?"

He wrapped his arms around his aunt and hugged her. "I thought you were at peace with his death?"

"I am. I am just not at peace with his last months. He worried over something and would never share whatever that burden was with me."

"You are a mere woman," he joked, trying to lighten his aunt's grief.

"Do not jest over this, Soren. He searched for something or someone. He mumbled in his sleep. He left in the morning and would not return. And he sang those songs, the ones he taught you and your father from the time you could speak."

"When do you leave here?" Soren asked. He felt the urge to get her away from this area. He'd seen this cottage burned to ash in his dreams and feared it was an omen of things to come.

"In a day or two. My niece is expecting soon and I want to be there for the birth. Now that winter is easing its grasp on the seas, I will go." She frowned now, searching his face. "Unless you wish me to stay."

"Nay, do not delay in getting to her. She lives on one of the northern isles?"

"Aye. You sound concerned. What are you keeping from this mere woman now?" she asked, touching his cheek.

"I know you are truly formidable, Aunt," he reassured her. Or attempted to. "I think you will enjoy being with your niece."

Ingeborg went back inside the cottage, asking no

more questions, which suited Soren. He had no answers for her and only fears about what was coming to Orkney. The winds whispered to him then, trying to ease his concerns but he was not soothed.

Death was coming. Fire was coming. War was coming.

Without more specific knowledge, Soren knew not from where or how. His dreams were filled with images of fire and war. And standing stones and brochs, like the ones that seemed to fascinate his grandfather.

He hoped that Ander had been able to decipher the strange words or images. His friend had sent him a message to come to Kirkwall that day. A hint of excitement in the words gave Soren a sense of optimism that he would finally have something tangible to follow to discover his grandfather's secrets and what they meant for him . . . and Ran.

Soren promised to send one of the workers from his farm to help Ingeborg pack when she was ready and he rode to Kirkwall.

"Where did you get this, Soren? Truly, it is a marvel." Ander looked up from his place at the large table and pointed to the parchment Soren had left with him. "You must tell me or I will not tell you what I have discovered about it." Priest or not, Ander could be ruthless when it mattered and he'd clearly decided it mattered now.

"This remains between the two of us?" Soren asked. Then he repeated it as a demand, his tone sharp enough that Ander blinked several times as he spoke. "This remains between us."

"Very well," Ander said in all seriousness.

"My grandfather."

Silence and a knowing expression met that admission.

"I would not share this with many, even without your orders, due to its very nature and content." Ander smiled and then put the sheet down on the table. Pointing to the top line, he nodded. "I did not recognize it at first, but comparing it to several other documents and manuscripts, it is actually Latin from a very specific place."

"Latin? It is no Latin I have ever seen," Soren said, leaning in closer and studying the shape of the letters. He'd been tutored in Latin, writing and reading, as part of his upbringing at his grandfather's hand.

"Not unless you do this," Ander advised as he lifted the parchment and held it up to the strong light coming in the window of the tower chamber.

The sun pierced through the parchment and the writing could be seen. It was Latin, clearly.

"Written backward?" Soren asked, reaching up to outline several of the letters and words.

"Aye. Here is the transcription of what it says." Ander held out a document to him.

On the sheet were two sections, one in Latin and the other in Norse. But as he compared one to the other, Soren saw that both said the same thing—

And in those days when the Old Ones were no longer worshipped, they left humanity in the care of those descended from their Bloodlines who would protect mankind from the one of Chaos and Fire.

If called upon, those Warriors of Destiny can rouse the winds and sea and earth and war and sun and beasts to their cause. Fire will serve both sides and will choose good or evil to triumph at the end.

Soren looked at Ander, who was grinning like a loon. He read the passage again.

"What does it mean?"

"It refers to old myths, passed down through the ages, of old gods, now superseded by the one true God. Your mention of *Taranis* was the clue I needed." Ander moved to one of the bookshelves in the corner and drew out an old book. "This is a history from an area on the continent, from before the downfall of Rome. It speaks of gods who governed those who lived there and worshipped their different forms."

"This sounds like blasphemy, Ander."

A sin and supreme offense of which Einar had been guilty. But this gave written proof to any claims made against his name now. Soren was glad his grandfather was already past the reach of those who would see to his downfall. But, having these kinds of documents in his possession could bring the same charges against him now.

"I prefer to call it a historical treatise on fanciful old customs. Similar to tales of the gods worshipped in error by the ancient Greeks or Romans in their day," Ander said as he put the book in front of Soren and motioned for him to sit. "Here is the list I found. *Taranis* is mentioned here." He pointed to it. "It is written in an archaic language, similar to ancient Greek and yet not."

"And you can read this?" Soren asked, moving the

book closer and looking at the indecipherable script on the page. If Ander said the word was *Taranis*, he would believe him.

"According to the bishop, I have an uncanny ability to discern old and unused languages as well as those we use now."

"Pride, Father Ander," he warned. But he was glad of his friend's gift at this moment. "Read on."

"Taranis is said to have controlled the sky with his power over storms and wind and lightning." Soren fought the urge to touch the lightning bolt mark on his arm. "Along with several other ancient gods, they managed to banish some evil one from the earth." Ander met his gaze now and smiled. "'Tis quite a wonderful story. Good against evil. Gods of the elements and nature."

"And who wins this battle of good against evil?" Soren asked, suspecting that this was no story at all but a historical record of a very real battle.

"According to this account, good did. But the ancients did not think evil would be defeated forever so they left their descendants with powers to return if needed. Descendants . . . bloodlines." Ander squinted as he read the words again.

"And how will the descendants defeat the evil if they need to?" Soren asked, trying to remain calm even as his breathing grew shallow and his heart pounded. Damn Ander! His careful studying of Soren's face told him he'd not fooled his friend at all.

"This does not say that. It ends with a warning to the faithful to be watchful and prepared at all times."

Soren got up and walked to the window, holding up the parchment and pretending to examine it.

"Is this tale a special one? In these types of fanciful stories?"

"Oh, nay. Every one of the ancient cultures and even our Bible, God's true word amongst us, tells of the final battle that will rage between good and evil at the end of days. This version has Taranis and other gods like"—Ander peered at the writing once more—"Sucellus and Belenus and Epona and Cernunnos and . . . Nantosuelta."

Ander closed the book and returned it to the shelf from whence it came. He was watching Soren too closely as though he suspected something more. "Strange that it does not mention the evil god they battle."

Just as a name had been scratched over on the other drawings. As though it was too frightening or dangerous to even give name to this evil.

"So, friend, now that I have revealed all that I discovered, will you share the other secrets you carry next to your heart?"

"Ah, I would, Ander, but I have left them home."

Although he tried to say it in a jesting manner, Ander was obviously not amused. Not even a bit.

"I am not happy with this turn of events, Soren. In good faith, I completed the task you set me to, only to discover that you will not keep your end of the bargain."

"I am not reneging on my *tacit* agreement, Ander. I simply left the other *two* documents at home," Soren began, knowing that Ander's curiosity at the thought of getting two more peculiar documents into his hands would ease whatever anger existed. "I will bring them to you in the morning?"

"Very well," Ander nodded. "I will wait in good faith to see what you have."

Soren left quickly after folding the document carefully and placing it inside his tunic. In the morning, he would send word of a delay and wait until he'd met with Ran before showing the others to Ander. There was every possibility that he would share the documents with her, if the letters she'd given him gave any information or knowledge from his grandfather.

Part of him—the part that had suffered greatly over the last two years to regain a semblance of normality back in his life—hoped it was a fruitless search and he could go his own way without Ran. But the other part—the one that loved her and wanted her for himself—took it as a challenge. That part relished the idea of her tearing away the calm and sanity in his life and returning to the ever-explosive passion they'd had before.

Soren had no doubt that he would discover the outcome very soon.

CHAPTER 8

Northwestern Scotland

William de Brus, now called Warblood, gathered the leaders of his company of warriors to discuss the final arrangements for transport north. He'd delayed their departure by several days to integrate those who now followed but had little or no battle experience amongst his more skilled fighters.

The battle would be between those who carried the bloodlines of the gods, and humans would not be part of that. But his human fighters were not easily detected by those they fought, so they were valuable for other uses and positions. Like the spies they'd sent out. And the searchers they'd sent on ahead. Everyone who pledged to him and their quest had a purpose in their battle against the evil one.

The priests used the time to strengthen the bond of their spirits that kept them connected to one another. This recent bonding had not been tested yet and so

Marcus and Aislinn continued to offer prayers and sacrifices to their gods in preparation of the next battle.

William's own life and world had been torn asunder and rebuilt into something very different in just the last month. From king's bastard son and a sworn man to a warrior made to protect humankind, William was completely altered from the man he had been. Now, the berserker warblood walked within him, waiting to be called forth.

"Do you think de Gifford knows the location yet?" Roger de Bardem asked. Roger now led the human army and had always been William's closest friend.

"Nay," Will replied. "When he boarded those boats, he was heard asking the one who captained it where there were ancient stones in Orkney. The last we knew, they were heading north of the Mainland to some of the other isles where older ruins lay."

"And we do not?" Roger asked.

"Aislinn believes we should sail directly to the Mainland. Even though some circles are known and most likely not the ones we search for, she says it's there."

The men all nodded in agreement. After seeing what the young priestess could do and her courage in the face of an enemy onslaught, no one would question her beliefs or pronouncements.

"So, we will leave in the morning. Prepare your supplies and organize those assigned to you."

Will nodded to Roger to remain as the others walked off to carry out their duties. Roger stood at his side and tilted his head in the direction of a lone warrior sitting at the edge of their encampment.

"And do we trust him?" Roger asked.

Brisbois de Gifford was born twin to their dark enemy but became a torturer and assassin for his brother when Hugh inherited all of the power in their bloodline and the titles and wealth and lands of the firstborn. Only in the last moments of the battle at the stone circle in Loanhead did he protect his niece and swear to her service.

"My wife says aye," Will said. "Brisbois is now her man."

Roger grumbled under his breath and Will understood his feelings. Brisbois had tortured one of the priests to gain information for his former lord. Corann had been rescued but had still not recovered from his injuries and could do little even for himself yet. The priests did not speak to or even look at Brisbois and the others trusted him little. But Brienne's word was good enough, and more so, for Will, so he did not allow the others to refuse him a place.

Brienne of Yester approached and Will watched as she glowed with the power of fire in her blood. An aura of orange surrounded her. It was her love that allowed him to control the awesome power that now seethed within him and his for her that gave her control over the fire. His blood heated for a different reason now as he felt the berserker rising and as his gaze turned red. She could bring it forth with but a word, calling to his blood.

"You still question his loyalty, Roger?" she asked as she replaced Roger at Will's side. Her touch brought warmth to his skin. "I vouch for him now."

"And that is the only reason he is tolerated, Brienne. You must know that," Roger explained.

"Aye. A time will come when all will see his loyalty, my love," she said to Will.

The words sounded almost as a prophecy, even Roger noticed it, and Will watched her face for some sign of a deeper meaning. It was there and gone as soon as he studied her. She knew more and kept it from him.

Their marriage, their trust in each other and their abilities were all new, and still growing and being tested. But Brienne absolutely knew something she was not telling him. The more important thing was that he trusted she would share it when she could.

"Are the women ready to sail?" he asked, as he wrapped his arm around her shoulders and walked with her toward their tent.

"Aye. All we need now is for the clear weather to continue. The priests offer their prayers for that now."

"So your duties are done then, wife?" he asked.

Before they began this next battle, one in which the outcome was in no way guaranteed, he needed his mate. Will and the warblood craved Brienne and the fire she bore. He needed to taste every inch of her skin and feel her release against his mouth. He needed to fill her body and mark her as his. He wanted to claim her in every way he could. His male flesh rose and his vision turned red once more.

"Everyone can see the change, husband," she said with a laugh. "And the warblood is loud."

"He wants his mate," the warblood replied, as Will's body grew larger. He tugged her closer, leaned over and inhaled her scent. He touched his mouth to her neck, tasting and smelling her arousal and whispered gruffly, "His mate wants to be claimed."

"Aye, she does. Come, Warblood, let us seek some privacy in the woods there."

William pulled the warblood back into his blood, wishing to join with Brienne as a man, as her husband. When he entered her body, he loved her as though it was their first and last time together. She opened her body and soul to him, giving him comfort and pleasure and her love. And he gave her all that he was—man, husband, lover, warrior, warblood.

By the early light of the approaching dawn, the warblood in him had been satiated and rejuvenated by the fire and passion and love of his mate. William watched as the boats were loaded and all of them readied for the battle of their lives.

Gods help them all.

North Sea between Papa Westray and Westray Islands

Hugh peered out over the flat piece of land and searched for any indication that the stone circle he needed to find was there. So far from a place where he could commune with the goddess and restore his powers, he worried to himself that he would not be able to sense it if they did arrive at the correct place.

But to those who were in his control, nothing appeared to be different. He waited as the man in charge brought the ship in as close as he could and dropped the weight to keep it here. They would have to use smaller boats to row into the shallow waters near the beach.

"You think this is the place?" Eudes asked from behind him.

"Svein reported several ancient ruins and possibilities."

He did not trust Svein Ragnarson at all. But the man could sail and owned the ships that brought them north. Hugh's message to the earl, or the earl's man since the earl wintered with his king in Norway, was that he sought those responsible for King Alexander's death.

Since he had the king's seal in his possession and was known as one of the king's councilors, the lie had been believed and he'd been granted access to all the islands. Only he knew that the men responsible for the king's death were already dead themselves and could never reveal the true plan of it.

Captain Ragnarson walked toward him now, hesitation in his step. Not the most optimistic of approaches. Ragnarson nodded to him.

"Well?" Hugh asked. "Any sign here of what I am seeking?"

"Just over that rise," the man said. "Some half-buried stones."

"I think you are leading me in circles, around these islands that you know well and I do not," Hugh said, pleased by the worried expression in the man's eyes.

"You asked me to take you where the ruins are. I have done that, my lord," Ragnarson said, trembling.

"I will kill one of your crew every time you take me to a place that is not what I am searching for." Hugh let the words sink in before nodding to Eudes. "Let us have a show of good faith now so you understand my meaning."

With a nod of his head, Hugh designated the one and Eudes stabbed him in the chest. As Ragnarson howled, Eudes dumped the body over the side. The captain charged at Hugh, but he used his other power, to compel people to his bidding, to stop him.

"That was not good faith," Ragnarson said through clenched jaws.

"But you understand what disobedience will bring now. As does your crew." Hugh walked to the side of the ship and prepared to climb down into the smaller boat. "Come, Ragnarson. Show me these ruins."

Although there was a hint of power in whatever lay beneath the thick peat layer, it was not the circle he sought. It took little time once they arrived there to determine that, so within an hour or so, they rowed back out to the ship. Only a few yards from the ship, the water began to swirl around them.

Hugh's blood heated and he laughed aloud. The waterblood was here! She. Her blood had risen! It had begun. Though he could not see her in the sea, he could feel her presence as she must feel his.

"Waterblood!" he called out. "Come, join me in this wondrous quest." Though the water moved around the boat, no one answered him. Probably too untrained to know how yet. "I can teach you how to use your powers, Waterblood." Silence. "You know me now, Daughter of the Sea. I carry the fire within my blood even as you carry the water. Find me when you wish an answer to your questions."

The sensation of another who carried a god's or goddess's blood moved away, deeper and farther, to the south, before disappearing completely. But that mattered not, for he'd learned several things.

The island he searched for, the stones he needed to find, were on an island to the south of this one.

The waterblood was a woman.

The waterblood was somehow connected to Svein Ragnarson.

His good mood was restored, for the battle was met and the players would now begin to take the field. Once he found the stormblood, who he knew was a man, he would persuade them to his side to open the portal and release their Goddess.

His laughter echoed across the water and chilled the heart of every man who heard it.

Within the sea

If it was possible, Ran shuddered. Carried swiftly south by the sea, she could not believe what had happened.

That man could see her! Or at the least, he knew she was there watching. He called her the same thing that the sea did and spoke to her about the power he carried. The orange aura surrounding him glowed fierce and bright, much more than Soren's did. Her blood wanted to answer his call, but she saw only her father in his grasp and felt his terror.

It took much to alarm Svein Ragnarson. Little frightened him. He faced down the earl or a torrential storm at sea with the same amount of comfort. But just now, abject terror filled him.

They crossed the miles swiftly, back to the Mainland.

Distraught and confused, she did not wish to return home. She needed help to free her father. Her brother was not here. There was no one she could call on for help.

Soren.

Dare she ask him for help? Would he help her father?

She knew he was keeping something from her and needed to find out what he knew. If he bore the mark. If he carried some power within him. If he could help her to rescue her father from this dangerous, powerful man who held him prisoner.

And who murdered without compunction. For she had been there watching at a distance when that man had ordered young Eigil's death. The sea had taken his body gently to the bottom, where she'd held him in a warm embrace until life left him.

Soren. Where would he be?

The currents changed direction and, in little time, the sea brought her to the broch. Placing her on the sandy beach near the tower, the water moved away but waited on her wishes, whispering her name. Standing, she shook out her gown and asked all the water to leave it now. Within a few moments, the water had trickled back into the sea.

He must be here, if the sea brought her here. She ran across the beach and up the path to the broch, pushing open the door and shouting his name. Her voice echoed in the empty chamber. Was he above?

Had he seen her come from the sea? It mattered not. Whether he was only a man or something more mattered not. She needed his help. Climbing the stairs, she found the first chamber empty. Continuing on and up, she nearly ran into him on the steps as she reached the top. Grabbing onto him, clutching his tunic so she did not fall, Ran looked up and met his eyes.

His very shocked expression.

His knowing gaze.

CHAPTER 9

Soren took hold of her shoulders so she did not fall backward. He could tell that Ran had not expected him to be coming down as she barreled her way up the stairs. If she had taken note, she would have noticed the way he shook as he held her there. The turquoise color that outlined her rippled, uneven and unusually bright.

Ran Sveinsdottir had just come out of the sea as an extension of the water and then turned into a woman.

He was not alone in experiencing the strange change that he had—she had as well. He was part of the storms and she was part of the sea. How this could be, he knew not.

"We must speak, Soren," she finally said, breaking the tension of the moment. "Please. I beg you."

She never begged. Headstrong and forthright, Ran spoke her mind. The only begging had been during moments of passion when she wanted more from him or when he delayed her pleasure.

Ran begged him now. He nodded and pointed down

to the floor below them. She turned and led the way. Once they stood facing each other, silence filled the space between them. He watched as she struggled with what to say and how to say it. Soren understood that she did not trust him and worried over sharing too much with him.

Mayhap if he began first, told her the truth now, she would begin to . . . Nay, she would never forgive him. He went on even realizing that.

"I saw you come from the sea," he admitted quietly to her. "I saw you change from water to the flesh and blood that you are now." She startled with each admission. He tugged his sleeve up, exposing the mark there. "I, too, am marked."

Her gaze moved over his arm and then she lifted hers and pulled her sleeve up until it was uncovered. Two waves burned into her skin; they moved like waves did in the sea. Peaking, falling and rising again. Over and over, they moved as he watched. Ran reached out to touch his mark and hissed when she did.

"Lightning?" she asked. "What does it mean?"

"I can call the storm. I can make the winds blow," he said, lifting his arm and watching as the bolt there flashed and another outside the tower answered. "I can command the lightning."

Her green eyes widened at his words. "And I can call the sea." She shook her head. "But why, Soren? Why us? Why can we do these things?"

"I think my grandfather knew about all of this," he said. He reached inside his tunic and took out the three parchment sheets. "He left these for me."

"What are they?" she asked, opening one.

"Ander translated it for me. Einar wrote it in Latin, backward, to make it difficult."

"More likely he did not wish it to fall into the wrong hands," Ran said, examining it closely. "So you told Ander about all this?"

"Nay," he explained, walking to her side after retrieving the wooden box from where he'd placed it. "I only gave him the one. No one has seen the others." Soren knelt then and held out his hand to her.

Ran knelt and placed the paper carefully on the floor, smoothing it out flat. A frown filled her brow as she studied the words.

"It tells a story about ancient gods who defeated an evil one and left behind their descendants to protect mankind." Soren waited as she read the Latin version. "If you lift it to the light, you can read it through from the other side." She did as he said and shook her head.

"This is written in Einar's style. How did he write it backward?" Ran asked.

"My grandfather had talents I knew not of," Soren answered. "And knowledge of many things forbidden and heretical."

"Ander could not be happy about seeing such as this." Ran held it out to him after she read it.

"I used his curiosity to overcome whatever objections he might have."

Soren folded it and opened the map. Ran stood and took it to the window. Turning, she matched the map with the sketches and marked locations. "Do you know what these squares and circles are?" She paused, studying it. "I can see the circles are those made of stones near Loch Stenness, but the squares near there?"

"I planned to travel there and see what he drew."

Ran faced him and held out the map to him. "I must find out what this is all about."

"What happened? You were frightened when you came in."

"My father is in danger, Soren. He is being held by a man . . . a man like us."

He wanted to ignore the fact that Svein might be in danger. That man's death would make his life safer. But Ran knew nothing of that. "How is this man like us? Is he from Orkney or an outlander?" he asked.

"He glows, as you do," she said. Her words startled him. "But with the hues of fire, not the silver that outlines your form. Yours is silver, like the lightning. Or like the storm clouds that build and layer in shades of silver and gray."

"You are surrounded by turquoise, the color of the water where the ocean and the sea meet around the islands." Soren needed to stop looking at her. He glanced away for a moment and then back. "This man has some power? You could tell?"

"I could feel it," she said, rubbing her hands up and down her arms as though chilled. "He said it, too. Said that he has fire in his blood. And that he could answer my questions."

"How did you see this?"

"I have worried over my father's absence. He should have returned almost a week ago and there's been no word. So I asked the sea if it knew where he was. The next thing I knew, I was there, in the water, watching this man as he killed one of my father's crew to force him to help in some way. He's looking for something. Stones or ruins. Somewhere here in Orkney."

"Your father is probably safe for now," Soren said. "If this man needs something from him, he will keep him alive."

"Will you help me then?" Ran asked.

How could he refuse her? If she knew what her father had done, it would tear her life and heart apart. To know how little regard Svein had for his daughter would be too cruel and she did not deserve that.

"Aye," he said, knowing he could not say otherwise. "Do you know where they are now?"

"They were north of Westray, in the strait between there and Papa Westray. Four of Papa's largest ships, carrying many fighting men and horses and supplies. And that man."

"He saw you?"

"Nay, I do not think he could see me in the water for I . . . blend in. But he could tell I was there somehow. Probably he felt the same strange sensation that I did. My blood raced and, for a moment, I wanted to go to him."

"I think that happened to me, Ran. When I saw you in the marketplace, you glowed. I could see little color in anyone else but you. And I could feel the same . . . pull."

She swallowed and blinked several times as though fighting with the notion. He'd wanted to go to her even knowing it was wrong. But then, the wanting had never stopped. Even when he'd betrayed her. No other woman held Soren in thrall as Ran did.

"I do not understand any of this," she said. "When did you know that something was happening to you?"

"The night before my grandfather passed. He told me I had the blood of the gods and their power." Soren laughed sadly. "I did not believe him. Only after he died, did I begin to think something was truly different with me." He paused to meet her gaze. "When the winds spoke to me, I could no longer ignore or deny it." Ran did not laugh as he would expect others to upon hearing such a thing.

"I fell over the railing on the ship coming here," she whispered. "The sea spoke to me. Rescued me." She shook her head in a furious manner. "What is this all about, Soren? Do I need to seek out that man to find answers? I think he is only using my father to use his ships, but something in his gaze as the sea took me away tells me otherwise." She shivered then, and her whole body shook with it. "I do not think he is someone I wish to seek out for any reason."

Then Soren suggested the very thing that he knew would offer him nothing but torment for every second of the endeavor.

"I think we should seek out the places on my grandfather's map and see if there are messages or signs left there for us." He let out a breath. "Einar clearly wanted us to know something."

"Us?"

"The letters he wrote—"

"—Are filled with more than simple greetings," she

finished his words. "I had not noticed it until I read them again the night before I gave them to you. Phrases that now seem to hold two meanings." Now it was she who turned away, contemplating their choices.

"If we are to help your father, if we are to understand what is happening, we must seek out more about these marks and these powers we have been given. There must be a reason for them."

Ran nodded and he knew his own personal hell was about to begin. To be in her presence, to be with her, all the while knowing how much she hated him, would be more penance on his soul.

"Gather some garments and tell your servants you will be visiting my aunt for several days," Soren said to her. "I'll see to things on my farm and meet you there, on the morrow."

"And Ander? He is your friend, Soren. Will you share this with him?"

The scuffling of leather on stone was his only warning before another voice entered their conversation.

"Aye, Soren. Will you share this with me?"

Father Ander Erlandson walked the rest of the way into the chamber and crossed his arms. Ran knew he and Soren had grown up together, until Ander was designated to enter the priesthood and sent off to be trained. That was when Soren and her brother Erik grew closer.

"Father," she greeted him with a respectful nod.

Father Ander was short and round, the complete opposite from tall and muscular Soren. And dark to his light features and coloring. His tonsured head and long black robes spoke of his calling.

"Ran, 'tis good to see you. You have been gone from our shores for too long. And how is Erik?" Father Ander asked in reply. Erik fit in between them in stature and complexion. She remembered the three as boys, rolling and playing and fighting. Always three. But now . . .

"He"—she paused and glanced at Soren—"he is well, Father."

"Soren," the priest said. Soren wore a guilty expression in his eyes now, like a boy caught committing some trespass. "I expected you in Kirkwall this morn." Soren tried to toughen his expression now and the resulting look was even guiltier.

"I had things to see to, Ander. I sent word," he explained. Clearly this banter between them involved something Soren did not want to do.

"Things like whatever it is you hide from my sight?" he asked, approaching Soren and holding his hand out. "You promised in good faith, my friend. Do not make me bring sin into this."

"How much did you overhear?" Soren asked.

"Enough? Not enough?" Father replied.

Soren looked over the priest's head at her before agreeing to anything. "Ran, this involves you and matters you may not want someone else to see. 'Tis your decision."

Father Ander faced her now, his face serious and solemn. "If Soren has not told you, my special gift is ancient and archaic languages, so you might find me helpful. But what he does not know is that a few weeks ago, something strange happened to me. I awoke one night from a terrible dream to find my arm on fire. Or so I thought."

The priest began to roll up his sleeve.

"My arm was not on fire but the skin was burning. A mark appeared. . . ." He tugged the wide sleeve up higher. Ran held her breath then. Did he . . . ? Could he . . . ?

"When Soren approached with his request for my help, it flared once more, becoming deeper and darker," he explained, gazing at her and then Soren, who stood now like stone. "As I held the parchment he shared with me, I knew it was part of the answer to my questions about what this mark is and what it means."

Ander walked across the chamber that now felt so small to her. Standing before her, he lifted his arm higher.

There it was! His mark was that of a small sticklike figure of a man. And like theirs, it undulated as if alive.

"Just now, as I entered and faced you, it burned again. Now, it moves like one alive. So, Ran, Soren, do either of you know what this means and why I have it?"

If Soren's reaction was a mirror of her own, her mouth would be hanging open in disbelief and shock at the sight. How could this priest be involved in something that was as ungodly an endeavor as there ever was? The three stood in this triangle for several heavy, silent seconds until Soren moved first, removing another packet from within his tunic and opening it before them on the floor.

Not the map she'd seen but some new piece, another drawing but this time only symbols.

"My grandfather drew this, too, Ander," he explained as they all moved closer and knelt around the parchment. "These symbols match mine"—Soren lifted his own sleeve to show the priest—"and Ran's." Soren nodded at her and she revealed her mark.

"The sea and the winds," Ander whispered. "As in the story. Can you truly rouse them?" The priest laughed aloud then, almost as an excited child would when discovering something wondrous.

"Aye," they answered as one. What would his reaction be to seeing her become the sea? Ran's gaze took in the other symbols.

"So there are four others?" she asked. She picked up the story translation and read it again.

> If called upon, those Warriors of Destiny can rouse the winds and sea and earth and war and sun and beasts to their cause. Fire will serve both sides and will choose good or evil to triumph at the end.

"If we are the winds and sea, then earth, war, sun and fire are out there somewhere?"

"Two firebloods?" Soren asked, pointing to the last of the words. "Fire will serve both sides. The man you saw—he said he was fire?"

"You have met another? Who is it?" Father Ander asked.

"The man who holds my father against his will, Father. He said he is fire."

"You saw him?"

"Aye," she nodded. "But he did not see me for I remained part of the sea."

The priest's eyes widened again and she could see he had more questions. Instead he turned his attention back to the drawing.

"There! There is the symbol I have. Outside the circle and along the edge. And there in it, near that hole."

A number of those stick figures lined the edges of the drawing. Ran reached out her hand toward the drawing. Soren took her hand.

"Have a care. When I touched it before . . ." He shuddered. "This is more than a drawing, I think."

Before he could be stopped, Father Ander touched the place in the center that had been completely blackened in. His body jerked and went still. His eyes rolled up into his head and he fell backward. She'd seen someone have a fit like this once—he had rolled on the ground and frothed at the mouth.

Ran moved quickly behind his head and held him steady on her lap, so he would not hurt himself on the floor. Soren folded the map up and put it aside, careful not to touch the center of it.

"Ander," he said. "Ander." The priest did not respond.

"Father," she said directly into his ear. Touching his cheek and then tapping it, Ran repeated his name a few more times.

Mayhap a cold cloth or a sip of water would help him? Looking around the empty chamber, she wondered if . . .

Ran looked at Soren and then placed her hand on the priest's forehead. Thinking of cold, clear water, she watched as her hand became that. Water dripped over his head and his cheek as she touched him there. Then, holding her hand higher, she let some drops trickle into his mouth.

Father Ander began to rouse. His eyes fluttered open and met hers just before he saw her hand. She changed it back to flesh and dropped it to her side. Soren reached out and helped his friend to sit. The priest shook his head and then shivered.

"My friends," he said. "We must find out what this means."

"Ander, wait. What happened?" Soren asked, pulling him to his feet. "You fell unconscious after touching that drawing."

"I saw. . . . I dreamed. . . ." He shuddered again and made the sign of the Cross over himself, several times, before continuing. "Evil. Pure, uncontrolled evil is coming. We must stop it. We must," he said. The vehemence in his words made her jump. "I saw everything burning. And I saw . . ." The priest seemed to lose himself in whatever he remembered for a few moments. "We must sort this out and find the way to stop her."

"Her?" Ran asked.

"The name crossed out on the drawing is that of a female, a goddess of such evil that her name should not be written down or even be uttered aloud." He blessed himself again and Ran wondered if he saw the irony of it.

"But Ran saw a man of power?" Soren said.

"Her unholy minion, that one. The one you saw. Her hand on earth, intent on freeing her," he said it quickly, like words learned by rote.

"How do you know this, Ander?" Soren asked.

"I know not, my friend. I know only that I must use what I have to find a way to stop her, as you two must use your gifts, your powers." The priest walked to the doorway, looking invigorated instead of the man who minutes ago had lain unconscious on the floor.

"Where are you going?" she asked, standing and walking to the doorway as he continued on his path.

"I am going back to the bishop's library to seek out more about the evil one," he stuttered out.

"Do you know her name?" Soren said. "Tell us."

"Nay, but I will seek it out. You go on with your plan to seek out the places on Einar's map." Father Ander stumbled down the steps and ran to his horse. Mounting it, he rode off toward Kirkwall, with the words of the prayer to the Lord's Holy Mother—*at the hour of our death*—echoing out behind him.

Ran realized he had been listening for longer than she'd first thought. He'd heard all they'd said. And he'd never once remonstrated either of them for discussing such heretical things as ancient gods and goddesses and powerful bloodlines. Even knowing that such stories or books or drawings existed was sinful in the eyes of the Church.

If anyone had known what Einar created or knew and reported it to the bishop, Soren's grandfather would have been in grave danger. Very grave. Indeed, his whole family would be suspect. And yet this priest seemed not bothered by it. He threw himself into whatever this endeavor was without hesitation and without question.

She felt Soren's heat at her back before he spoke. Thinking on it, she knew where he was and even if he was looking at her. Her body had not forgotten his touch and wanted it even now in the midst of this new and dangerous situation. And she wanted his strength and his comfort. If she could have commanded her memory to forget what he had done, what he had cost her and what she'd promised herself, Ran would have faced him and walked back into his embrace.

And would never leave it.

That thought scared her. Two years of pain and humiliation and her heart could ignore it at the sight and nearness of him. Would she never learn?

When he stepped closer and placed his hand on the frame of the door, watching Father Ander riding away, she ducked low and passed under it, moving to the other side of the chamber.

"So, we meet at Ingeborg's cottage in the morn then?" she asked. Ran retrieved the wooden box of letters and waited for a reply.

"Aye." He said nothing else and watched as she left the tower. Only then did she remember how she'd traveled to the broch.

"Keep these safe for me? Tell Ingeborg to read them if she wishes." Ran handed the box back to Soren. Heading to the beach, she heard him call out to her.

"Ran, we need to slow them down or they will reach the Mainland before we have found a way to stop her," he said. "I will slow the winds in their sails. You might calm the waters?"

Smiling at the way he made it sound commonplace, she nodded. "I will."

"And have a care and stay a safe distance so he does not know you watch."

How had he known she would seek out the man and watch over her father?

Because they knew each other well. They were two halves of one whole. Or they had been before he broke them in two. She nodded once more and made her way to the beach.

"On the morrow," she said before diving into the sea, becoming water before she hit the surface and merging with the rest of it.

CHAPTER 10

The first decision Soren made was to travel to the places on the map. Unsure of his—their—powers, he readied the horses. One to ride, one for supplies.

"What are you not telling me?" Ingeborg asked.

"Are you leaving on the morrow as you'd planned?" he asked instead of answering. His grandfather would want her protected.

"I know there is more to this than you are saying. Something that those papers revealed to you. You inherited that streak of stubbornness from Einar, Soren." She turned to go back inside.

"Ingeborg," he said softly. "I do not know much and have more questions than knowledge. I know where you will be and I will send word to you when I understand."

She did not look at him as she nodded and went inside. If his dreams were correct, this house would not stand for long. If Ander was correct, Ingeborg would not be safe, even on the northern isles. No one—no man, woman or child—would be safe from this great evil. But it gave him some peace to know his aunt would not be *here*.

A sound drew his attention and he watched as Ran approached. She rode like a proud warrior maiden of old, in a gown over breeches. He remembered the feel of those legs wrapped around his waist as they'd joined. His mouth even watered as he remembered the taste of her skin and her mouth. His own breeches grew tight at such memories, so he turned away and finished tying the canvas that covered the supplies.

"Good day, Soren," she said as she climbed down from the horse. "Is Ingeborg within?"

"Aye," Soren said, taking the reins of her horse. "We will go after you've spoken to her." He watched her enter the cottage after knocking on the door.

In a shorter time than he thought it would have taken, Ran and Ingeborg walked out, arm in arm, and stopped in front of the cottage. With their heads together and whispering quietly, he thought them plotting something against him. They'd done that before. Before . . .

"I am ready, Soren," Ran said. "No need to frown." She took the reins and mounted, seating herself quickly.

Soren walked to his aunt and hugged her. "Travel safe," he whispered to her.

"Swear to me that you will save her, Soren. Swear it!" Ingeborg clung to his sleeves, holding him close. "Choose no one, choose nothing, over her." With that, Ingeborg released him and stepped back. Dabbing at her eyes, she called out her farewell to Ran and then met his eyes.

Whether Ran had told her or whether she'd gleaned

it from reading Einar's letters, Ingeborg knew that something bad was coming. And that they were at the center of it. When he glanced at Ran, her expression remained open.

His aunt began to sing softly, so that only he could hear it. Without thinking, he joined her . . . in one of the songs that Einar had taught him. When the words ended, she smiled.

"It is a prayer, Soren. A prayer to the Old Ones to watch over you and bless you." His mouth dropped open at her words. She knew? "Some mere women learn much by listening, you know."

Did she know anything more?

"Einar told you to sing them when you needed help. Or guidance. Remember that, Soren. It is important." She stepped inside and turned to close the door. "Gods be with you."

Nothing in his life was as it seemed only weeks before.

As he walked to his horse, he felt Ran studying him. The words, those last words, that Ingeborg spoke had shaken him to his soul.

He'd always thought he'd been defending Einar against false charges, but the more he discovered, the more he began to realize that his grandfather was truly a heretic. If Soren held powers he believed were granted by an ancient god, did that make him an apostate as well?

Soren felt the entire world beneath his feet shift in that moment. He was not the man he thought himself to be. He would not lead the life he thought he would. His relatives were not what he thought them to be.

"Are you well, Soren?" Ran asked.

"I think not," he replied. What else could he say to her?

"What did Ingeborg say to you?" She guided her horse closer.

"Her words matter not. She simply made me realize that we are crossing a line in doing this. Everything we were raised to believe in our lives was wrong. Now we will seek to learn what the truth is."

"A good thing, seeking the truth?" she asked, watching him closely. Her green eyes narrowed and he knew exactly what she was thinking about then.

"In this? I am not certain, Ran," he admitted, mounting the horse and guiding it over next to hers. "But it does not appear that we have a choice in this. 'Tis either go and find it or it will find us."

"I am not good at waiting," she said. Which, to him, referred to several different matters.

She was impatient when something needed to be done. She was worse when it came to waiting for something to be done. Worst though was her impatience in passion. He had to look away then, for he was certain the lust would be on his face and she would know what he was thinking about.

"Let us go then," Soren said, urging his horse forward, down the road toward the Bay of Firth and then west toward Hamnavoe, the harbor town. The first hours passed by in silence.

The winds that shaped Orkney whipped around them as they did most days. Very few stands of trees could survive because of the strength of those winds.

He asked them to ease for now and they did. Ran noticed the change.

"Did you do that?" she asked. He nodded. "What else can you do?"

"I have not tried too many things," he admitted. "Not knowing if there are limits or an amount of this power, I did not want to use it up." He slowed his pace. "I can control the winds and clouds and storms. I can make lightning. And I was able to fly with the winds."

"I would have never imagined speaking of such things in a calm manner, but it is how I feel about what has happened to me," Ran said. "I thought that the sea was dragging me along with it, somehow keeping me alive and breathing in it. But then, I held up my hand," she said, doing that. "And I could see through it."

Her hand, once flesh and bone, now turned again to water in the shape it should be. Just as she'd done when Ander lay unconscious on her lap. She was looking at him and did not even realize it. Soren nodded at it and she followed his gaze.

"Like this!" she said, excited at the sight of it.

"How far can that go? When you are not in the sea?" Soren asked. The sound of a rider approaching stopped them from finding out.

"Do you know who it is?" Ran asked, turning around and shielding her eyes from the sun to see.

"Looks like a boy," Soren said. As that boy grew closer, he recognized the lad. "A servant in the bishop's household."

"Mayhap Father Ander sent him?"

"Most likely," Soren answered.

It took but a few minutes for the boy to catch up with them. Soren waved to the young servant and called him over.

"Father Ander sent me to find you," the boy said, out of breath from the riding.

"How did you find us?" Soren asked, waiting for the boy to regain his breath.

"Father sent me to your aunt's cottage and she said you headed in this direction. Toward the lakes."

Soren took out the skin holding water and held it out to the boy. "What is your name?"

"Kelsig," the boy answered, before taking a deep pull of the skin.

"Rolf's son?"

"Aye, Rolf the miller." A good man and one who wanted his son to succeed in life. Serving in the bishop's household could lead to an education and training in the Church. Since Bishop Dolgfinnr answered to the Archbishop of Trondheim in Norway, there was travel and many other opportunities for those in his service.

"So, Kelsig Rolfson, what message did Father Ander send you to tell me? Or did you bring one?"

"He said he would meet you in two days' time on the coast. Near the squares. He said you would know what that meant." Kelsig paused and looked from Soren to Ran and back again. "You do know what that means, do you not?" he asked. When Soren did not respond quickly enough, the boy continued. "Because I do not want to have to come back all this way and tell you."

Ran burst out laughing at the aggrieved tone and

Soren smiled, nodding at Kelsig. "I am glad to tell you that I do understand the message and you will not have to ride to me again."

And, within minutes of reaching them, young Kelsig Rolfson was riding back to Kirkwall. Once he was out of sight, Soren took out the map and opened it, holding it so Ran could see it.

"I know of nothing on the coast there," Soren said. "I have been there and passed by the area by boat and nothing is built there."

"I wonder what the squares are or what they mean?" Ran asked. "If we take this same road north, we will pass between the two lakes and can explore the squares Einar marked there."

Soren agreed. "I know that this circle is the old burial cairn. Then this one would be the stones near the southern edge of Loch Harray, to the east of Loch Stenness."

Stone circles and burial cairns were scattered across all the islands of Orkney. Sometimes the stones were appropriated away for other needs, but the grave sites, some thought to be haunted, were usually left untouched.

"But those squares make no sense to me," Ran said. "Unless something has been built there—barns or storage buildings—since I left?"

"Nay," Soren said. "Well, we will see when we arrive there."

Soren felt the silence between them, as they rode, as they ate, and as they arrived at the burial cairn. Words had never been a problem for them in the past. They'd spent hours talking and planning their life together. And in this moment, he missed that the most. They were facing unknown dangers and she was willing to do that, but she could not simply talk to him.

Ran felt his gaze on her. She knew he watched her closely. As they passed places familiar to them, Soren would begin to say something to her and then stop, realizing how uncomfortable she was. Reminding her of their past only brought the bad memories with any good ones. She hardened her heart dozens of times since their journey began and she suspected she would need to strengthen her resolve in the matter of Soren Thorson many, many more times before they parted ways.

As they would need to.

Whether or not they were able to return to their lives after they rescued her father and saw an end to whatever was happening to them, she and Soren could never return to what they had been.

But her body did not or would not hear those words of wisdom and reacted to every touch or glance. When he'd helped her down from her horse and touched her back and arm, her body ached to feel his touch everywhere. When he reached past her to get the sack holding their meal, her breasts ached for his hands to caress them. The worst was the way her mouth watered when he smiled or touched his tongue to the edge of his lower lip.

All those nights of pain and heartbreak suffered would be forgotten in an instant if her body made the decisions.

As they finished their meal and rode toward the first of the stone circles on Einar's map—near the southernmost part of Loch Stenness—a sense of unease filled her. The horses felt something too and became skittish as the distance between them and the stones decreased.

"Why are they so disturbed?" she asked, looking around the area for the cause. No one else approached. No animals were there. The sky was clear and Soren kept the strong winds under control. "I see nothing."

"But you feel it as well?" he asked.

The low humming. The slight vibration from below the ground and even through the air. She nodded. "I hear something. You?"

"Aye. Like the buzzing of thousands of bees or insects. Let us move closer and see if it changes."

The horses balked when they urged them forward, so Soren suggested leaving them there, closer to the road, and that they approach on foot. As Ran adjusted her cloak, she saw Soren remove a sword from his pack. She raised an eyebrow as he slid it into a scabbard on his belt and walked to the edge of the field where the stones stood.

Ran had a dagger inside her boot for protection, but she wondered if those weapons could fight against the evil that Father Ander spoke of. They made their way across the empty field to the slight rising where the huge stones sat in a sort of circle. Though the reasons and uses of such things had been lost in the passage of time, they never ceased to impress her.

These stones by Loch Stenness were the tallest in the area, taller even than the ones farther up the road called Brodgar's Ring. Stories told that several stones had been toppled and taken in pieces so that only eight of the original eleven stones remained in place. Smaller ones lay inside the circle, in the center of it. Looking back across the distance, she could see the burial cairn they'd passed and several other stones, separated but close enough that she knew they were somehow connected.

"I wonder what these were for?" she asked aloud. Walking around the stones, she looked for any markings and found none.

"Legends are all the explanation we have," Soren said. "Some have noticed that they align with the sunrise on the solstice. Others claim they are ancient temples." He ran his hands over the surface of the one closest to him as he walked past it and she had to look away. "I see nothing on the stones."

"Nor I," she said, following him into the center of the circle. She could see an indentation in the ground, but no other sign of Einar's knowledge or presence. "Should we ride on? Look elsewhere?"

Soren pulled the map out and held it up before them.

"There are some squares in that field, between here and the lake. Come. We can search before we leave."

When she stepped into a boggy spot in the field, Soren held out his hand to her. Even knowing it was not a good thing to do, she took it and he pulled her free. A few paces later, he did it again, but that time, she noticed, he did not release it. Ran told herself it was necessary. His height and strength would keep her from falling. She told herself many things in the next few minutes as they walked toward the water's edge.

And when he released her, she told herself she had not enjoyed the feeling of his hand, his skin, against hers and knew it for the lie it was. They found nothing in the area of the squares on the map, with the exception of a strange vibration from the ground and the voices.

"Do you hear that?" she asked, walking toward the sounds. "Whispers."

"The voices you hear when the sea calls you?" he asked. "I hear nothing more than the buzzing."

"This is different, lower in tone and quieter than the sea. The sea sounds like happy children, chattering my name."

When she glanced at him, Ran saw his curiosity. "It's how they sound when I am with them." Walking toward this new sound, she realized it came from the lake. Leaning over, she put her hand into the water of the lake and listened. At the touch of the water, the voices began, pulling her toward them and the lake. But these voices, this voice, was dark and dangerous.

Ran. Daughter of the sea. Daughter of the waters.

All the waters heed your call.

I need you. Help me.

It was only when Soren wrapped his arms around her and pulled her back that she realized that something was wrong.

"What happened?" she asked, pushing her hair from her face and facing Soren.

"You were moaning, as in pain. And then you were being pulled into the lake." He released her then and she stumbled. Grabbing her, he lifted her into his arms and carried her out of the field away from the water. "You did not change to water. Something was pulling you in and you were fighting it."

With his long paces, they were back on the road quickly.

"Ran, I am sorry," he said as he placed her on her feet. "I felt the danger. I had to stop you." He stepped away, putting space between them. "Otherwise, I would not have touched you."

Ran needed to tell him something. A warning. Something was . . . wrong. She did not know she was shaking until he took her by the shoulders once more. "What ails you, Ran?"

Her teeth chattered and he wrapped her cloak more tightly around her. She could not put into words what she'd felt as she put her hand in the water. Something was wrong with the water.

"Something . . . I touched . . . Wrong . . ."

A shock traced a path through her then, as she realized what had happened. The dark voice echoed in her mind like a siren's call, forcing her to move.

"We need to get away from here, Soren," she said as she pulled the reins of her horse free from under the rock where Soren had secured them. "We must leave now."

Soren put his hands out and helped her mount quickly. Securing his sword, he was on his horse and leading the other one that carried their supplies a second later. They followed the road until it narrowed where the two lakes almost met. She sent out a plea to the water to separate and let them pass.

When Soren stared at her, she nodded and he led them across the strip of now-dry land. As they approached Brodgar's Ring, the bad feeling eased and Ran felt as though she could take a breath without shaking. Soren eased the pace and brought them to a halt. He climbed down from his horse and walked to her.

"Are you well now, Ran? Can you tell me what happened?" he asked. He let out a breath and dragged his hands through his hair. She'd seen him do that same motion hundreds of times in the past; it meant he was worried. His eyes looked haunted when he said his next words. "I thought I had lost . . . you . . . again."

From the pauses, though, she was certain he was thinking of a different woman. The other woman he'd lost. The one who had fallen or jumped off the cliff not far from here. She cleared her throat and met his gaze.

"I felt evil, Soren. I heard evil," she whispered. "It is not coming. It is already here."

CHAPTER 11

Soren believed her.

It took but one look at the intensity in her eyes, the paleness of her skin or the shaking of her hands to know Ran truly believed it, too. She was not a woman given to histrionics. When she'd discovered what her father wanted her to see—Soren and Aslaug naked in bed together—she had simply studied him for a very long moment and then walked out. And he'd never heard about her reacting with tears or an emotional collapse.

Ran evaluated every person, every situation, with a cool, clear look. If she said that she had touched and heard this evil, he believed her. The sight of her being pulled into the dark water was enough to prove it to him.

For a moment, he had seen something else. Someone else.

Aslaug.

Had she leaned over, reaching for something, and slipped, as they'd told everyone? Or had she been pulled over the side by the lure of evil? Or desperation?

He shook off these heavy thoughts and looked at

Ran now that they'd stopped. The sun had begun its slide down toward night and they needed shelter. Ran needed shelter. Soren had planned to stay with a friend farther up the road but he did not think Ran would make it that far now. There was a small shepherd's hut on the other side of the stones, near the numerous cairns that lay around Brodgar's Ring.

The winds whirled above and around them, whipping their cloaks and sending dust and dirt at them in waves. Something was indeed wrong here and now.

"Come. We will seek shelter there," he said, pointing off in the distance.

He gathered his reins and hers and walked the three horses across the rising to the hut. She did not fight him on it; indeed, she gave little reaction at all. The fear sat deep in her eyes now. The winds tried to rise against them now, and it took more concentration to make them ease their force. By the time they arrived at the small shelter, Soren wondered if something was happening to his powers.

He cleared out the hut and tossed a thick blanket on the ground. Helping Ran down, he settled her there and then saw to the animals. Soren offered her the skin filled with ale, but she refused it. Once he saw to setting things in place and had them in a covered place, he sat next to her. Taking a breath and letting it out, he told the winds to protect them.

This time, they obeyed him without resistance. Strange that.

"I had planned to reach Digby's farm before stopping for the night," he explained. "You do not look as though you could ride much farther."

"D-D-Digby?" she stuttered out.

"His father passed just over a year ago and Digby inherited the farm," he told her. "I am surprised that Einar did not tell you that."

"Are you angry that he wrote to me?" she asked, shifting to face him in the growing twilight.

"Nay. Just surprised. The first truly in what looks to be a long series of surprises about my grandfather."

"Sometimes, people are simply not who we think they are," Ran said softly.

"That sounds like an accusation." The words were out before he could stop them. It was a subject he did not want to discuss. It was a topic that could only cause trouble. More trouble than they already had before them. He shook his head. "That is a topic for another day."

She watched him without responding and then stared off as the winds blew some distance away.

"We have not discussed how we will free my father from that man." Ran met his gaze. "If he serves the evil I felt in that water, we may not be able to rescue him."

He wanted to take her in his arms and hold her. To ease her fears or at least hold them at bay. But he could do neither. Not now. Not here. *Not yet.*

"I know what I saw. Tell me what you heard and felt."

Ran gathered her legs up under her skirts and rubbed her hands on the fabric as if to remove some dirt or soil from them.

"The words were similar to what the sea says to me. *Daughter of the sea.* Telling me the water heeds my commands." She shook her head and shivered. "The tone of the words carried an ominous feel. That was the first warning I had that it was not the sea speaking to me."

"Is that when you moaned?" The sound of it terrified him for it came from the depths of her soul. Worse than the moan of someone in pain, this sound was one of desolation and desperation . . . and hopelessness. Soren hoped he'd never hear such a thing again, but suspected he would.

"The voice asked me to help them. They said they needed me."

"They? More than one, like the voices you hear in the sea?" He always heard the winds as a group, never just one voice.

"At first, it sounded like a woman's voice, and then a man spoke as well. Then, well, then I could not tell. They blended together and begged me to help them . . . her."

"Could it have been your father's voice? Or did they say how you could help them? Or her?" he probed.

"Nay," she said. Then she shook her head. "Nay, not him. And they did not say what they needed in words," she explained. "I could sense that they are trapped. That they could not come to me so I needed to go to them."

"Go . . . ?" he began until she held up her hand and shrugged.

"I know not. Just that they needed my help."

He thought on her explanation and hoped Ander would catch up with them sooner than the two days hence he'd said. Surely he would give good counsel about what these strange things meant. Before he could ask another question, she shook her head.

"It was one voice. A woman's voice. Distorted somehow, mayhap by the water? And the pain she suffers being imprisoned." She let out a breath filled with frustration and confusion. "I hope Father Ander has found out more about all of this."

He nodded and watched as she turned and leaned against the wooden frame of the hut, exhausted by what had happened. The sun was setting quickly and the air grew colder. Between the shelter and their nearness and the lack of cold wind, they would not be too uncomfortable through the night. A fire would have helped, but the ground and grass were too damp to sustain one, and he had nothing to burn as fuel.

"She said something else. Something I have suspected but this is all so new and strange," Ran said. She sat up once more. "The voice said *all the waters heed my call.* All the waters."

"You already know that. You do that." He knew it. He'd seen it as he watched her become flesh and blood from the window of the tower. "You made the water leave your garments."

"I did." She shifted around. "I did!"

"If you doubt your abilities, attempt something now. Make the water leave where we sit before our blanket and our arses are wet," he suggested.

Before the words had finished being spoken, the earth beneath them dried out. He smiled and nodded at her. So little effort and so much power. Soren could feel it just before she used it. Why could he feel it?

"So, you can. You already have more experience at this than I do," he admitted. "You found your father by asking the water. You became the water. You can command the water even if it's not the sea or river or lake."

"I need to find out if my father is still well. That man cannot be happy that he is being prevented from reaching the Mainland."

"Let me go. He might have sensed you because of your connection to your father. I have none," he said, standing. At her nod and as she watched, he let go of his human form with but a thought, becoming the wind.

Take me.

Take me to Svein Ragnarson.

The voices began, welcoming him and guiding him higher into the night's sky as he became part of them. His body changed to currents of air. He marveled at the view he had of the sun setting in the west as he rose higher and higher. The appearance of the land below was nothing that he could have predicted. Here and there, a fire burned or a croft or cottage could be seen. Lochs and rivers reflected back the light of the now-rising half-moon.

In a shorter time than could be possible for a man, they soared over the water separating the mainland from Rousay, which lay in almost complete darkness. He continued crossing that island then a bigger expanse of water until he reached Westray.

Slower now. Once across the strait, he slowed even more and flew lower. If this man, this minion of evil, could sense another with power, could Soren sense him as well?

Suddenly, Soren felt the air change around him. It

grew thicker, denser somehow. And hotter. Waves of heat washed over him. The winds that carried him chattered, whispering warnings in their hissing voices.

Danger, Stormblood.

Caution, Soren, son of the storms.

The fireblood. Danger.

He stopped and searched the area below him. In the distance, off the shores of Westray, sat four ships. Even with their sails open, they did not move.

"If you do not release my ships, Stormblood, I will burn her father bit by bit." The voice came out of nowhere and struck him as though a blow. "My sacrifices will not go unanswered and you and the waterblood will pay for this. And their deaths."

Soren looked down on the beach of Papa Westray, the isle closest to the ships, and was horrified to see piles of half-burned bodies. And a line of men, immobilized somehow, awaiting the same fate. There, watching it all and unable to stop it, from his expression, stood Svein, Ran's father.

So, the man knew that Svein was Ran's father. And was not above using that as leverage, though he suspected it would be more effective against Ran than Svein.

"Speak to me, Stormblood. Do not run away like the woman, hiding behind this new form. Speak to me like a man of honor does." His voice now was cultured and refined. He spoke in Norn but with the accent of a foreigner. A nobleman?

"Stop the burning," Soren said, shocked that he could speak in this manner, "and I will meet with you." He waited to see if his challenge would be answered.

The fire went out, gone in an instant. With a flick of

his hand, the men waiting roused and another flick saw them scatter back toward the ships. The winds put Soren down on the beach and he was human again.

Svein lost any color he still retained as he saw to whom the man had been talking. Most likely because he knew his chance for mercy at the hands of Soren Thorson was less than this stranger offered.

"Who are you?" he asked.

"I am Hugh de Gifford, councilor to the late King Alexander of Scotland," the fireblood said. "I come on another's business though."

"Late king?"

"Alas, the king died several weeks ago. A fall from his horse." The sarcasm in his voice told Soren that the manner of the king's death was not something as simple as the fall from a horse. "His death is only a part of this plan," de Gifford said, speaking boldly. "You can join me and reap the rewards, Stormblood."

"How do you know me?" Soren asked.

"I know many things, Stormblood. You carry the winds within you. You can command storms and the sky and the lightning. You bear its mark on your arm," the nobleman said. Holding his own arm out, he continued. "As I bear the mark of my power, my goddess."

Flames. Two flames burned and melted together only to re-form and do it again. Soren could feel the heat of it and then his own mark answered, the bolt sizzling in and on and under his skin. He hissed in pain and de Gifford smiled.

"It can be pleasurable if you allow it to be."

As Soren watched, the flames grew larger and burned the skin around them; the scent of searing flesh filled the air. Soren grimaced at the smell while de Gifford seemed to enjoy it. His face wore the expression of arousal.

"Nay? Mayhap the release of your power will give you that pleasure?" With those words, de Gifford narrowed his gaze on Soren and sent a fireball at him.

All he could think in that moment was *nay*. The winds swirled around him and pushed the fireball back. At the same time, his fingers and hands heated and he lifted them, aiming at the fire. A bolt of lightning struck the fire, the ensuing explosion lit the whole beach and the crash of it rumbled out across the sound and to the other island. If he thought de Gifford would be alarmed, he was wrong. The man stood, arms across his chest, nodding.

"Feel it race through your body, your blood. Feel it in your flesh," he urged in a smooth voice that echoed inside his thoughts somehow. "Power is pleasure," he said.

For a moment, Soren felt it as he described. The lightning came not just from his hands, but from deep within him. In his blood. It pushed power throughout his body; his flesh reacted. Then he remembered the sight that had greeted him—a certain sign of power abused.

"Why are you here?" Soren asked, letting the power calm. "What do you seek?" He knew part of it but wanted de Gifford to declare it to him.

"Our power comes from the old gods and goddesses—you know that, do you not?" Soren nodded. "My family knew the goddess would return and has prepared for generations for this day. I have been bred to carry her power, to open her way, back into the world."

So, just as his grandfather had known, other families did as well. If only his grandfather had shared the knowledge sooner.

"I seek a circle of stones," de Gifford said.

"There are many here in Orkney. Every island has them. The ancient people who lived here built many of them."

"Ah, but only one is the doorway to be opened, Stormblood," the man said. "I seek the true one amongst those built to hide and deceive."

"Then go in peace to find your circle," Soren said, goading the man for more information.

"I also need the two gatekeepers' help," de Gifford admitted. "Here in Orkney, it is the stormblood and the waterblood who hold the key." He approached Soren. "Join me. Be at my side when the goddess returns. She will reward her faithful ones."

Something was inside his mind, pushing him, pushing him to accept this offer. He could not breathe now. Pain exploded in his head.

"Even as she punishes those who do not serve her," he said, staring into Soren's eyes. The pain grew more with each passing moment, until Soren broke free with one thought.

Ran.

He became the winds and tore away from the fireblood. De Gifford screamed out in anger and set everything on the beach and the surrounding area on fire.

"You will come to me. She will come to me," he shouted as Soren flew higher. "Chaela will be served!"

Some force rippled through the air as de Gifford screamed out the name of the one he served. The name had its own power.

After sending a message to Svein on the whispering winds, Soren raced back across the sea and the islands to Ran. Forming his body before her, he met her startled gaze and knelt before her.

"'Tis worse than we thought, much worse," he said.

Hugh tried to keep hold of the stormblood, but he could not. His powers lessened day by day because for too long he was too far away from a place where he could commune with the goddess. If he was to defeat the Warriors of Destiny and bring these two to his side, he needed to find a place that opened to the void.

The one thing working in his favor was that the gatekeepers here were so new to their powers that they still thought in human ways. That would slow them down and give him time to do what he must do. He turned and walked to Svein.

"You will take me to the place where they are," he ordered. Pushing his will into the human, he repeated the order. "You will take me there."

Svein blinked several times and moaned as the pain of resisting heightened. Hugh pushed again and once more until blood began to drip from the man's nose and eyes.

"Why do you resist so?" he asked, walking up to him. Staring into his bloody gaze, Hugh asked again. "To resist is pain and death, human. I can cause it. You have seen it, so doubt not my intention. So why do you resist my wishes?" He needed this man or Hugh would have caused his head to explode as he usually did to those who disobeyed.

"Ran," Svein whispered.

The same word that the stormblood had uttered before he escaped. But it was not a word, was it? It was a name.

"Your daughter?" he asked. Svein could only close his eyes. De Gifford released him and the man fell to the sands, gasping for air and in agony.

Hugh smiled. Both Svein and the stormblood were linked to the waterblood—one by blood, the other by desire. He'd felt that connection as soon as the stormblood realized the pleasure in exercising his power. Controlling her would be much easier now that he understood the stormblood's weakness.

He had no doubt that the winds and sea would release the ships momentarily, just as he did not doubt that Svein would take him to the island where the other bloods were. He closed his eyes and spread his senses out, seeking the other Warriors who would oppose him. Ripples on the edges of his senses warned of their approach.

"Take him to his men, Eudes. We will leave as soon as the winds and sea let go of their hold on the ships."

Take us to your home, he ordered with a thought. *Directly there*, he pushed.

Blood gushed from Svein's head. Hugh cared not. As long as someone could hold him up and the man could mumble, he was of use. As soon as his usefulness ended, so would his life.

The thought of so much destruction and death ahead brightened Hugh's mood. Knowing that he would control the storm and seas in a very short time made him smile.

Chaela, I will free you soon, my Goddess, he whispered. Soon.

CHAPTER 12

"I fear we must release the ships, Ran," Soren said to her as he knelt before her. "He is torturing innocent men until we let him go his way."

"And my father? Does he yet live?" she asked, hoping their actions had not resulted in his death along with the others.

"He lives. The man, Lord Hugh de Gifford, knows you are Svein's daughter." Soren took her hands and she did not resist. He had some terrible news to tell her, she knew. "He will keep Svein alive as long as there is a use for him. At this moment, his usefulness is related to you, Ran."

"So he stays alive as long as Hugh de Gifford thinks to control me through him?"

Soren confirmed her words with a nod.

Ran had seen the way men worked and how men of power controlled. Watching as her father plied his business over the last two years had exposed her to the corruption and dealings of men who wanted something. If she had been naive when she'd left, she did not remain that way for long. It was the type of marriage in which she would find herself, if they all survived.

The truth of the matter sank into her soul. Unless they could come up with a way to defeat this evil man and the entity he served, her father would die. Chances were that he would die before they could defeat Hugh. The tears began before she realized it.

Soren reached out as though to wipe them but he stopped himself. Instead he lifted the hem of her cloak and handed it to her to use.

"What do we do now, Soren? Do we give in to this evil and keep my father alive, knowing we endanger so many more by doing so?" she asked. Soren looked startled by her words.

"I think he will be busy searching for the stone circle he believes is here in Orkney. Releasing the ships and him gives us time to find a way to stop them. If it is your intention to do that?"

He watched her with those deep, blue eyes, waiting for her answer. Two years ago, that intense stare would have melted her heart and given him whatever he wanted of her. But now, now she wondered what it meant.

"Do we have a choice?" she asked him. "These powers did not just appear for no reason. If we believe the story Father Ander found, we are part of a group of people who can stop this evil. The only ones who can." She let out a sigh.

Just weeks ago, her intention had been to have a short visit home before leaving on the journey to a new land, a marriage and a new life. At that time, everything in her life was settled and the pain of the past eased for the first time in two years.

Now, she sat here looking at the one man she could not trust being asked to put her trust in him and in some ancient plan begun eons ago. If there was an old god in charge of this, it had to be Loki, the Norse trickster god who disrupted with guile and deception.

"Are you ready to loose the winds and I will release him from the sea's grasp?" she asked, climbing to her feet with his help. Ran glanced around the area. "I know not how to influence the sea without being near it or in it," she admitted.

"The evil one said you command all the water," Soren said. "So the water that hides in the ground and runs to the lakes and sea is also yours to control. Give your order and I will give mine."

Release the ships, she said in her thoughts as she closed her eyes. *Release my father's ships.*

After a few minutes of silence, she opened her eyes and found Soren staring at her. The expression she recognized. Two years might have passed, but she knew that look and what it meant. And the worst thing was that she was certain she returned it.

Oh God, how she wanted him! Whether it was more intense because of the danger or if she'd simply lied to herself all along, she knew now that she wanted him with every muscle and fiber in her body. Ran could imagine what would happen if she gave in—the passion between them would soar and be that much stronger and more explosive for their time apart. Her body ached for him. Her body readied for him. Her body . . .

She stumbled back away, making the next step impossible. Ran wiped her lips even though there was no kiss to wipe away. Passion and its play were not difficult for them. Nay, their bodies spoke the same language from the first time they'd touched. Lying with Soren had been a joyful thing. And though her body would be exhausted and sometimes sore from his strength and relentless bed play, it would welcome him in the next instant.

It could not happen. It could not happen again.

"I need . . . my . . . from the pack," she stuttered as she walked away from him and over to where the horses were. Walking anywhere but into his embrace. He let her go but his eyes followed her every step. She moved over to the packs and found hers, tugging the ties loose and looking inside it.

For nothing. For anything. She looked for something that would give her an opportunity to regain control over her wayward self. How was she going to manage being so close to him, risking everything at his side, and not give in to the terrible, complete need for him?

"Do you need help?" Soren called out.

"Nay," she said, "I have found it." She pulled a woolen blanket from the pack and walked back to the hut. Unfolding it, she tossed it on the one they were sitting on. "A bit more if we're to sleep on it," she explained.

"Go ahead then," Soren said, pointing to the spot sheltered by the wooden frame. "I will watch for a while."

"Are we in danger?" she asked.

"I think not, but I would rather be certain. Go. Rest."

When she finally was able to look at him directly, she recognized his own discomfort in this situation. At his friend's farm, he could have slept in a separate place from her. Now, they would pass the night in close confines. She nodded and sought a place on the blankets while he stood outside.

"Soren?"

"Aye?"

"What will we do next?" she asked. They needed a plan, something that made sense.

"De Gifford does not know where the circle is," he said. "He said something about it being hidden from sight. It being disguised by the other circles built to hide its location."

Lying on her back, she thought on it. "So it would not be the ones here then?"

"I think not, but there are other places marked on my grandfather's drawing."

"Or in clues he left at those places?"

"Aye. So I think we should continue to search as we'd planned. And when we meet Ander at the coast, he may have more answers for us."

"I agree," she said.

She sank back into the silence, watching by the light of the half-moon as he paced slowly between the hut and the lake. His movements, even paces back and forth, eased her into a sleep she did not think she would get. Sometime in the night, he crept into the shelter and lay down on the blanket at her side, close but not touching at all.

The next thing she knew, Ran opened her eyes and found Soren watching her sleep. His gaze was on her mouth then and she heard him groan when she licked across the bottom lip in reaction. It mattered not, she repeated to herself.

They were different people now, with different lives.

So why did she pray he would kiss her?

"Ran," he whispered in that tone she loved.

Mayhap one kiss would prove it was over? Mayhap one kiss would release the tension and let her move on? Even knowing she was lying to herself, she took the next step.

"Kiss me, Soren."

And he did.

The only thing it proved was how foolish she truly was.

Soren touched their mouths together, sliding his over hers.

But then she leaned in and opened to him.

Like a man dying of thirst, he drank her in. If his hand moved to her waist and drew her closer, he remembered not. If she reached up to take hold of his shoulders, he could not tell. All Soren knew was that she was in his arms.

He tasted her, slid his tongue inside her mouth and teased hers until she touched him back. The kiss changed from touch to possession and he moved on top of her to show her that he'd not forgotten anything of their passion.

She opened to him, sucking on his tongue now and cupping his arse as he ground into her. Her thighs welcomed him and he eased between them, sinking in close to her. The fabric of her garments prevented him from anything more intimate, but she shifted her leg so that his cock was rubbing her deeply.

His body hardened. Hell, he'd been erect since the first time he'd seen her in the marketplace. Now, though, his flesh thickened and readied and he prayed for her touch there.

When Ran moved her hands up to tangle in his hair, pulling his mouth to hers, Soren cupped her breasts, sliding his thumbs over the nipples he knew were dark pink and full. She arched against him, causing a friction between their bodies where his cock touched her. Her nipples were always so sensitive and her body responded to his touch as it always had.

A moment later, she pushed at him and they rolled so that she lay on top of him. Straddling his hips, she sat back and reached up to gather her hair out of their way. It made her back arch and her breasts angled right into his waiting hands. Her breasts pleased him, filling his hands and responding to every caress. Her nipples hardened—he could feel them through the gown she wore—so he pleasured them.

He wanted her mouth. He wanted her tongue in his mouth. Sliding his hands around her, he drew her down to him—hair be damned. She placed her hands on either side of his head and balanced there, kissing him, kissing him back, sucking on his tongue.

Then, as quickly as it had begun, it ended.

Ran pulled herself up, still sitting over his cock, and stared at him. Shaking her head, she slid off him to sit at his side. His erect flesh no secret, it pulsed within his breeches as she moved away. Soren took in several deep breaths, fighting the urge, the urges, his body was screaming about.

"I . . ." Ran began. "It cannot be. This"—she glanced at his cock, which pulsed under her gaze— "cannot happen between us."

He wanted to ease her feelings and confusion, but he had no words to offer about that. The only thing standing in their way was her father. And considering that Svein needed Soren's ungodly help, he doubted Svein would object at all. More likely, Svein would give Ran to him in exchange for his help if he asked for her. Nothing was more important to Svein Ragnarson than himself.

"Go to sleep, Ran," he said, climbing to his feet. He would get no more rest this night so he walked over to the lake's edge and sat there, trying to convince his body that there would be no more of her.

It took a long time for his body to accept the truth of it and to calm. The sun's light crept over the southeastern horizon then and Soren knew that another day of torment was just beginning. He would pay for his sins one way or another.

Marcus stood near the front of the ship, watching as the sun rose in the east and greeting it with prayers he knew so well. He felt Aislinn at his side as he finished his prayers. With a final word of praise, he turned to face her.

"Aislinn," he said. "Are you well?"

She nodded and smiled. "I had the most interesting dream, Marcus. You will not believe what happened."

So little in these last days and weeks had been good, and from her expression and her light tone of voice, he suspected this bit of news would bring all of them joy.

Marcus took her hands in his and nodded. "Tell me. Was it a prophecy?"

"I met another priest. He lives here on Orkney. He awaits us in the bay where we will arrive."

"A priest?" Marcus asked.

William approached, but waited a short distance from them until he was invited closer. The warblood was always respectful of the conversations between the priests. "Aislinn has seen a priest, already on Orkney."

"Aislinn, what did you learn of him?" William asked. Aislinn's dreamwalking had saved Brienne's life and William had been part of it, so he respected that, too. "Did you send someone on ahead, Marcus?"

"Nay. I know of none in our line here." He and William looked at Aislinn for an explanation.

"He did not know until the mark rose and the dreams began," she explained. "And, Marcus, he is a priest in the Church. The Church of Rome."

"How can that be?" William asked before Marcus could. William had been raised in that faith. "Catholic priests are not usually open to heresy."

In lands where the Church ruled, talk of other gods or other faiths brought up charges of heresy, damning anyone accused of that to torture and a fiery death.

"I saw him. He wears the robe and cross and his hair is cut in the manner of a priest. He said his name is Ander. Father Ander."

He and William exchanged glances and shrugged. William's own faith had been tested and shifted from the belief in one God to the possibility of others in this endeavor.

"He knows both of them. The stormblood and the waterblood are known to him and their powers are rising."

Aislinn's dreams and prophecies had pointed them north to Orkney and to the one island called the Mainland. But they expected to go and search for signs of the stormblood and waterblood. Now, though, this priest had given her wonderful news. Marcus shook off his shock first and nodded.

"Gods be praised!" Marcus called out. The others gathered around them. "We have a brethren priest awaiting us ahead."

The excitement spread and it brought about a lifting of spirits that they all needed. William even called to the other ships and told them. The winds were kind to them and soon they approached the northwest corner of the main island. With the knowledge and instructions given in her dreams, Aislinn was able to direct them to the bay closest to where Ander would await them.

By afternoon, the ships approached as closely as they could and anchored. It took several more hours to unload the people, horses, supplies and weapons. By dark, the encampment was set up and they awaited the arrival of their newest priest.

CHAPTER 13

The only good thing about that day was that the weather was fair. Lack of sleep and the need to hold his control in a tight grip made him bad-tempered throughout the day. Ran never looked askance or commented, but she knew to give him some distance this day.

It did not matter, truly, whether she was near or far, he could not get her out of his mind. They split apart, each going in a different direction around Brodgar's ring of stones, looking for signs or clues. But every time he glanced over at her, she was looking at him. They spent the morning examining each of the more than thirty stones, and then searched the cairns that lay in all directions around the circle. Most of the cairns were simple mounds or small hills with no stones or places to leave clues. Some, a very few, had flat stones or raised ones nearby.

They shared a simple meal and headed north again. It would take a few hours to reach the coast and the place designated by Ander. How the priest was traveling there, he knew not, but he worried not about that.

If Ander said he would meet them, he would. As they approached the Loch of Skaill, they found Ander waiting for them on the main road to the bay called by the same name.

"My friends," the priest called out.

"Ander," Soren greeted him.

"Father," Ran said.

"Have you found any clues left behind by Einar?" Ander asked, as he fell in with them.

"None," Soren answered. "Though we have learned much since we saw you last."

As they rode past the loch, Soren and Ran explained what had happened in their encounter with Hugh de Gifford and what he was searching for. Ander seemed at ease with everything they told him, which disturbed Soren in some manner.

"Should you not object to such things, Ander? Or tell us the cost to our immortal souls for pursuing knowledge of false gods?" he asked finally.

"In my travels and work for the bishop, I have seen and read and learned many things, Soren. I have learned that it is the sacred duty of good people to battle evil whenever and however they encounter it. It is what God's Son teaches us. And if our Almighty Father allows there to exist other lesser deities or beings to aid in His cause and is not threatened by their presence, who am I to tell Him otherwise?"

Soren considered the words of explanation for a minute and could not decide if Ander was jesting or not. Ran shrugged, unwilling to argue with the priest.

"When you say it in that manner, it makes sense," he admitted.

"Well, my friend, I heard your words, declaring the powers you now have, but I admit that I would be more comfortable if I witnessed it."

"You wish to see a display, Ander?" Soren asked.

"You saw my hand change, Father," Ran said.

"Ah, I did. But it was as I lay delirious. I may have dreamt it."

"O ye of little faith," Soren muttered as he looked to Ran. She nodded and walked to the edge of the loch. He waited for her to go first.

In an instant, Ran became water. Then she let her form go and seeped into the ground under her feet. A minute later, she rose out of the surface of the loch and took her human shape once more. When she reached his side, Ander nodded at him. As he considered what to do, he noticed that the priest kept poking Ran as though testing her to see if she was real.

Soren let go of his body and changed into a cloud. Whirling around them, he floated up above them. He spread out in a thin layer and then gathered again, changing to wind in a moment. Ander let out a laugh, appreciating the sight before him. As he soared around them, Soren saw something he could not have seen from the ground.

Behind a small hill and outcropping of rocks, four people stood—two men and two women. He dropped to the ground behind them and took his human shape before they turned around. His hands tingled as the lightning built within them.

"Who are you?" he called out.

His voice sounded like thunder as he spoke. Ander and Ran rushed to his side. The priest reached out to stop him from casting a bolt at them. But one man, the larger man who was clearly a warrior, changed into something else as he sensed the threat of Soren's power. Something even larger. Something blue. If Soren's voice was like thunder, this creature's was an explosion and war cry in one. He prepared to charge Soren but was stopped when one of the women—one who glowed in the hot metal orange of fire—stepped in front of him and placed her hand on his arm, calling him by name.

"William, he is a friend, not a threat," she said. The creature growled loudly and seemed to grumble as he stepped back, allowing the woman forward.

"I am Brienne of Yester," she said. "We mean you no harm, Stormblood." She glanced over at the creature and he changed back into the warrior. A blue haze outlined the muscular body of a trained fighter. A knight mayhap? "This is my husband, William de Brus," she said. "Lately of Scotland."

"Why were you hiding here?" Soren asked, lowering his hands and letting the lightning go back into his blood.

"That was my idea, Soren. I wanted them to see you and meet you. And this is Aislinn and Marcus, their priests," Ander explained.

A woman priest? Soren's shock must have shown, for the young woman stepped closer and said something only to him. "The Old Ones did not worry over women serving them like this new one seems to," she said.

Soren looked at the much older man and nodded in greeting. Ander introduced Ran and Soren by their names and heard the priests whisper "Waterblood" and "Stormblood" in wonderment and awe.

"Will you return with us to our encampment so that we might speak?" Brienne asked them.

Soren remembered part of the story Ander told him about the bloodlines and their powers. He looked at each one, knowing that William must be the warblood, and Aislinn and Marcus already acknowledged their priesthood. Staring at Brienne, he tried to figure out if she could be fire, the one linked to the war hammer on the drawing. The color around her remained aglow in the shades of fire.

And if she was, was she related somehow to the fireblood they'd met? The one holding Svein prisoner and doing unspeakable things to others? As though she'd read his thoughts, she held out her arm and tugged her sleeve out of the way.

Two flames, entwined, burning.

"Fireblood," Soren said.

"We have met the other one," Ran said, stepping closer to look at the mark. "Hugh de Gifford."

At the name, the warblood came out once more, growling and pulling Brienne behind him. "De Gifford," the blue berserker growled. Though Ran startled at the sight and sound, she did not move away.

"You have?" Aislinn, Marcus and Brienne asked in one voice.

"He has my father. And his ships," Ran admitted.

Ander stepped in and put up his hand.

"We should not discuss such matters on the open road. Soren, Ran, come back to the camp with us and we can discuss all manner of subjects."

"With us?" Soren asked.

"I was led to them by dreams, Soren," Ander admitted in a quiet voice. "I can explain."

Although he was leery of going with these strangers, Ander's vouching for them convinced him. Ran nodded her agreement and they waited for them to retrieve their horses.

In little time, they crossed over the last hill before reaching the shore and Soren blinked several times before believing the number of men, fighting men and others on that beach.

Suddenly, it was not the two or three of them fighting this great evil and her minions. It was a large number of trained fighting men, priests and others involved.

Soren smiled at Ran then, relieved that she might not be placed in the danger that Ingeborg warned him about.

"They might even know more than Einar," he whispered to her, as they walked through the area, greeting people as they passed.

"At least they can tell us more," she replied, more at ease now than she had been all day.

They joined a small group made up of, as it turned out, the leaders of this army against evil. In addition to the fireblood and warblood, there were the priests and a few other fighters—human warriors—considered as the leaders. Everyone in the camp followed their orders, but Ran was fascinated by their attitude toward the young woman priest.

It was clear to see that they favored her. As Aislinn passed, everyone greeted her. They asked her questions. They all tried to find a way to speak to her. She was held in esteem, that much was apparent to Ran as they walked through the camp.

Questions filled her mind as they gathered to speak. Even as introductions were being made, Ran tried to concentrate on them, rather than the man who remained close at her side now.

Last night's folly made the light of morning very uncomfortable for her, for them. Part of her wanted nothing more than to dissolve into the ground and spend the day with the sea and rivers instead of facing Soren. Now, surrounded by dozens of others, it was easier not to look at him. Not to blush in embarrassment for what she'd said and, worse, what she'd done with him. To be amongst others made it possible to pretend it had not happened.

But, if they were to give her father and his men, many of whom she'd grown up with or sailed with, a chance at survival, she needed to learn more about this nobleman who served an ancient evil.

"Aislinn, do you want to speak first?" William asked.

"You must be overwhelmed by all of this, all of us," the lovely young woman said. Her eyes seemed to glow and there was a faint color, like moonlight, around her. "Marcus and I and the other priests, save yours"— she nodded at Ander—"have lived apart on a small island off the southwest of Scotland for a long time. We have studied the ancient legends and Old Ones. We worship them in man's place, keeping the rituals alive."

"Aislinn is the strongest seer ever to come amongst us," Marcus added. "Some months ago, her dreams grew stronger and more prophetic. Then one night, our own blood rose, as did our marks, and we knew the evil one was trying to reenter the world."

"That is the story I told you," Ander added. "I found many more versions of that same one in other books. It is an ancient battle fought many times."

"But how is this all possible?" Soren asked as he took her hand in his. It was a comforting gesture that felt right to her for now. "You have been trained for this, spent your lives studying. How did we get this power? How did they?" He nodded at Brienne and William.

"My father was bred for it," Brienne said. "His family has remained faithful to the evil one through the centuries."

Ran stared at her and realized the similarities to the nobleman who held her father. The same black hair. The same amber eyes. "Hugh de Gifford is your father?"

"Aye. But my existence and inheritance of the power was an unplanned surprise for him," she explained with a soft glance at her husband. "He tried to pass his power to a noble daughter, but the gods had a different plan."

She was a bastard.

"I was sent by the king to investigate the strange stories. He feared that Hugh de Gifford was involved in sedition. What I found was more, so much more than that," William said softly. He lifted the hand he'd entwined with Brienne's and kissed hers. The love between them was difficult to watch, considering the love lost between her and Soren. She pulled her hand from his.

"I had no idea that I would find Brienne or the power I have or the rest. And we are still learning about our powers," William said and looked at her and Soren.

"Now you are facing the same decision we had to make but know you are not alone."

"Tell us how you discovered the truth," Aislinn said. Soren nodded at Ran.

"I have always lived with the sea, sailed it," Ran said. "Then, on my journey here, I fell from the ship and I heard voices in the sea. When I survived, I knew something was happening but had no idea of what or how." Ran smiled at each as she spoke. They understood the confusion and fear she'd felt.

"Then the mark rose and I knew I was different. When I next saw Soren and could see the aura of color around him, I suspected he was somehow involved."

"How fortuitous that you two were already known to each other," Marcus said.

"And lovers," Brienne said. At Ran's frown, the woman changed her words. "In love."

"Nay!" she protested at the same time Soren did. Standing, she moved away from Soren so there could be no mistake.

"We are not . . ."

"Our families each knew the other," Soren explained. "In Orkney, many families have been here for centuries. Some from even before the Norse took control."

An awkward silence took hold. The men, Ran saw, were clearly uncomfortable. The women, well, their gazes filled with sympathy as they met her eyes.

"I beg your pardon," Brienne said. "I misunderstood your connection and did not mean to speak of such personal things." But the knowing look in her gaze belied her words. As did the exact same one in Aislinn's.

"My grandfather knew about the Old Ones," Soren

said, breaking the tension and while looking at everyone else but Ran. "He had told me stories since I was a child. I did not understand what they were until he passed. That was when things changed for me."

The sadness and loss in his voice tore at her heart. He reached inside his tunic and brought out his last connection to Einar, holding them out to the group. Ander nodded to the other priests.

"He told me that I carried the blood and power of the god of the sky and storms. Taranis, he said. I did not believe him until it was too late to tell him so."

"We have all lost much," William said. "Friends, family, possessions and our lives. All given to this cause. Hugh killed my father to ease his path." William stood then and pulled Brienne to his side. "But we have gained much in this quest. I have gained much," he said. "The question is: will you fight the evil one who attempts to come back to our world and destroy it?"

All Ran had wanted was to marry the man she loved and live the expected life—home, children and contentedness. Ran knew that no matter the choice, no matter her actions, that expected future was already gone, shattered along with her dreams.

"I need to free my father. If you will help me do that, I will do what you need of me," Ran said. She knew the meaning of the sad glances she received. She understood that the odds in this particular gamble were against her father, but the whole endeavor was risky at best and deadly at worst.

Suddenly she could take no more talking. No more powers. No more. Ran turned and walked down to the water's edge, away from all the planning. More confused than the day she'd found out about Soren's betrayal, she crouched down and touched the water, seeking some solace.

Ran had emptied her mind of thoughts and fears as she touched the water. It was as though they accepted all of it and allowed her a moment of peace. The emptiness did not help her sort out her feelings or plans, but it was exactly what she needed.

After some time had passed, she understood that she needed to return to the others and sort through the turmoil, so she thanked the sea and stood up. Turning toward the camp, she found Soren standing a short distance away.

"Do you know how long you have sought the sea for comfort? Whenever you are near it, you touch the water. In a boat or on a ship, you lean over and stare into it. Water has always been in your life."

She walked toward him. "And have storms always been part of your life, Soren?" she asked. Then, before he could reply, she nodded. "Ah, they have. As a farmer, and a sailor before that, storms have always controlled your life. Too much rain or too much wind and the crops fail. The same with sailing. Both too much and too little can harm your efforts."

"True," he said. "But I never could have conceived of something like this. That I could call them forth. I thought myself simply a farmer, with a farmer's life ahead of me. And I was content with that, Ran."

His words matched her thoughts exactly. Again they were in harmony. And yet, not at all.

"Soren, I know that my father's life is most likely forfeit. I know that Hugh de Gifford intends his death."

She walked up to him and met his gaze directly. "But I must try. I must try."

He nodded and looked over her head for a moment, to where the others waited. Ran knew that there had been something between Soren and her father. Something bad. But now, without him, her father stood no chance.

She'd walked out of Soren's life, never expecting to see him again. Ran had asked for no explanations of his side of their sad ending and had given him no chance to offer one. Now, she asked him to help her in something that might even cost his life in addition to hers.

"Your father does not expect my help, Ran. There is ill will between us," he began, still not looking at her.

When she would have pursued what he'd said, he forestalled her with the stubborn jut of his chin and his fierce blue gaze. "I cannot speak of it, but he will think himself forsaken if the decision were left to me."

"And is he forsaken, Soren?"

"Nay," he said on an exhalation. "I will help you, Ran."

Ran knew she would get no more than that from him. His agreement to help was all she needed. She would have told him that she was grateful. That she would find a way to repay him or to show him how much it meant to her.

Somehow.

"I think we need to know where they are. If we loosened our hold on them the night before last, they could be anywhere," Soren said.

It made sense.

"I will go and find them."

"Ran?" Soren touched her arm as she moved past him toward the sea. "Have a care. He is a dangerous man."

As she melted into the sea and sought her father, Ran realized that she did not know if Soren spoke of Hugh de Gifford or her father . . . or both.

She thought it was the latter.

CHAPTER 14

Ran approached the ships slowly this time, trying to observe before moving closer. The ships traveled in an orderly line, coming from Westray and taking the outside channel around the islands. From their heading and speed, she guessed Father was taking them around the southern approach and through and into Scapa Flow.

As though he was going home.

It was the course set to return to Orphir.

"Come, Waterblood!" Hugh de Gifford stood at the side of her father's ship, inviting her aboard. "Come and speak with us."

"Ran! Get away!" her father yelled as he ran along the side of the ship. "If it is you, go! Go now!"

He could not see her as part of the sea. De Gifford now could.

"Svein, lucky for you, your daughter will not be so foolish as to leave without hearing my offer."

She watched as de Gifford took hold of her father's

arm with a hand that glowed like the metal in a smith's fire. Her father screamed at the agony of such a hold.

Ran moved like a wave toward the ship and placed herself on the deck before changing her form. She ran to her father and touched de Gifford's hand, sending plumes of steam into the air. No matter how much water she put on it, the burning did not stop.

"I am here," she yelled, stepping away, now fully in her human body. "Stop, I pray you. Stop."

Now horror replaced the pain on her father's face as she walked toward him. When de Gifford let go his grasp and Ran tried to help him, her father recoiled from her touch.

"What are you?" he asked. "Are you some perversion like he is? An ungodly creature?"

The words cut into her heart. But he was in terrible condition and had suffered at this evil one's orders. Ran looked around at the other crew members and saw the same horror and fear in their gazes.

"Bjorn," she said, walking to the older man. He backed away from her and then made the Sign of the Cross over himself, as most of them did. Askell would not even meet her eyes.

A part of her died then, realizing that they would never accept her as Ran Sveinsdottir again. Well, if she was waterblood, she would do what she could to protect them. It was the reason the old gods set up their bloodlines—to protect mankind. She faced de Gifford and studied him for a moment, now seeing the coloring of Brienne in his face.

"What is it that you want of me?" she asked. She

noticed that his black hair was now more gray than black. A change since she'd seen him the first time. He seemed older now.

"I want you to take your rightful place in the order of things," he said. "You have powers that they cannot understand or accept." He nodded to the men who had just rebuffed her approach. "At my side, you will learn the full extent of them." De Gifford walked closer and whispered. "You have no idea of what you can truly do."

His voice grew soft and enticing. Within it was a compulsion to follow him. He was deep within her thoughts now, whispering his temptation.

"Chaela is unlike anything you can imagine, Ran. And she will give you more powers when she is freed from the place she was imprisoned by the traitors who turned on her. She is the strongest of the Old Ones, the only one still in existence. Help me open the circle and she will grant you your every desire."

Ran tried to fight it, but there was something stopping her. She could not move now. Could not speak. Could not turn to water. Had he done this to Soren? How had Soren escaped?

"Come with me," he said without speaking. "Once he helps us open the gateway, you will have him for eternity. And I will show you ways to punish him for his betrayal. Torment to last an eternity, Ran. For his faithlessness. For fucking your brother's woman and then pushing her from the cliff."

She gasped, horrified by the words. Were they the truth? How would he know such things? Her gaze alone moved, looking across at her father. Had her father revealed such things to this evil man?

The sibilant temptation began again and Ran wanted to accept it. She wanted to give him what he wanted. All of it. To pay Soren back for his actions. To make him suffer, not for two years, as she had, but forever.

She would take the life from him bit by bit, sucking the water from his bones and marrow and muscle. She could do that. She could take the water from him. Make him feel the painful loss of each drop until he was nothing.

Nothing but dust beneath her feet.

"Ran."

Ran opened her eyes. She had taken hold of one of the sailors without even knowing it and had . . . had . . .

She had taken every bit of water from his body.

The man's desiccated body now crumbled under her touch.

Silence reigned; not a sound was made. Only the sound of one man moving toward her.

"This is only one of your powers. You control the water in this world. Take your place of honor and we will rid ourselves of those who opposed us."

The voice was real now. The temptation more so.

"Soren will rue the day he betrayed you. He will regret not accepting his place with me. Soren will . . ."

She heard nothing but his name now and her heart pounded at the sound of it. Soren did not deserve such a fate. No one did. But as de Gifford now touched her, she saw the destruction and the ultimate chaos of all she loved.

That would be the result of freeing this Chaela.

"Soren!" she screamed out.

The sea around them bucked, the ship tilted and de

Gifford lost his hold on her. She joined with the sea and escaped the ship, tearing through the water and screaming. The seas boiled as de Gifford sent his terrible fire into it, but after rising in steam, the water always returned to its home.

In confusion, she went with the water, in circles, deep and then shallow, moving, always moving, until the last whispers of his temptation left her. But the fact that she'd murdered a man with her touch did not. Tormented by what she'd done, she could not go back to the others and face them. Instead of protecting, she had destroyed.

Ran swam away from Orkney, out into the larger ocean to the west where no ships sailed, racing through the cold water, away from her homeland, and screaming out her rage and horror and guilt. Forcing herself up into the air, she released the wave and crashed back into the sea, trying to punish herself for the heinous act. Crying and sobbing, she whipped the water into currents and whirlpools.

When she was finally exhausted, she turned herself over to the sea, hoping it would let her die there. Better that than to live to kill again. Especially if she killed Soren.

For in spite of his betrayal, in spite of her anger and hurt, she loved him. She'd never stopped loving him and she knew that now. And she knew she would die first before harming him.

She loved him.

The sea gentled around her, warming and caressing her. It carried her for hours and she cared not where. Night or day mattered not.

Only when the sea placed her on a beach did she rouse, pushing back her hair and rising to kneel. The place looked familiar to her. Standing, she knew it at once.

The Brough of Birsay, a tidal isle on the northern edge of the Mainland. For now, separated from the rest by the swiftly moving channel, but at low tide, the land bridge would be open. It was morning, for the sun was just creeping over the horizon and sending shards of light across the land. It was peaceful here. If she did not think too much, she could imagine herself here in earlier days, exploring the empty buildings of the abandoned monastery.

Centuries before, this place had been sacred ground for the Church. And before that, the ancient Picts claimed it as theirs. She'd not visited here for years. Had the sea brought her here because it remained a sanctuary, untouched by evil?

During her last visit, she'd gotten trapped on the island for the better part of a day, waiting for the tide to go out and reveal the causeway. Now, that would not keep her from leaving.

But, where should she go?

The evil one needed her to open the gate to the place where she was imprisoned.

The others wanted her to help find that same gateway, in a hidden circle of stones, and seal it.

Her father wanted to be rescued.

She wanted . . .

Ran sat back down on the ground and watched the sun rise higher in the sky. Piercing through gray clouds that floated low and thick on that horizon, she could think of only one thing she wanted.

Soren.

As though she'd conjured him out of nothing but his name, the winds swirled before her and became him.

"Ran," he said, running to her. He fell to his knees before her and searched her face. "I have been searching for you. I asked the winds to find you and they could not. Not until now. Are you injured? Did he harm you?"

"I cannot think about him, Soren."

"We were terrified when you did not return," he said. "I know how convincing he can be; he tried his deception with me. And with your father his prisoner, I feared he had drawn you in." He dragged his hands through his hair and shook his head. "When you did not return in two days' time, I feared you were dead."

"Two days?" Time mattered not when she was in the sea. "I did not know. I did not know where to go."

"What happened?" He moved closer and touched her cheek.

In that moment, she knew how she'd escaped. It was thoughts of Soren that broke the evil one's hold on her soul and her heart. Because . . .

"You gave me the strength in that terrible moment, Soren. When he'd torn my heart open and tried to burn his way in, you were there, standing in his way." She reached out and stroked his face. "I have been lying to myself and to everyone around me. I did not stop loving you. Not then, not now. When I realized that, I had the strength to break his hold and get away."

"Ran," he began, but she placed her hand over his mouth to stop him from making any promises.

"I have seen what Chaela plans to do when she is

free and I cannot allow it. But I am empty, Soren. Emptied by what I . . ." She could not finish the words. She could not admit that dark sin to him. "I need you, Soren. I need your strength. I need your love."

"I need to tell you the truth of it, Ran," he said, tugging her hand free.

She knew then that the truth did not matter. She'd seen too many truths in the way evil worked. Right now she wanted only him.

"Nay. Nothing but love in this holy place. Love me, Soren."

And he did.

Not only because she'd asked, but also because he always had and it was what he'd wanted to do for more than two years. If loving her would help her in some way, he would. And he would answer to the rest later.

Soren leaned over and began with a simple kiss, an innocent one compared to many others they'd share. Gently rubbing his mouth against hers, he moved closer and pulled her to him so that their bodies touched.

He sensed her weakened spirit and emptiness. There had been some injury to her soul and she had emptied herself of everything to deal with it. Though he could have asked the winds to show him what had happened, he did not. She did not want him to know, but he could imagine the feeling of violation her soul suffered.

"Aw, Ran," he said, cupping her face in his hands. When she met his gaze tears filled her green eyes. "Nay, no tears."

"I love you, Soren," she said.

The simple declaration almost unmanned him. He

would not use the words or bind her to himself when he knew she still doubted him. But he could give her his love without the words.

He kissed her eyes, tasting the saltiness of those tears. And he touched their mouths once more and felt her arch against him. "I want to touch you, Ran. Let me?"

She nodded then and, after tossing his cloak behind her, he guided her back to lie on the ground. With a wish for warm winds, he untied the laces of her gown and loosened it. Soren moved slowly, undressing her bit by bit and kissing every inch of her skin as he did so.

It took no time at all for him to arouse her; he felt the heat moving through her body. Each touch brought a sigh. Each kiss or touch of his mouth and she arched against him. Ran dug her fingers into the ground as though trying to keep from touching him.

Finally, she lay naked before him, clad only in her stockings, and he drank in the sight of her body. He'd missed the way the nipples of her breasts puckered when he blew against them. And the inclination of her belly down to the curls between her legs. He rolled her to her belly and began a new path down her back, over the globes of her arse and onto her thighs. The place behind her knees still made her laugh.

He paused only long enough to remove his tunic and breeches. Then he moved behind her, sliding his arm around to cup her breast as he slipped his cock between her legs. He drew out each caress, each taste, each kiss, trying to be gentle. She arched back against him, their bodies spooned together as he kissed and bit and licked the place on her neck that was sensitive.

"Soren," she whispered. "I need your strength now.

Take me." She turned in his embrace and met his gaze. The turquoise aura pulsed brightly around her and her eyes changed to that color. "Fill me with your love, Soren. I am empty."

She reached between their bodies and took his cock in her hands, tearing away any control he had. Their joinings had never been quiet and easy. They joined like a storm, full of thunder and shattering release. He pulled her to him, sliding one leg between hers and lifting hers over his hip, opening her to his touch.

She held him with two hands, sliding one under his bollocks and the other moved up and down his shaft. Soren rubbed the inside of her thigh, watching as her mouth opened and she breathed in shallow, quick breaths as he moved ever closer to the place where he wanted to be. When he turned his hand and slid it along the cleft of her flesh, she moaned, clutching his erection even harder.

He wanted to make her scream. He needed to feel her scream. He needed to taste her release against his mouth.

Soren pulled himself free and pushed her onto her back, climbing over her and pushing his legs between her knees. She opened to him, to his gaze, to his touch, closing her eyes and arching before he even did as he'd planned.

"Do not move," he growled.

He kissed and suckled the tips of her breasts, rubbing his face against her as he did. Soren took the puckered buds between his teeth, one then the other, and tugged on them, loving the sounds of her pleasure when he did. He hungrily kissed and sucked his way up and down her body until she lay trembling with need beneath him. If she arched up against him, he pressed her down with his palm over her mons. Using but one finger, he teased her flesh, making her shake and quiver for more.

Then, even though his own flesh could bear no more, he moved between her legs, his mouth on the sensitive skin on the inside of her thighs. Ever closer to the heated core of her, he slowed if she moved against him. She'd liked these games of time and pleasure and her body response and wetness told him she remembered them well.

Knowing she was past ready, he lay between her thighs, opened her wider with his shoulders against her knees and kissed her intimately. His tongue outlined her glistening cleft and he slid his finger deep within her. Smiling against her flesh, he licked her hard, using his tongue to find the tight nub at the top of it.

When he drew that between his teeth and began rubbing it with the end of his tongue, her body began to open in response. With his mouth there, he pushed his tongue deep inside her, mimicking what his prick would do, rubbing the sensitive flesh until he felt her body begin to release against his mouth. Sucking the now-erect bud, he tasted her arousal and her release, the sound of it made it only sweeter. Her hands slid into his hair now, pushing him against her as she arched and pressed against his mouth.

Soren sucked and licked and bit until she screamed and writhed, her body pouring out its release. As he felt the shudders lessen, he moved, climbing up onto his knees and lifting her hips.

"Fill me."

She did not have to ask him for that; he thrust into her in one deep push, filling her with his hardened flesh. His cock lengthened and widened, as the tightness gripped him.

"Again."

It was an order and so he laughed. She knew what she wanted and told him. And he plowed her more deeply.

"More," she whispered, her voice filled with arousal. "Deeper."

He drew back until he was almost out of her body and then, using the muscles of his thighs and his arse, he thrust back in so hard that he moved them along the ground. If he worried that he'd been too rough, her body and her words told him otherwise.

"Ahhhh." She let out a long sigh and tilted her hips under him. "Now, Soren Stormblood," she whispered, meeting his gaze. "Take me."

And he was lost. His body responded to her call, thrusting deep and hard, over and over. She wrapped her legs around his waist and met every thrust, drawing him in and clenching around his flesh to make his withdrawal more difficult. The feel of it, the way her deep muscles tightened on him, brought his own release ever closer.

But not until she did.

Leaning down, he took her mouth, thrusting his tongue inside, deep, and shared the taste of her own essence with her. She grew tighter and tighter around his flesh until she arched and screamed out her release. He did not relent, he did not stop, plunging completely into her and feeling the ripples of her peak. Only when she was done, when her flesh inside relaxed, did he allow his release. His body tensed and his seed sprayed against her womb in wave after wave of heated wetness.

He stayed within her, listening to her breathing until it grew slow-paced and even. Then, rolling onto his side, he took her with him, keeping his cock within her for every possible last moment. She tucked her head under his chin and against his chest and he felt her every breath on his skin.

If God or the gods were merciful, this would not be the last time they shared this physical bond. If they had any mercy, Soren would be able to claim her as his own and keep her for all their lives.

But, as with other gods—the Greeks or Romans— the gods liked to play . . . god with humans. And he feared that this would end badly.

CHAPTER 15

She wanted him back inside her as soon as he'd withdrawn.

Ran's body ached, with need, from use, from pleasure, and yet, she wanted him to do that again and again. She could never get enough of his strong body within her. If truth be told, it was like an unending craving in her for him—a need that was never satisfied, always grew and never stopped. So, having him once would only make it worse. Her body begged her for more.

Lying here in his arms, she could almost imagine that all was right in the world. That they were once again together. That they would be. Easing her arm from under him, she gathered her hair and tried to pull it from his grasp. With his eyes closed and his breathing deep and even, she thought him asleep.

She reached over and moved his hair from his eyes. Those eyes opened and met her gaze.

Ran was not ready for this to be over, so she leaned up on one elbow, her hand holding her head, and traced his mouth with a finger. That little caress began their next joining, as different from the first as it could be.

Gentle and quiet.

Slow-paced.

Marked with sighs and caresses and releases that both fulfilled their need and created it anew.

Only later when she realized the sun had reached its midday point in the sky above them did she know they had to leave. She released the sea from keeping the island separate and he released the warm winds with the same reluctance. They took time dressing, helping each other with laces and ties and boots.

Ran watched the waters swirling around the circular island's edge and something bothered her. Everything important in Orkney's ancient history involved circles. The standing stones were in circles. This island would be a perfect circle except that part of it had been cut away by the water's currents over time. Even the old church near her home in Orphir was circular, the only one she'd ever seen in that shape.

And the first circle that Einar had mentioned was the broch.

"Soren," she began, finishing tying off her braid. "What have the others been doing while I have been . . . away?"

"They have been searching for the hidden circle. And keeping watch for Hugh," he said. "They discovered that de Gifford can sense those with power easier than he can humans. So their soldiers keep watch and follow his moves."

"Did they find anything? Any sign yet?"

Soren walked over to her. "Nay. Why? What are you thinking?"

"I think we need to search the broch again. Do you have Einar's map?"

"Nay," he said. "I left it with the other drawing and the passage with the others. Their priests wanted to study it," he explained.

"Can you get it and meet me at the broch?"

"We could both return so they can see you are unharmed," he suggested.

She still felt fragile, not ready to face their new allies and the multitude of questions they would have. Or the knowing glances of Brienne and Aislinn. Not yet. Ran shook her head.

"Wait for me," he said as he disappeared into the sky.

She nodded and walked to the highest point on the island, not very far at all, to look across the water to the Mainland. Where was the circle they needed? She'd not asked what they were supposed to do once they found it. Knowing priests, it most likely involved some kind of ritual.

She closed her eyes and tried to remember the map Einar had drawn. The broch was a large place on it, yet they'd seen nothing there. Some empty chambers, on several stories leading to the roof.

Soren reappeared in front of her and held out his hand.

"Come. I will carry you there," he offered.

"Can you do that?" she asked. He shrugged.

"The first time I traveled with the winds, I kept my

human form. If I can do that, I can hold you." He took her hand and tugged her closer. "And if it does not work, you will drop in the sea and all will be well."

How strange a thing to consider, Ran thought, as she moved closer and Soren lifted her in his arms. In the next moment, she was high in the air over the island, looking down at the water.

"This is extraordinary," she said. "I have never seen the like."

"Everything looks so different from up above," he agreed. "This must be what birds see as they fly."

It took little time at all for them to reach the outcropping of land on which the broch sat. Much like other brochs all across Orkney, it was round and had thick walls. Many believed brochs were defensive towers, where people in centuries past could gather if under attack. Their wooden steps could be pushed away and the door sealed.

When Soren put her down, she looked at the entrance and realized what had bothered her. The steps led up to the first story.

"What is beneath the floor?" she asked, walking up the steps.

"I think it is only the earth," Soren answered. "My grandfather never mentioned any cellar or storage room."

They opened the door and went within. The steps that led up sat within the inner and outer walls. Soren pointed at the floor adjacent to the stairs. It was a different color wood and did not fit well into the space. Ran stepped aside and he reached down and pried one of the slats free.

Then another one. And the last, which exposed a set of steps that led down. She smiled at Soren, knowing that this hidden chamber must be significant. Einar must have left something behind for them.

A torch sat in a sconce at the top of this newly found stairway, so Soren found a piece of flint and lit it. Holding it out before them, Soren led the way down the stairs.

The air was damp and dank as though water regularly filled in from the nearby strait. But when they reached the bottom, the dirt floor was hard packed and dry. Lifting the torch to light the room, Soren's expression spoke of some great discovery. She climbed down from the last steep step and turned around to look.

Not an inch of the wall around this chamber was empty.

Most images were sketched in black, charcoal most likely, but some others had colors around them, too. Some symbols matched ones they knew—like the marks that she, Soren, Brienne and William carried on their arms. The one marking Ander and the priests and the other man Roger appeared all across the drawings. The most amazing part of it was the perspective, for this seemed to be an elaborate map left for them.

"Soren, this is a map," she said, pointing to the way the mainland and islands appeared.

"Different though," Soren said. "Almost as if he's looking out in each direction with this as his focal point. Look. See here," he said, pointing to one wall where a large city was drawn. "If we were to break the walls down and lay each out flat, it works clearly."

"But this is different from the one on parchment,"

she said. He took it out, opened it up and they both studied it. "See here? There's much more detail on the wall than on this."

Soren nodded, comparing the sketch to the wall. "Not so much to the north or even south, but out to the southwest, there are markings for places I do not remember. Mayhap this was his practice piece? Or his notes for the wall?"

"I think we need to show this to Aislinn and Marcus," she said. "They have scribes who can copy this so it can be examined and deciphered."

"I will bring them here or it will take days for them to travel here."

He left, climbing carefully up the narrow steps as she remained there studying the marks. She would not know what they meant until the priests looked at them, but she noticed several things quickly.

There were eight different marks around the perimeter and ones like those of the priests scattered about. The eight marks were placed around the chamber and they were somehow imbued with magic or power. She could feel it when she touched the one matching hers. And Soren's was exactly opposite of hers. The war hammer lay opposite the flames. The sun and the tree lay opposite of each other. The last two—the horse and the moon—as well.

Aislinn carried the crescent moon on her arm.

If all was as it seemed, Aislinn would be called to close one of the circles. Did she know that?

Ran heard someone above and climbed the stairs, leaving the torch in a sconce in the stairway. And she found the female priest waiting there.

"It is both frightening and exciting being carried that way," the young woman said in a breathless voice. "It was almost how I see things when I am dreamwalking."

"Dreamwalking?"

"It is something I can do. A gift from the gods. I travel in my dreams, walking to find places or people," Aislinn explained.

"Down this way," Ran directed, going first down the steps. "We have only one torch so it is not very bright." She heard the fast intake of breath behind her when Aislinn first glimpsed the chamber.

"Do you feel it?" Aislinn asked, holding her hands out as she turned round and round the chamber. "Do you?"

"Only if I touch that one," she said, pointing to her mark on the wall.

Aislinn walked around the perimeter of the chamber, not touching the drawings and marks, but simply gliding her hand in the air near them.

"There is power here. Power and . . . magic," she said, awe filling her voice. "Someone very powerful did this."

"Einar Brandrson, Soren's grandfather," Ran said.

"It would have to be a priest of immense ability, Ran. These are not simply drawn or sketched. They are imbued in each stroke with blessings and spells. Very few of us could create such a thing. I doubt Marcus even," Aislinn said.

"You doubt I could what?" Marcus asked, coming down the steps with Soren behind him.

Neither of the women said a word; they waited only

for Marcus to see the chamber. His first expression was of surprise, but then the older man's eyes rolled up into his head and he pitched forward. Soren managed to grab his cloak and keep him from hitting the dirt floor. Unlike when Father Ander fainted, Marcus did not fall to the ground.

He began chanting and walking around the chamber, stopping, Ran noticed, at each of the eight marks. His words blended together and became like a song, the tune of which Soren began humming under his breath. When she glanced at him, he shrugged.

"My grandfather taught me words and songs," he said. "I know not what they mean. I never have."

The three watched Marcus for several minutes until he slowed and then stopped completely. Aislinn walked to his side.

"Marcus, are you well?" she asked.

Marcus blinked over and over and then wiped his forehead and shook his head. "What happened?" Then he looked at Aislinn. "Do you feel it, Aislinn? It is wondrous, truly wondrous."

"What is it, Marcus? A map certainly, but what made you do that?" Soren asked, motioning with his hand in a circular pattern.

"These are the signs of each of the Warriors of Destiny, you know those," Marcus explained. "But these words are the blessing the gods needed to seal the gateway. And these, these"—he pointed at words scattered all around the chamber—"these are the words the ancients used to capture the evil one."

"Chaela?" Ran asked.

Marcus spit on the floor and whispered something

like a curse before saying anything to her. "I will not speak her name. To use the names of the gods gives them power but to say hers is to call her attention. We never want her aware of us." He pointed at the marks around the chamber.

"See there. Every time a name is written it gives power to the symbol. But see those? The priest destroyed her name to avoid saying it."

"And you can read these words? Understand them?" Ran asked.

"Only when the gods allow me to," Marcus said. "But now? Nay. Not a one. But the priest who created this would have."

"Why do you keep saying that Einar was a priest? If I am a stormblood, would he not have been one, too?" Soren asked.

"In days long ago, when the bloodlines were created, each was kept separate from the others. To keep them pure and keep their power undiluted. But when the gods sent the bloodlines out into the human world, they did not remain separate."

Marcus looked at her and Soren. "Your families intermarried, here and in other communities until their powers mixed. Only in some generations are there purebloods strong enough to call on their powers."

"Like this generation?" Soren asked.

"The gods are good to those who believe, Soren. We priests have long believed that when needed, the Warriors of Destiny are created to battle this evil who can be contained but not destroyed."

"And old Einar?" she asked.

"He was a generation ahead of the rising," Marcus

explained. "He collected much wisdom and heard the call of the gods, but did not teach you as he should have, Soren." Turning to face her, he added, "Or you, Ran. Great priests such as Einar are sent to teach."

"What do we do now, Marcus?" Aislinn asked. "So much of our history is told through stories and not written down."

"I think we should copy all of this so we can study it. The time is coming and we need to find the gateway. These drawings"—he motioned around the walls—"are clues and signposts for us. They are an immense source of knowledge not to be ignored."

They left the chamber and snuffed out the torch. With care, Soren replaced the wooden slats covering the secret steps. If someone happened along and entered the broch, they would not find the chamber easily.

Outside, Soren and Marcus decided which priests would be needed and Soren brought them using his stormblood powers. It took several trips, and on each one he brought a nervous priest, writing supplies and torches. Soon, everyone who needed to be brought or taken was seen to and only Soren and Ran remained.

"They know," Ran whispered to Soren.

"And are you embarrassed?" He took her chin and studied her face. "You never worried over it before," he said. "Should I disavow the declaration you made to me in passion just hours ago?"

"Passion does not answer all the questions yet standing between us, Soren," she said.

"No it does not," he said. "We will see to those other questions, Ran. I owe you an explanation but it is not

time for that. First, we must see to your father's safety
and to this matter we are caught up in."

She had not even realized that he'd lifted her up
and returned her to the camp on the other side of the
island while they conversed. Soren put her on her feet
and changed form. Before she could let go of him, William
and his man Roger strode up to them.

"Ander has gone missing," William announced.

"He was here this morn," Soren said. "I spoke with
him."

"He received a missive; an emergency arose with the
bishop and he was called back to Kirkwall," Roger explained.

"The bishop is not in Kirkwall," Soren said.

William's grim expression spoke volumes without
saying a word. He nodded at Soren and the two walked
off, whispering and planning something.

"He will not survive," Roger warned her. "He is too
full of godly spirit to survive de Gifford's care."

"Mayhap that will be his protection against the
evil?" she whispered as she followed the men back
toward the tents.

How many deaths would she carry on her soul if
they did not find a way to defeat this fireblood? How
many?

CHAPTER 16

After delays and disappointments, things were beginning to go his way. Hugh was furious when he lost control over the waterblood, but he still held her father. Even the man's reaction to seeing his daughter as she truly was would not harden a loyal, loving daughter's heart to his suffering.

The seas worked against his journey after she disappeared screaming into it. Hugh thought it was not something she did apurpose at all. More likely, it was the reaction of the sea and an untrained waterblood to his attack and her fury and guilt. He would use that when the time came. Her expression when she realized she held someone in her grip as he convinced her to kill him was something he would remember and rejoice in for a long, long time.

At least until he killed her. And her stupid, stubborn father. And, now, an added pleasure—the priest.

Hugh walked down the stone steps of the round church. He'd felt the presence of the chamber as they approached Orphir. At first, he mistook the feeling as the one he experienced when coming in contact with something of a sacred nature. A church was consecrated and holy, made so by the bones of the saint in the altar stone. Whether he believed in that God or his saints, the power was there. Once he'd forced the Roman priest to remove the altar stone and its relics, he felt the building tremble from the power beneath it.

Here was the portal through which he could worship his goddess.

Through which she could touch him with her fire and purify him.

Through which his own powers would be strengthened for the coming battle.

He laughed now, following the corridor to the end and pushing open the last door that stood between him and Chaela.

"Good Father," he said, passing the priest who stood immobilized against the wall. "You carried out your task well. I shall make your death—when it comes—a swift one in honor of that service."

The priest, not an old one, did not meet his gaze; he never had. He only prayed under his breath, relentlessly. Over and over the same Christian prayer. *At the hour of our death.* Well, he would be at the hour of his death shortly.

The other one chained there said nothing. Hugh was not certain whether Svein Ragnarson had lost his mind, for the waterblood's father reacted to nothing now—not pain or pleasure nor words or threats. It mattered not to Hugh. Less resistance now was one thing he would not have to worry over when the ceremony was ready.

Neither of them matter now. Nothing mattered.

Hugh disrobed and stood there, waiting for the opening to reveal itself. He spoke the words of worship and praise over and over until the heat burst into the chamber . . . from the floor. Hugh walked around it, outlining it, memorizing it, honoring it. His body, now showing the ravages of his true age, ached with every step.

But soon, soon, his goddess would come to him.

A scratching at the door dragged his attention from the portal. Eudes opened it and dragged in one of the sailors from Svein's ship. Hugh pointed to a place and Eudes pushed the man there and left. Crouching before the gagged and bespelled man, he placed his hands on the man's head and spoke within his thoughts.

You are privileged as few are. You will be my sacrifice to the goddess. Do not die too quickly.

All was in readiness. He knelt and then prostrated himself over the portal, preparing himself for the agony of Chaela's blessing. When it came he knew that nothing could have prepared him for it, especially in his weakened form. His skin burned and he screamed as she touched him.

"Hugh, my faithful one," the goddess whispered through the portal. "Always faithful."

"Chaela, I beg your favor and have brought a sacrifice to please you."

A terrible shriek echoed through the chamber and bursts of fire heated the floor where he would once again touch her. Looking into the darkness, he tried to see her but could not. Not yet.

"Accept my gift, O my goddess."

Hugh lifted the man up and held him over the opening. Slitting his throat first, Hugh lowered him slowly into the void. With his throat cut, the man could not scream as the anguishing fire destroyed him, but that did not stop him from trying. The blood gurgled out, dripping on the floor all over the chamber, as the goddess consumed him. Hugh released him and listened until all he could hear were the goddess's exhalations.

He created a wave of fire there on the floor, covering the portal, and called out to her again. Barely able to kneel from the agony of her first touch, he spoke again. There was so much more coming.

"If I have pleased you, grant me your favor, my goddess."

Crawling forward, he thrust his hand into the portal and waited. The fire melted his skin and his hand turned like molten metal. His body burned in torment . . . and pleasure. He screamed and screamed at the pain of this joining with his goddess. When his voice was gone, she still did not let go.

"You failed me, Hugh," she said. "I must be freed. You must free me!" she screamed from the void. The stone walls shook at the sound. "The gateway is nearby. Water."

"I will," he gasped out, trying to understand her words. His skin was engulfed in flames and burned, melting and reforming only to burn again. There was no pleasure now, only relentless suffering without an end.

"Free me," she whispered. "And there will be much favor for you, my faithful one," she promised.

Now her touch changed and his body reacted. His prick hardened and he neared a sexual release. His skin burned but now pleasure raced through his blood as she sent waves of bliss through him. His seed spent, he fell back when she released him. The sound of wings fluttering was all he could hear as she moved away.

Rolling away from the portal, he waited for his body to recover from this encounter. She had punished him this time. He felt her anger and her disappointment. As he waited for his skin to mend, the whispers began anew. The priest was praying again.

"You will carry out the ritual, priest," Hugh said when his throat finally healed. "And then you will be the first offering to the goddess when she is free," he warned. Rolling to his side and then pushing up onto his knees, he laughed at this one.

"It will be a great honor," Hugh said. "You will not live to enjoy it, but you will be remembered by the faithful."

Standing now, he straightened up, running his hands over his flesh. Resilient. Renewed. Younger. He pulled his robe on and opened the door. The chamber was empty and silent now, the portal closed. Eudes waited there. Other than a quick glance at Hugh's hair, now black again no doubt, Eudes did not react.

"Bring them along," Hugh ordered.

Climbing the steps out of the lower chamber, he found the day half gone. Time did not pass at the same speed when he communed with the goddess as it did when he was not in her presence. He'd lost hours in the agony she gave him. Hours of being undone and re-made. Of pain and torment. Of pleasure and release.

Now, he needed to find the circle. The goddess had said "water" during their joining. Was the circle near the water? From what he'd learned, most of the stone circles here were close to two big lakes in the center of the island. Or did she mean something else?

This was not as easy as finding the first circle. His father had done so much of the searching and preparation for that. He'd known the location before the others did. Now, in this strange land, he had to search for it. Or . . .

He could simply wait for the other bloodlines to find it and then use the waterblood and stormblood to open it to save her father and their friend.

They were not the only ones using human spies to keep watch. His men reported back often. That was how he'd captured the priest. Funny, a Roman priest who also knew the old gods. Ironic too that he would be the one praying the ritual to free Chaela.

As they left the church grounds, Hugh decided to use Svein's house while they waited. He was not opposed to a bit of luxury and a few good meals while he gathered knowledge for the next step.

And the housekeeper learned her place quite quickly with the right incentives. Bruised, bloodied and on her knees before him was his favorite.

He gave the few women to his men to reward them and to keep them busy while he waited. A bit of sexual pleasure held a man's loyalty and Hugh used it on those he needed. Soon all the servants there learned that they did not answer to the old master.

And never would again.

Soren went back to the broch the next morning. The priests had made great progress in copying the symbols and drawings as rapidly as possible, working without stopping even through the night. Precious parchment sheets lay strewn around the main chamber, placed there as they were finished. Studying them, side by side, he looked for anything he might recognize. Or a symbol or sign that might indicate the hiding place of the circle they needed.

Efforts to locate Ander were unsuccessful, but Soren did not doubt that de Gifford had him. Word was that he and his men were at Svein's house in Orphir waiting. Waiting for what they knew not. Tension grew in the camp as preparations were made for so many different schemes and scenarios. Roger had the fighting men well in hand, but William did not think they would be needed, as in the first battle.

Marcus did not think that Ander possessed the knowledge to perform the ritual, so William ordered more guards on all the priests. Only Aislinn with her own personal hulking guard was permitted any freedom. The warrior was not well liked, Soren could tell, and most of the priests scattered at his approach. But the man answered only to Brienne and did whatever she asked of him—protecting Aislinn was his only duty now.

"Soren," Ran called from below. He walked down into the lower chamber to answer her call.

"Look at this part," she said, pointing to a section of the wall in the direction of the main stone circles. "So many signs and symbols there, and there." She outlined several of the strange ones. "Einar had squares drawn there on his other map."

"That is where you had that strange experience. You became ill. I thought you were going to fall or be pulled into the water." She paled at the memory.

"Aye, there. That is on Loch Harray. The markings are on the other side, near the Watchstone and its mate."

"We did not search because you were ill," Soren said.

"Mayhap we need to look there? We might have missed whatever this symbol means?" Then she touched a place near Brodgar's Ring—the drawing showed a smaller stone or monument. "We may not have been careful when we searched the stones for any signs or messages."

Ran had a keen mind and could pick up patterns quickly. And he did not miss her reference to their distraction the morning after their first day and night together.

"Should we look closer?" she asked.

"Let us first speak with William. He asks that we tell him of our plans and movements."

Soren gathered up the completed copies and rolled them. Handing them to Ran, they left the chamber and the broch and walked out. They did not wish to draw attention to their presence there or to give Hugh any sign that the broch held some significance. So only three priests worked in the chamber at a time, with another keeping watch from over the rise near the road.

The main responsibility of the watchman was to close up the stairway if anyone approached and to leave. Soren had spent most of this last day overseeing both transporting the necessary priests and keeping watch over them and the broch. From up high, Soren could see anyone on the north road miles before they grew close.

Marcus estimated that they would finish their work here in one more day. Then the whole of the knowledge shared by Einar would be ready for their study. Soren was continually surprised by everything he learned about his grandfather.

A priest? And that of great power and abilities?

And he had grown up believing his grandfather was just a little daft and held some questionable philosophies. Had Soren's own resistance been the reason Einar had delayed in sharing this knowledge? He would never know now.

They stood in the shadow of the broch, hidden from prying eyes, when he held his hand out to Ran. She accepted his touch more easily now, but there remained a divide between them. They had not lain together since that morning on Birsay. She slept in the women's tent and he barely slept anywhere he laid his head.

Reunited in a manner but still very separate, he thought, as if she held some secret from him even as he held his own critical one from her. Love was not the issue for them—he doubted not that their love remained even after his betrayal and two years of separation. Now, trust was the challenge.

She did not trust him.

Soren squeezed her hand and took her in his arms. It took only moments to take her to the encampment and though he became the wind, he could feel her body within his embrace. If he did not put her on her feet immediately, well . . .

"Ah, you have returned." William approached with Aislinn and her ever-present guard.

Ran held out the rolled parchments to William.

"They are quite effective at this task," William said, nodding to Aislinn.

"It is strange for us to have a written document of our beliefs," Aislinn said. "Our faith has been handed down from generation to generation through prayers and songs and stories. To see these"—she nodded at the vellum sheets—"is strange and wondrous."

"I think we may have missed something at Stenness or Brodgar," Ran said. "There are many markings in that area that we do not understand yet."

"Ran wants to go and make a closer examination of the Watchstone and the smaller stone just outside Brodgar's Ring," Soren explained.

"Two priests are there now," William said. "Tell them what you seek and they can help."

"Once Marcus and the others examine these, we should make our plan." Aislinn looked from William to him. "Brienne said Hugh has touched the goddess. Her own powers have flared uncontrollably." This development did not sit well with the warrior.

"Where is she?" he asked.

"Away from us, in the hills, until she can gain control," Aislinn explained.

"Damn it," William shouted. "Damn him to hell!" His skin began to shift to blue and his eyes blazed. The warblood was very close. He strode off, calling out orders and growling as he went.

"He will seek her out," Aislinn explained. Soren

knew from the look in the man's and the warblood's eyes that his mate would not be alone for long.

"How does he do that?" Ran asked. "Change into that creature and yet keep control."

"Love." He turned at the single-word reply. She continued. "His love for her and hers for him enables them both to retain their humanity even while in their bloodline form."

He shook his head. Before he could say anything, Aislinn touched his hand.

"You have had that ability from the beginning of your powers because of the love that already existed between you two," Aislinn said. "It is most powerful."

Ran made a soft noise and he glanced at her. Her discomfort at this topic was there on her face. She might have accepted that something still existed between them, but she was not ready to speak of such things to strangers.

"If you are ready then, Ran?" Soren interrupted, holding out his hand once more. Aislinn nodded and stepped away.

"I would speak with you when you return, Ran," the young priestess said.

Soren scooped her into his arms and lifted her high in the air. It was very peaceful up here and he found that he stopped and just floated many times just to enjoy it. He did that now, allowing Ran to see everything beneath them.

"The coastline looks so very different from here," she whispered. "And even more so when I am in the water."

"Have a look," he said, holding her still. "There is

the Bay of Skaill. And look how the layers of rock change at the sea's edge."

He'd climbed on many rock outcroppings, risking falling into the dangerous waters. It was something boys did to challenge themselves.

If he dawdled now, enjoying the feel of her in his embrace, with no one else around them, he refused to feel guilt over it. Since meeting up with these outsiders, they had barely a moment without others around. The priests liked to ask them questions. The others—the warblood and fireblood—spoke of powers and plans. Even Roger and the other men drew his attention away from where he wanted it—on Ran.

"I think I would remain up if I had this power," she said as they flew south.

"Do you feel that way when you are with the sea?"

"Aye. I feel safe there. It is my refuge."

Her voice was not that of the strong woman he knew. She had been injured, so injured that she sought the sea and him to recover from it.

"I am here for you, Ran," he whispered. She looked at him and said nothing. "But you do not trust me. You love me, but you do not trust."

She sighed and he carried it away on the winds.

"I cannot simply change what I feel or I would," she explained, her gaze still on the ground and not on him.

She would have let go of the love she had for him, if she could have. Soren understood it.

"Nor can I," he said. "I do not expect that you should. I would just tell you that I will prove myself to you, if you will give me the chance."

Ran neither agreed to nor denied his plea. Considering how long she had been convinced he'd betrayed her, it came as no surprise to him. He was also certain that her father added to her anger and humiliation. Erik being involved did not help either. All because Soren had not stood up to her father's ludicrous demands.

All to protect a man who truly was a heretic and who believed in other gods. Worse, those gods were not as false as they'd been taught to believe.

But she had let Soren close, let him inside her, and she had sought him out for help when her father was in danger. That must mean that there was some chance to rebuild the trust lost. When this was over, there would be time to sort out the rest.

If they survived at all.

CHAPTER 17

From this height, Ran could see the mysterious mounds scattered all across the land. As Soren took her closer to the slip of land between the two large lakes, she saw that the number of mounds increased. Around Brodgar, she could count at least a dozen. More trailed north to the henge called Bookan. And more spread south toward and around Stenness.

Whatever the reason for them, it was clear that this area was held to be special by the ancient builders who erected these circles of stone and the cairns and mounds around them. Ran had visited most of the larger islands of Orkney and knew that these structures existed on all of them, but none had as many as the Mainland.

Only Kirkwall and the immediate area had none.

This area of the island meant something special. The stone circles and brochs and burial cairns and mounds spoke to it. As did the other darker feelings Ran had when she stood near the edge of Loch Harray, where Einar's first map marked it with those squares.

Soren set her down near Stenness, where they'd first

felt something around them. The two priests were there, examining the stones. They stood and stared as Soren took his human shape again. Ran could not fault them for their curiosity, for it must be extraordinary to see proof of their beliefs right before their eyes.

"Stormblood. Waterblood," the priests said in voices filled with awe and respect. "How may we serve you?" the older one asked, bowing low before them.

"William said you might help us search for symbols or markings," Ran said, walking toward them. Soren handed her the map he always held close now and she unfolded it. "Here. And here," Ran pointed at the two places she was curious about.

"Of course, Waterblood," the priest said, bowing again. "We will do whatever is required to serve you."

At first, the bowing and the glances had been complimentary. Now though, they made her uncomfortable, as they also made Soren, if his expression was any indication.

"I pray you, please call me Ran. And this is Soren," she nodded at him. "And you are called . . . ?"

The astonishment on their faces surprised her. But one priest looked at the other and then back to them, apparently not willing to disobey a descendant of their gods.

"I am called Aleron and this is Kester," the younger priest offered.

After a few minutes of awkwardness, with the priests continuing to bow at their every word or request, the two grew more at ease with them. The bad feeling was gone now, but the buzzing grew as they neared the stones.

"Do you see that there are eight stones remaining in place, Soren?" she asked him. He glanced around, counting them and studying their places.

"This looks like the same alignment that Einar drew around the chamber. Look how these stones are shaped," he pointed out. Walking to the middle of the circle, he looked again and nodded. "The one marked with your symbol would be that one," he indicated the one to the west. "The one that matches mine would be this one." Soren walked over to that stone.

Ran walked to the one he'd pointed out to her and realized he was correct. Einar had drawn this arrangement in the broch. The low noise grew and she leaned closer to determine whether the sound came from the stone or something else. Ran placed her hands on the stone . . .

. . . and the world she knew disappeared.

The circle appeared as though freshly hewn and placed on the ground near the lakes. But this land was wider and the lakes smaller in size. Eleven stones stood in place, and people wearing white robes danced around them. Bells and drums filled the air along with the whispered chants and songs of the priests.

Then two priests led a woman into the circle and stood her within a smaller circle of three smaller stones positioned there. She swayed to the beat of the drums, her eyes closed, her arms extended to the sky. The people gathered around the outside of the circle, the music and sounds growing raucous now.

The scene continued before Ran as though she was not there.

Two priestesses led a man into the circle now and

stood him before the woman. Ran realized that the woman was drunk, for she seemed unaware of those around her. The priests took hold of her arms and pulled her down to the ground there, stripping the thin gown off her as they did.

She must help her. Ran let go of the stone and made her way to the center where the woman lay writhing on the ground, being stroked by the two men holding her there. Ran shouted but no one seemed to hear her.

Then the priestesses tore off the small garment the man wore around his waist and began to pleasure him with their hands and mouths, until his prick grew long and thick and hard. They led him to the woman. All six fell to the ground, their bodies rubbing and pressing against one another. The people around the circle began chanting some words. As she watched, unable to stop them or make them hear her, the priests and priestesses rose and surrounded the couple still on the ground.

They were . . . rutting.

The chanting grew louder and louder, the tone and timing of it sexual in nature and the man paced his thrusts into the woman to those chants. The woman moaned in pleasure, still on the ground, as the man plowed deep into her.

Ran looked away and then saw an old man carrying a large dagger into the circle. He walked seven times around the circle in one direction, then another seven times in the other, stopping before the couple on the ground in the center. The chanting and prayers reached a feverish pitch as the man threw back his head and screamed out as his seed released into the woman. They moved in unison as he emptied into her.

Then, quicker than she thought possible, the old man straddled the couple, grabbed the man's head and slashed into his neck. The woman kept screaming out her release as the blood poured over her. The priests took hold of the dying man and lifted him out and away from the woman, allowing his blood to cover her. As she lay shuddering with her own release, the people fell to their knees and touched their heads to the ground.

Unable to breathe or move, Ran watched in horror as the priests and priestesses dipped branches in the man's blood and blessed all those around the circle with it. The naked woman climbed to her feet, following them, and allowed the people to touch her, taking the blood of her lover to smear on themselves.

"May she be fertile!" the old priest called out.

"May she be fertile!" the crowd answered.

The woman laughed and shouted, "May I be fertile!"

Raising the dagger, the priest shouted again to those watching. "Or her blood will nourish the soil!"

"Her blood . . . life to our soil!" the people yelled.

"My blood for the soil!" she laughed out, falling to the ground now.

A fertility ritual? Here at the stones?

Ran turned looking around at the area. The crowd waited and watched as the woman was brought once more to the center where the man's dead body now lay on a pile of wooden branches dipped in tar. The old priest gave her a burning torch and she lit the pyre aflame, watching as the fire consumed the man whose seed yet ran down her legs and mixed with his blood.

Stumbling back, Ran noticed people she had not seen

before. As the old priest took a place before one of the stones, these four men and three women did so, too. Dressed in costly garments and gemstones and crowns, they glowed, each surrounded by a bright color—turquoise, silver, molten orange, red, green, blue and yellow gold. The woman clothed in a gown that flowed like the sea met Ran's gaze and smiled at her before turning back to the others. The priest glowed like moonlight as he spoke more words to the people. The seven touched the stones and became them, growing taller and leaning to meet over the sacrifice.

And then everything was gone and she stood holding on to the stone.

The gods? Had she just seen the gods?

Three women and four men. The woman in turquoise? Was that the goddess who ruled the sea? Her own ancestor?

A fertility ritual and a sacrifice to please them? In their honor? Here on the field of Stenness?

When?

Ran staggered into the circle and began to fall. She heard Soren screaming her name as she landed in the center, in the same place they had just burned their sacrifice to the gods.

Soren scooped her up and carried her out of the circle. She did not respond at all, no sounds, no movements. He laid her on the ground as the priests came running.

"Ran!" he called, rubbing her hands and tapping her cheeks. "Ran, wake up," he said.

She'd walked to the stone opposite of where he was and laid her hands on it. Her body had jerked and jerked, and then she pulled away and stumbled to the center, where she fell.

When she did not wake after several minutes, Soren decided to take her to the priests in the camp. Mayhap Aislinn knew what was wrong? Lifting her gently and leaning her head against his chest, he asked the winds to take them. Ran did not rouse even as they approached the encampment.

Soren remembered her words about the sea and knew that he must give her to the sea. To revive her. To protect her. Going north past the shoreline, he dipped down until he could glide within inches of the surface of the water. Carefully, so carefully, he stopped and let her slip into the sea under him.

He watched as her body disappeared into the water. Her human form dissipated within seconds of his placing her there. Soren floated above, watching and waiting for any sign of her.

"Come back to me, Ran," he whispered, the winds carrying his voice into the water. He stayed above the sea, watching and waiting for her. The sea was her refuge, it had saved her before.

What had happened? What had she seen or touched?

He and the priests were in and out of the circle, touching all of the stones and searching for clues, and nothing happened to them. But Ran reacted to something there, just as she had the first time. Was she somehow connected to those places?

Soon, a whirlpool formed beneath him. It spun the water around and around until a huge wave rose. As though it could see his form, the wave rolled toward him and then crashed into him. He laughed and threw the winds at her, creating thousands of water droplets that rained down on the sea. Ran rose in her human form and waited for him to carry her.

"I think I saw the beginning," she said. "I think I know where the circle is."

"A vision?" he asked, turning toward the coast and the encampment.

"When I touched the stone, I saw it. I saw them."

"Them?"

"The gods. The seven Old Ones. They lived here. They existed with the humans who worshipped them, Soren."

Excitement filled her voice, which was not what he expected to hear.

"You scared me. I saw you convulse and then collapse in the circle," he said, leaning his head against hers. "Do not do that again." It was a mixture of a command and a plea.

"Take me to the broch," she said. "I want to show you first."

They reached the broch and entered the chamber. The priests had finished copying the drawings and were gathering up their supplies to return to the camp. He took them back and returned to Ran.

She walked around the perimeter of the broch's lower chamber, reaching out but not touching the drawings. Then she stood in the center and faced one side. Faced the southwest.

"When I was there, when the stones were first sanctified, the land and water were very different from now," she explained. "The water was much lower and more land, here"—she pointed—"and here was above the water."

"And you think the circle we are looking for is . . ."

Could it be? Had they been standing right on top of it, or been part of it already?

"Under the water?" he asked. She smiled again and nodded, walking closer to the wall but still not touching it.

"Here, I think. See how the land curves right there in his drawings? When I was there, it was in the distance, a huge circle that sat between Brodgar and the land that projects into the lake from the west."

He was astounded. Even the map hinted at its presence. Einar had known.

"So, how do we get to it?" He turned to her. "If it's under the water, how do we perform the ritual they said we must do to close the gateway?"

"I am not certain. I hope that the priests can tell us that when we show them this," she said. "I do not think the water of the lake there will heed my call."

"But you control all water, Ran," he said. "Why would it not obey you?"

"I think I heard the evil goddess that first time. I think she is there, beneath whatever this gate is, waiting for it to be opened. So when I touched the water, it was her voice speaking to me."

"But her man must be able to open the gate to free her. So how will he get to it if it's under the water?"

"I think the others may know," she said. "We should talk to them now."

He followed her to the stairway and was surprised

when she stopped and turned to him. It put her face level with his own.

"My thanks for saving me," she said, touching his mouth in a quick, fierce kiss. She rested her arms on his shoulders and touched her forehead to his. "I could feel your strength around me, Soren. I knew you were there."

He slid his hands around her waist and pulled her close, kissing her mouth and tasting her deeply. She tasted salty like the sea. She leaned against him and ran her fingers through his hair. Cupping his head in her hands, she tilted her face and offered herself to him. He took it, sucking in her lower lip and grazing it between his teeth. She leaned her head back and he pressed his mouth on the tender skin of her neck, nipping up to the edge of her ear and biting it.

She arched against him, her breasts pressing into his chest and her hips grinding on his. Soren reached down and gathered the length of her skirt in his hand, teasing the curls he found with the back of it while holding her in place. With the other hand, he stroked between her legs, moving his hand over the soft skin of her inner thighs and then up in between. She gasped but did not move away.

Staring into her eyes, he pleasured her until she was wet and panting. Then he unlaced his breeches and took out his cock. Pressing forward, he found the place he wanted and entered her in one thrust. He guided her hips down and she hissed as she slid down his length, seating him deep within her.

"I have noticed," Soren said as he withdrew and thrust again. "You want me after you have been in the sea," he whispered. Leaning forward until she was sitting on the stairs, he shifted so that he could enter her by driving his flesh up and back into her.

She arched up against him then, her flesh grabbing and holding him, creating a marvelous friction as he moved in and out of her. If his weight on her bothered her, she said nothing. Always she opened for him and allowed him his way.

Within the tight area of the steps, Soren could not move the way he wanted to, so he took hold of her and walked up to the main chamber. She laughed when he nearly dropped her, but her legs around his hips kept him seated within her. As soon as they were out of the stairway, he knelt down and settled deep inside of her with a moan. One she matched.

And then he took her the way she liked him to—thrusting deep, pulling out and plunging back in, hard. He reached up and tried to unlace the ties of her gown. He wanted his hands on her breasts. He wanted to kiss them and bite the nipples and make her scream. When the ties resisted, he tore them apart as she laughed.

"I would have loosened them," she said as he covered one nipple, sucking it into his mouth and teasing the tip with his teeth.

"It was taking too long, Ran."

Kiss, lick, suck, bite. Then listen to her release a sigh or moan deep in her throat. He left marks this time, small red love bites along the undersides of her breasts that she would see when she dressed or bathed. Kiss, lick, suck, bite. She arched against him, clutching her strong legs around him, trying to keep him buried in her.

"You are taking too long, Soren," she whispered.

"Is that a challenge? Should we see who finishes first?"

Her laugh turned to moans and gasps and then screams as he plundered her. He would make her come first. Rolling to one side, he slid one hand down her back and slipped his thickest finger against the puckered opening. He did not enter, just pressed against it as though he would.

"Soren," she yelled out.

"You made the wager," he whispered, sliding his other hand down between her legs and against the little bud of flesh that was most sensitive. Hooking his finger against the bud, he held her tightly in his grip. If she moved or squirmed, she pushed him in deeper, either his fingers or his cock.

He knew the moment she gave in, thrusting herself against the hand in front, so that his cock moved, too. Enough play, he decided. Taking his hands from pleasuring her, he rolled her to her back and held her arse tightly. Then he counted his thrusts—an old game between them.

"One." He thrust deep and pulled back with a shift of his hips.

"Two." Another thrust, sliding them along the floor.

"Three." She shuddered then, it began deep inside around his cock and then took over her body.

"Four, five, six." Her body clenched tightly around his flesh and continued to spasm as she peaked.

He gentled his movements then and continued until she softened around him. Then he allowed himself to find release.

"I remember when you could hold out until the

eighth or ninth one," he said against her hair, when he could breathe again.

"I do also," she agreed. He lifted off her and she slid back. She was thoroughly taken and tousled. Her hair was a mess, her lips were swollen and her breasts exposed to him through the opening in her gown. The reddened marks would blossom by morning, reminding her of his attentions.

"You look . . . well pleasured." He knelt and leaned over, kissing her gently. "Are you well pleasured?"

"Aye, truly," she whispered back.

"Ran . . ." he began.

He wanted to tell her he'd loved no one else but her. That he taken no one else to his bed since she'd left it. And none before. But that would mean exposing her father's sins at a time when she most needed to believe him blameless. He could not do that to her, not even to make his path with her easier.

"Nay, Soren," she said, slipping from his grasp and standing. "I do not wish to hear about the past. We have now, this day, and we know not how many more. If we are successful, if we survive this ungodly challenge, then we can speak of the past."

It was probably best, considering that he had no other reason to rescue or attempt to rescue Svein than the man's place in Ran's heart. He would do it for her.

But he needed to find a way to rescue Ander for himself.

They would have made it back to the camp in time for the evening meal, if she had not issued another challenge. And having won that one, she offered him the chance to break their tie. That third time he would remember for a very long time and he would smile when he did.

They arrived to find the camp settling down for the night, but the leaders waited for them. Though the night and the shadows cast by the fires hid Ran's becoming blushing, there was not a man or woman in that camp who did not know what they'd been doing and why they were so late.

Or what he would do again as soon as they could manage a few minutes of privacy.

CHAPTER 18

Ran could not meet any of the gazes that now focused on her around the unlit fire. But for now she must. Knowing where the circle was meant that they needed to come up with a plan to get to it and seal it.

In doing that she was condemning her father to death, one not of his choosing or fault. And though he was guilty of many, many things, none of them deserved this ending. Hugh de Gifford was torturing him, both by physical means and using his men, his ships and her against his mind and heart.

And now another innocent, truly an innocent man of God, would pay for sins he did not commit.

All as evil pursued its own course.

Ran explained what she'd seen, blushing through the description of the fertility ritual. With Aislinn's help she was able to concentrate on everything else going on around the ceremony and describe the location and appearance of the circle that now lay under the water.

The priests were fascinated by her descriptions of the old gods they worshipped. To hear of their human embodiment and the worship, even the ritual she'd witnessed, gave them more knowledge about their gods than they had before.

"But that is what happened in our ritual," Brienne said. Still thinking about the couple rutting in front of everyone, Ran startled. "Not that part," Brienne admonished with a teasing tone. "The stones we consecrated with our blood grew impossibly tall and met in the middle over the void. And I saw something, someone, in the sky above us," she added.

"Living stones?" Aislinn asked. "Could each of the circles actually have the gods within them?"

"Marcus, tell us what you know of their leave-taking," Soren said to the priest.

Did he notice that Soren moved closer to her and touched her as they talked? His hand on hers. His leg against hers. His eyes on her. Ran forced herself back to the conversation.

"The legends say that after the evil one's betrayal and imprisonment, the gods decided to leave humanity behind. They had long been familiar with humans, so they strengthened the bloodlines of their descendants to carry the powers needed to defeat her if she ever rose again. There has never been a mention of how they left or if they actually remained here."

"But many generations spoke of them still being here, did they not?" Aislinn asked.

"Aye," Marcus nodded. "Some thought them so enamored of humans that they would never have left. Some said the gods still spoke to them. Some stories of their accomplishments and traditions have been appropriated by other gods." Marcus looked at William and the other Christians in the group and then at those of Norse descent.

"Will the ritual be the same at each circle, Marcus?" Roger asked. Roger's men had been instrumental in defeating Hugh de Gifford's human forces and preventing more of the priests from being killed.

"I, we, know that the blood of the two must be mixed on the altar with that of the third, the priest. Then the prayers must be said and they must sanctify the stone that bears their mark with the blood." Marcus looked to William and Brienne and Aislinn, who nodded in agreement. "If the blood is spilled together on the ground and touches the barrier before the three touch the stones, it will tear open the void and she will escape. If the altar stone is broken after the blood mixes and spills on the ground without the stones being blessed, she will win." All of the priests mumbled several words under their breath when he said that.

"But what will make this time different," Aislinn said softly, looking at Ran and Soren, "is that neither of those who must enter is the fireblood. So Hugh cannot do this himself."

"So we are safe because he needs us?" she asked.

"No one is safe, Ran," Marcus said, with a sad smile. "Once the three are within the circle, it closes itself so none can enter. But if the wrong prayers are spoken, all within will be destroyed." He met their gazes then. "All three within would be destroyed, leaving Hugh alive to find the next gate and leaving us without two of the bloodlines."

"But the gate would be sealed?" she asked. More and more it sounded as though a sacrifice of some kind must be made to overcome this evil. A sacrifice of their own lives.

"The gate would be useless, but not sealed. And we will have lost three valuable people of power with two more gates where he could succeed," Aislinn added.

"But if he is not within and cannot enter, then Soren and I and Aislinn or Marcus can finish the ritual and seal it closed."

"Hugh will not allow us to come out unscathed," William said. "He and his men killed a number of our fighting men and our priests. We cannot afford such a loss again," he warned.

"So Hugh will have to believe he controls someone or two or all three of those who go in?" Ran asked.

"He would not trust any of you to do his bidding," Soren suggested. "That is why he took Ander. He will torture him until he follows his orders and then send him in to say the prayers."

"But he is not practiced in our worship!" Marcus objected. "He knows not the prayers or the ceremonies or how to bond with us."

"The gods have marked him, Marcus. As they decided that Einar would have powers and knowledge such as he had," Aislinn added. "Already Ander has learned much through dreams and visions."

They grew quiet, taking all of this into consideration.

"Ander is a faithful servant of his God," Marcus said. "Would he not rather give up his mortal life to save his immortal soul?"

"Aye, Marcus, he would," Soren agreed. "Unless he thought he *was* fighting evil." His voice had dropped so low it had been difficult to hear him.

With a quick signal, William motioned to all of them to cease talking. Ran watched as glances were shared and nods of assent went through the group. She thought she understood what was happening, but she wanted to speak to Soren in private.

"'Tis late and there is much to think on," William announced. "We will make our plans on the morrow." Standing, he held out his arm to his wife. "Brienne?"

Everyone watched as they left and walked toward their tent. Marcus and Roger remained, speaking about some matter. Aislinn told her of the uneasy friendship between the two—one who relied only on what he could see or know and the other who had faith only in the unknown and unseen.

She and Soren had been sleeping apart, but she did not want that now. A sense of impending disaster grew within her with each passing hour and day, and she wanted to be with him.

"I will walk you to your tent," Soren said, waiting for her. "Come."

"Ran," Aislinn touched her arm before she could walk away. "I have moved my things to another tent, so that you may . . ." Aislinn looked at Soren and back at her; now the priestess was the one to blush. "I thought you would like to be together."

Ran smiled as the young woman rushed away. As always, the brutish Norman soldier dogged her steps. Hand in hand, Ran and Soren walked to the tent positioned nearest the water and entered. As soon as they did, the winds began to swirl and blow outside.

"I thought you were controlling them?"

"I am," he said, with a mysterious smile.

Did he plan to take her again now? Did his hunger match hers? She began to unlace the strung-together laces of her gown, hoping to save them from further damage, when he placed his hand on hers and shook his head.

"The winds will cover all manner of noise this night," he whispered, as he put his finger to his lips. "Fog would be a welcomed help."

A minute passed and then the back flap of the tent lifted and William entered. With a nod to her, they sat down in the dark tent and discussed a plan of Soren's that he had hinted at.

The night that she thought would be spent in his arms was instead spent with a parade of visitors, whose arrivals and departures were covered by the winds whipping outside or by the fog that formed and dissipated several times through that night.

"So what is the plan then, William Warblood?" Marcus asked.

Ran walked out of their tent to find the discussion going on in the center of the camp. Loud enough for everyone to hear.

"The same we used before, the two go into the circle with the priest and perform the ritual. The rest of us will deal with whatever Hugh brings against us outside the circle." William glanced at Marcus and Aislinn. "Once you reveal and open the circle."

"It will not work," Soren said, walking up and sending the discussion into an uproar. "I know you are the trained knight and warblood, but we need to attempt something different. He will use whatever and whomever he can against us—against Ran and me. He has her father and all his men. He has my friend."

"And how do you think it should work, Soren?" William asked. Ran winced at his belligerent tone. When he crossed his arms over his massive chest and his gaze grew red, everyone but Brienne became nervous. "You do not know this man. There are no limitations to his evildoing. He will crush your friend and then destroy all of us."

Soren stood and went toe to toe with the warblood then. Not a good idea from the growling sounds the slightly blue warrior was making. Brienne stepped between them, whispering furiously to her husband, who once again was his human self. Letting out a breath, William spoke calmly now.

"How do you think this should be handled?"

"I think that I will make a bargain with de Gifford to protect all that is important to me." His gaze fell on Ran and she felt the heat of a blush in her cheeks once more.

"You are not with us, Stormblood?" Marcus asked.

"I do not know any of you. Why should I accept your word on this?" Soren said, indignantly. "Lord de Gifford has offered safety for me and those I care for. I can protect my lands and retain my power when his goddess comes."

"When did he offer this to you?" William asked.

"I went searching for Ran's father. Lord Hugh and I spoke." Ran winced again, knowing full well it was not a discussion. But for their purposes here and now, she did not contradict him.

"You think to trust him? Do not, Soren," said Brienne.

"I do not trust him, but I know not all of you. You arrived on our island and began giving me orders. Tell me why I must do what you say." Soren crossed his arms now and shook his head. "I will speak to him and see if I can trust him."

"You cannot unleash this evil on the world, no matter what promise he makes you," Roger argued. "Believe not a word he says."

"As I said, I will make my own judgment."

"And when he destroys you and everyone and everything you hold dear? How are we supposed to stop him then?" Brienne asked. "He is my father, Soren. I know him. Do not trust him."

Soren stood alone in the middle of them, each one trying to convince him to stay. It was time for her to play her role.

"Soren, what do you mean to do?"

"I told you, Ran. These people are the strangers here. I am going back to speak with Lord Hugh. To strike a bargain," Soren said.

"But he holds my father and Ander, demanding our compliance," she said. "We cannot bargain to let evil return to this world."

"I think if we give him what he wants, he will leave our lands and our lives can go back to what they were," Soren said.

"What life would that be, Soren? The one we planned to have together? The one that you destroyed by seducing my brother's betrothed? Or the one you have now? You have none because the woman you seduced and was forced to marry died."

Try as she might to say these things as though in a

play, the bitterness that lived within her seeped into the words. Aislinn, Brienne and Soren watched her closely and she knew they'd heard the truth within the planned words.

"I think you should go, Soren," she said, turning away from him.

He disappeared in a second.

A strong wind wound its way through the camp, pulling up tents and stirring up the sands. When it moved out over the sea, she could feel him touching the water.

"What will we do now, William?" she asked. Ran did not know the next step, only that they would wait for Hugh to communicate with Soren.

"We should move our camp to be closer to the circle. We must be there to help however we can," he said. Raising his voice, he continued. "We have to hope he comes to his senses and realizes he cannot bargain with the devil and think to win."

She nodded and watched the warblood walk off. She felt sick—her stomach roiled and her head hurt, almost as though they had truly fought. Even knowing most of it had been a performance meant for the spies sent by Hugh, all she wanted to do was go to the sea. But to do so now would look as though she chased after Soren.

She would, though not yet.

So she went to find Aislinn and hoped the young priestess could share more of her knowledge about the old gods with her.

CHAPTER 19

Soren followed the winds as they encircled the island, allowing them to lead him. In spite of knowing they'd planned it all out to give de Gifford's spies something to report, he did not like it.

Most of all, he hated saying what he had to Ran and hearing her words about their separation. Under those words lay the betrayal that would never ease between them. For even if he explained and she believed him, there was still the fact that he had not chosen her. And worse, it was not his bairn that Aslaug took to her death, but Ran's brother's. Another secret he kept from her.

He laughed then, bitterness now filling his heart.

All for naught. All for naught.

Well, his grandfather would have died a terrible death, so he was grateful it had never come to that.

And if these powers had risen at the time they were together and promised one to the other, how differently this might end.

Soren followed the winds higher and higher until he could look down on all of Orkney in one view. Going lower and lower until he was over the two largest of the Mainland's lakes, he searched the place where they believed the circle was. From up here, Soren could see the faint outline of it out in the middle of the lake. The size was immense, bigger than any henge of earth or stone he'd ever seen. Easily it was twice as large as nearby Brodgar's Ring.

How low had the water been for men to build such a wonder? Considering how far out in the lake it was, he could not estimate the number of years since its creation. He knew of other stones and walls that now lay under the sea because of changes to the coastline from decades or centuries of relentless storms and currents. Had that happened here?

Swirling lower, he noticed the way the earth pitched near it, making it look as though the whole of the circle simply slid off the edge of the land into the water.

Had it? Had those gods Ran had witnessed had enough power to accomplish such a thing? If the powers they imbued into their bloodlines were any indication, he would have to say that they did have enough to cause such a thing to happen.

And what power would it take to raise it from the lake bed? Or to move the water away and hold it until they performed the ritual? Would they have enough power to do both? All while fending off both the other warriors and de Gifford's men?

Soaring high again, he knew he would need to wait at least a day before seeking out de Gifford. His reason to go to him would be to confirm Ander's imprisonment and to seek information about his friend's condition. He had no doubt that de Gifford would try to lure him in. Soren knew he must not be too arrogant in his ability to fool this man. Pride must have no place in this or he would fail, as would they all.

Unable to seek out Ran, Soren returned to his own farm, changing where no one could see him and walking his lands. He spoke to those who worked the lands for him and his cousin who oversaw it now. For a few hours, it was like returning to the life he thought would be his.

He worked alongside them through the day and shared their meal. With nowhere to go, he slept in his own bed, for what he knew would be the last time and morning found him well rested. Soren wrote out a document turning all of his property over to his cousin and left it there. He took some time to write a letter to his aunt, hoping to explain more about what he'd learned since seeing her last. He prayed that she had traveled north.

Finally, the time came for him to seek out the one man who could be the death of everyone he knew . . . if de Gifford succeeded. When he arrived in Orphir, Soren was determined that he would stop the man and the evil he worshipped from ever entering his world.

Soren found nothing to be as he expected it.

After the scene on the ships at Westray, he expected chaos and disarray. He expected a desperate force of men enslaved against their will.

Instead he found a well-ordered encampment surrounding Svein's house. The ships were farther out in the bay, but repairs were being made to them. Men training at arms. Men organizing supplies. Men preparing food.

He walked along the path from the road and was greeted by one of the guards. If the man thought that someone appearing out of the air was an oddity, he said nothing and did nothing other than point him in the direction where his lord could be found. The surroundings were clean and the atmosphere calm, though as he walked closer to the house, he felt some tension growing.

The last time he'd visited this place was over two years ago. Svein had summoned him and Aslaug as though he were king and they his subjects. Soren had mistakenly thought the subject to be discussed would be upcoming marriages. He expected Ran and her brother to arrive at any time. He expected his request to marry Svein's daughter would be taken seriously.

He'd left, they'd left, bound in a terrible plot that, meant to save the ones they loved, cost too much. If Soren had only known the truth then. If he'd known about Einar's faith. If he'd known what the results would be, he might have had the strength to stand against her father.

Soren took in and then let out a deep breath as he approached the doorway. This house was modest for a man of Svein's tastes. Instead of a fortress to defend him and his family, he'd chosen a stone house near the water. Svein's reputation for ruthlessness kept any petty thieves away. His connections to the bishop through generous contributions of prayer and gold and his connection by kin to the now-absent earl stood him in good stead.

But Lord Hugh de Gifford cared nothing for Svein's position or connections; he simply wanted to use the man for whatever he could. And he had.

"You look like a man considering choices."

Soren looked up into the very face of evil.

He'd seen and heard de Gifford only once before and the man from that encounter and this man were completely at odds. Instead of the person he'd seen before, he found a man he thought now too young to be Brienne's father. Vitality shone from the man's face and stature. He wore the costly garments and jewels of a wealthy nobleman. His name spoke of a French or Norman background though his accent gave neither away.

"I am," Soren replied.

De Gifford motioned for him to follow and led him to the chamber Svein had used during their discussion. Had he chosen this room intentionally? When de Gifford smiled, Soren knew the answer.

"So the dealings with Svein you have had in the past—they happened here?"

He had already decided that the truth about this would be his best weapon, so he glanced around the room and nodded.

"He forced you to disavow your beloved, marry his son's betrothed and live a lie or he would destroy your family." He knew it all, probably from Svein's own lips.

"Aye," Soren said. "And Aslaug's family as well."

"And the bairn she carried." De Gifford knew it all from the expression in his eyes. Soren nodded again, watching and waiting for de Gifford's first move. Well, second, since bringing him to the place of his failure and humiliation was the first.

"And you want to save him?" de Gifford asked, sitting in the large chair used only by Svein.

"I do not wish to save him," Soren admitted. "She wishes to save him."

"Ahhh. The daughter who has let you back into her . . . well, certainly not bed, for that is the one place where you haven't fucked her yet."

Soren struggled to keep an even temperament. Control was essential now.

"Women can be forgiving," Soren said, smiling at the man. "Very, very forgiving."

"So I can kill him now?" Hugh asked calmly.

Soren held back from the word he wanted to say. He could not appear too eager.

"I do not want to save him, but I do not want you to kill him. I want him to know his failure. I want him to confess his crimes against me to his daughter and then I will kill him. In front of her." Soren turned away and stared out the window at the sea. "If you kill him, he becomes a martyr. Svein can be no martyr."

"For a simple farmer, Stormblood, you have interesting friends and enemies. In this moment, I cannot decide which it is better to be."

"But I am not a simple farmer, am I, my lord?" Soren used the honorific for the first time. "Nor was my grandfather before me. Marcus said he was the strongest priest ever born of the blood."

"Old Einar. The target of Svein's persecution."

Soren faced the nobleman and walked toward him.

"When I first encountered you, I had no idea of the magnitude of this situation," Soren explained. "And now? Surely you have been told about the broch? And Einar's drawings? The location of the other bloodlines?" Soren offered.

Hugh's eyes flared at the mention of the last, turning the color of molten metal for a single moment before returning to normal. "By her father, that priest and others," he replied.

His spies might have told him about the broch and the drawings, but the location of the other three bloodlines and the priestess' place in the rituals to come had been kept a secret. Marcus himself had seen to copying that particular panel of the wall. And then he'd had it whitewashed so none would see it.

"I know now about the old gods and my place as their descendant. I am tired of having others decide my fate," Soren said quietly. "I already know you need me to open the gateway, so tell me of your plans and my place in them."

De Gifford studied him for several long moments before reacting. Then he nodded. Standing, de Gifford walked to a table in the corner of the room and filled two goblets with a rich, reddish liquid. He walked back and held one out to Soren before taking his seat again. Soren held his cup to his host and then tried it.

"A comfort I allow myself. 'Tis from the bishop's own supply."

It was a richer wine than anything he'd ever tasted. Smooth and full of flavor, it warmed his throat and stomach. Soren could tell it was potent, too. De Gifford probably wanted to loosen his tongue. Another sip and he complimented with a raised cup.

"If you help me in opening this gateway, the goddess will be very pleased. She was the most powerful amongst them, you know. She can give you powers and a position of great importance in her new kingdom," de Gifford promised.

"I want the two you hold and Ran," Soren stated calmly.

"Why the good father?"

"We have a bond since childhood. I owe him much," Soren said, once again speaking the truth.

"I have plans for Ran," de Gifford began. "She offers such . . ."

"I want the priest, Svein and his daughter when this is done," Soren repeated. "I am certain I will want other . . . comforts," he held up the cup and smiled. "Before I agree, I want your word on this."

"We plan to breed the bloodlines and produce other powerful people to serve the goddess. Once she is freed, they will all be at our mercy," de Gifford explained. "Even the daughter of my flesh will once more have some use." He glanced away for a moment and then turned back with a smile, a lecherous one. "Ran Waterblood is extremely powerful; her blood is strong." Soren could see the man becoming aroused as he spoke of Ran.

"She is mine," Soren said forcefully. "She owes me three years. And sons I should have had. So first, I will breed sons on her to serve the goddess," he said, pausing to take a mouthful of the wine. "Then, once she has paid her penance for believing her father's lies, I am not opposed to allowing others . . ."

Soren let the words drift off and slid his hand down and touched his cock. De Gifford's lust was apparent. The man laughed aloud and drank down a good portion of his wine.

"This all depends on you bringing her to our cause. Will she open the gateway? Will you?"

"She thinks I will save her father for her. She's begged me to do so—and she begs so prettily when she needs to," Soren smiled. "I told her I would find a way." He drank the rest of the wine and put the cup down and nodded. "If you have a priest to carry out the ritual, I will open the gate."

Hugh stood from the chair quickly and threw his cup against the wall, screaming out. Soren tried to be patient and waited on his show of fury to pass.

"The damned priests die before I can turn them to my purpose," he ground out through clenched teeth. "They live like sheep, dragged onward by Marcus and fed nothing but his lies and his will." He stopped and took several deep, rapid breaths, regaining his control. "The last one, with the last one, they broke the bond they had forged amongst themselves and let him die." Hugh took one last breath and met his gaze. "The only one I have now is your priest. The one of the Christian god with no training in the old ways."

Did he dare? Soren knew this was the dangerous part of the bargain, but it could be the only way to make this all work.

"If you can turn him to our cause, I can give him the words during the ritual." Knowing it was a huge risk to Ander, to his soul, to sanity and his life, Soren let the words settle.

"How is that possible? You are the stormblood, descended from Taranis the Terrible," de Gifford said. "A priest must be trained. A priest must learn the spells and the chants—"

Soren leaned his head back and began to hum the first song Einar had taught him. When de Gifford just stared in disbelief, he added the words. After a few lines of the chant, the ground began to shake beneath them, tremors coming from somewhere away from the water and moving through the house.

From wherever the portal to hell opened into this world.

He stopped and waited for de Gifford's reaction. The nobleman grabbed his arm and pulled Soren's sleeve up, searching for the mark of his bloodline. It was there, the lightning bolt surging now, sending bursts of power into his body and blood.

"How can this be?" Hugh asked, staring at the mark. "Only priests can learn the spells and rituals."

"I told you—Einar Brandrson, my grandfather, was the most powerful priest the Old Ones created. I carry his blood, too. He has taught me the words and the sounds since I was a boy. I only realized it when I saw those words carved into the walls of the broch. 'One to open, one to close' he would say as he sang them to me."

Silence filled the chamber as he waited for a reaction.

Hugh leaned his head back and screamed, making the walls shudder and creak. Throwing his hands into the air, he began calling out words Soren did not recognize. He heard the goddess's name several times and he watched as de Gifford changed into living fire.

Ablaze, no longer man but creature of the evil one, he was terrifying to watch. Only the eyes and mouth appeared like those of a man. The heat of it knocked Soren back a few paces and he worried that the house would burn. Then, an instant later, he was human again.

"I will want to see you use your powers," de Gifford ordered. "Then I must see to tasks undone."

"The priest?" Soren asked.

"He has little will but much heart. So far, he has refused my offers. Now. Now I have so much more reason to bring him into our fold, as the good Christians say."

"I want him alive," Soren said. "When this is done."

"Alive? Alive can mean so many things."

Soren crossed his arms over his chest and waited.

"Very well, the priest alive. Svein alive for your use. The woman to pay for her sins." De Gifford laughed under his breath and then spoke. "They will all wish they were dead."

"So, are we agreed then, my lord?"

De Gifford stopped and stared at him. "You do not trust me, Soren Stormblood."

"And you do not trust me, my lord. This will be an interesting arrangement."

He followed de Gifford outside to the training yard his men had set up and for the next hours, he allowed the fireblood to guide him in using the powers he held. Surprisingly, never did he feel endangered or threatened. Instead, Hugh de Gifford was a patient instructor, showing him all manner of things he could do with wind and storm and lightning.

Which made Soren very ill at ease.

They parted, each with tasks to complete, and agreed that they would attempt to open the circle in two days' time during the fullness of the moon. Two days during which Soren must play his part as a willing accomplice, convince Ran to trust him enough to play her part and fool the most dangerous man, or creature, on earth.

And yet, as he rose into the sky, searching the island below him, Soren was invigorated. And hopeful. For the first time since the changes within him began, he felt hope.

CHAPTER 20

Hugh entered the stairway and followed it down under the old, round church to the portal below. He'd left both the Christian priest and Ran's father chained there, allowing them to witness more than their human minds could probably comprehend. Hugh had found that torture along with deprivation made most men more amiable to his demands.

But he also knew that most Christian priests were subjected to various practices that were or were very close to torture during their religious training. Oh, they'd be horrified to think of it as such, but the Church understood very clearly how to break men down and rebuild them into the fanatical, ruthless priests needed to carry out their duties. This Father Ander would have suffered such treatment and might be harder to break.

Though neither he nor his father and grandfather before him had been believers in the Roman Church, he'd learned their teachings and carried out their ceremonies of worship while waiting for the time when he could act on his true beliefs. Waiting until their wealth and power and *powers* could keep them safe from censure . . . or worse. Now was the time for his rise and, with the goddess's help, he would be successful. First though, the goddess demanded her due.

As Hugh approached the door to the chamber, the walls began to shake and the ground rumbled beneath his feet—Chaela was hungry. Lifting the latch, he pushed open the door and entered. Father Ander was conscious and saying those damned prayers. Relentlessly, the priest murmured the same one over and over again. Hugh knew it and knew it well, for part of his preparations. The priest's fingers moved as though holding his beads and his lips unceasingly whispered the words. Only a slight hesitation occurred when the roar came from below the stone floor.

"Hail Mary," the priest began again, closing his eyes. His words faltered when Hugh approached him. Hugh waited for him to finish this rendition before stepping closer and laughing at his efforts.

"At the hour of your death. Amen," Hugh offered the last words, mocking the priest. "How many times have you said that prayer, Ander? One hundred? Two? A thousand?" Crouching before him, Hugh leaned closer even as the priest tried to lean away. "Mayhap your prayers have been answered?"

Father Ander's words came to a stuttering stop.

"Aye, good father," Hugh continued. "Your savior has arrived to help you." He laughed then. "Oh, I see your confusion. Not *the* Savior, but yours. Soren Thorson has claimed your soul and your life."

"Soren?" Father Ander asked, his dry lips bleeding as he tried to speak aloud.

"Soren Stormblood has seen the right path and will open the gateway for Chaela."

The shrieking that came from below them at his declaration made the chamber quake. Ander tried to press his arms against his ears to block it. "He cannot," Ander whispered. "He will not."

Hugh grabbed the man's hair and slammed Ander's head back against the wall over and over until he was almost unconscious.

"A pity you feel that way. With this kind of devotion, you could be the new high priest to Chaela. You could begin your own new church, choose your own supplicants."

Hugh walked to the door and opened it. Motioning to Eudes, who stood waiting outside, Hugh stepped aside and watched as Eudes dragged the chosen sacrifice and tossed him on the floor. Ander began to struggle to turn away and began his prayer again.

"Hail—" Hugh grabbed his face, forced open his mouth and thrust a finger of flame against his tongue. Ander screamed against the agony.

"The only reason you still have that tongue is that I need you to say the prayers aloud. But when you have fulfilled your duty, I will tear it out and burn it before I burn you to the goddess." He released Ander and stepped to the center of the chamber. "Silence!" he yelled.

As the priest lost the last vestiges of control and sought any oblivion he could find, Hugh wondered if he yet prayed those words to himself. Then the goddess called to him and the priest was of little concern to Hugh. His own prayers echoed through the chamber, mingling with the screams of the sacrifice and honoring his death.

In the end, the goddess was placated, the priest was an empty vessel waiting to be filled and Hugh moved one step closer to succeeding.

Brienne had said her father could travel from fire to fire, using any form of it to move from place to place. That was how Hugh could watch and know so much. And why Marcus had made them finish using them so quickly to light the chamber beneath the broch. Once the fireblood knew of them, he could travel to them.

Or just go in search of them.

So, Ran had promised to meet Soren on Birsay the next night. They had much to discuss and decide, but if she did not trust him, if she could not play her part, they would fail.

She wanted to believe she could, but the words spoken aloud yesterday stirred up her doubts. Ran loved him, she knew he loved her. Love was not their problem. Lovemaking was certainly not.

Traveling through the sea, she remained in her watery form when she moved onto the beach like a wave. Soren lay there, a hand thrown across his brow, his breathing slow and even. Asleep.

As she watched him, she noticed injuries and burns on his arms. He said he would do what was necessary for Hugh to believe his defection, but she had not thought that part through.

Seawater healed. Seawater soothed.

She flowed up around him and then, changing from cold to a soothing warmth, she covered his body like a blanket and held him. He moaned as the warmth penetrated his skin. She washed over the bruises and the burns and offered him relief from the pain.

"What . . ." he said. Waking, he lifted his head and realized it was her.

"I wanted to ease your pain and your injuries," she said. "My waters heal skin."

He lay back and did not resist, allowing her to caress his skin and soothe the tears and the burns.

"What are they from?" she asked, flowing gently over him. "What has he done to you?"

"He is testing me—testing my loyalty, testing my resolve," he said. He lifted his head and glanced as she spread across him.

"And will you be loyal?" she asked.

"I am only loyal to you, Ran. I know you will not understand this, but I have only ever been loyal to you."

Ran felt the truth of his declaration to her soul and let it ease some of the bitterness still residing there.

"But what we face, what he plans, I cannot do unless I know that you trust me and will be loyal to me. No matter what he says, no matter how he tempts or threatens us or the others, I need to know if you will be with me."

She knew she loved him and now she must trust him.

She did trust him. She knew it in that moment.

"I am with you," she said. "I am."

He did not say anything then; he just lay still as she flowed around and over him. "I love you, Ran Sveinsdottir. Forever and always. You are the only one in my heart."

"I love you, Soren Thorson," she whispered.

They remained like that for a time.

"You are talking to me. Your voice sounds lovely when you are the water."

"I am," she said, realizing that she had not done that before. She'd spoken to the sea, she'd screamed in it, but had not tried to send her voice out of it. "Is it lovely?"

"I think it's the soft voice that calls to sailors, beckoning them in the depths."

His voice was soft and sleepy. She laughed until he spoke again. "Beckon me in, Ran Waterblood. Beckon me into your depths."

His words called to her. She reached out her hand and pulled him to stand. Though still water, she held her form, keeping together almost as human skin. Then she moved around him, removing his garments one by one until he stood naked before her. She covered him in warmth and caressed him, touching his back and his wonderfully muscled back and arse. Then she stroked his cock, using her watery hand to encircle it and massage it.

His head fell back and he let out a deep, soft sigh. She guided him back down to the sand and covered him, sliding over him, pressing, caressing, stroking him until he gasped. Then she took human form and straddled him, sliding his length into her. He opened his eyes and held out his hands to her. With entwined fingers, she balanced on him as she moved up and down his flesh.

"I cannot decide—water or woman," he whispered, pulling up and wrapping his arms around her to hold her close. The hair on his chest teased her breasts and made the tips tighten. She rocked her hips, sliding in and out a bit, waiting for him to take control.

He did not. He let her set the pace for their joining. And though she loved it when he thrust hard and deep, this easy pace suited her this night. Soren tilted his head and kissed along the fullness of her breasts. Lifting and arching her back, she pushed her breasts closer to his mouth.

He took one in his mouth and laved it with his tongue. The roughness made her ache deep inside. Each slide of his tongue brought about another throbbing within her core. And still he did not take her.

He slid his hands down around her arse and guided her rocking pace. This was the time when he would roll her on her back and fill her. Not this time.

"Are you anxious, Ran? Hurried?" he whispered against her neck as he kissed his way up to her ear, stopping several times to taste her mouth. "I like the gentle pace of the sea," he teased.

Her body wanted to explode beneath him. Everything within her had tightened and tightened and now she wanted to come undone. She wanted the storm.

"Soren Stormblood," she whispered. "Take me."

In less time than she could have imagined, he changed into a storm, pushing her back and thrusting deep. His winds moved over her skin, their brisk chafing teasing her breast as his tongue had. She arched up to meet each thrust of his flesh. Ran could see him and then not, as he became something else, something human and yet not. Something more. Something different than he'd ever been.

"Ran Waterblood," he called from within the winds. "Come with me."

His voice turned her to water and she was held within the winds as they rose and rose into the sky. Lightning bolts coursed around them, and each one shattered her until the water and winds reformed. Thunder rumbled through the skies as they, storm-blood and waterblood, merged into one.

Then they burst, together as the lightning struck again—water and wind, man and woman, stormblood and waterblood. Lovers until the next bolt that shattered them apart. Over and over, through the sky, on the sand, in the clouds and in the water, they became one and shattered, joined and shattered into pieces. Water and air mixed together, carried by the winds, across and in the sea, until with a burst they fell apart, each falling back to the beach where it all began.

They lay on the beach, trying to ease their racing hearts. Soren reached over and took her hand, pulling her to him. Power rushed through her body, pushing through her veins and arteries, into her muscles and bone and marrow. When she looked at him, she could see he was filled with it, glowing silver even more than before.

"I do not know what happened, but I think that is how we will uncover the circle and defeat Hugh de Gifford."

It was a long while before they spoke, and then Soren told her his plan. She understood that they or any of the warriors or their people could die in this endeavor. More than that, Ran understood that this battle was in her blood and connected now to her, their, powers.

By the time morning came and they parted, Ran knew that Soren was already a part of her as she'd left part of herself behind in him.

Marcus liked to pray in the dark silence of the night. Oh, he enjoyed the time of common prayer where his community of priests would gather and pray together. But there was something special about listening to the sounds only present in the dark.

So this night he walked several miles down the beach until he found the place where the gods wished him to be. The outcropping jetted north into the ocean and sat high up so he could see miles in all directions. Kneeling and closing his eyes, he began his ritual.

The silence was filled with words from the gods. He let them seep into his soul and sought the truth he needed to know from among the clamor of the messages.

He could feel the fear of his faithful priests.

He felt the doubt of the other warriors.

He knew the dread that the other men felt, facing the coming battle with an evil they could not from the way in which they were trained.

But those thoughts and fears and prayers were not what the gods had brought him here to see. The flashes of lightning sparking against the huge storm to the north was.

Pillars of clouds collided high in the sky, filled with wind and rain and lightning flashes and crashing thunder. As he watched the storm grew and circled the tidal island, and Marcus understood what he was seeing.

The waterblood and stormblood had merged! Praise be! His soul cried out in joy at the sight of it and at being gifted by the gods to witness such a thing. In a way he could not have anticipated, the two had joined, not only their hearts and bodies but now their souls and spirits. Whatever strife had kept them apart had melted in the strength of their love.

Praise be!

As the storm, lightning, winds and rain dissipated, Marcus fell to the ground, prostrating himself and opening himself to the gods for their directions.

When morning came and a bright sun rose into a cloudless sky, Marcus understood what he must do. Returning to the camp, he went to the tent of the healers where Corann yet recovered from his ordeal with Lord Hugh. He waited in patience and prayer until his old friend opened his eyes and then he merged with him, sharing his thoughts.

Corann shook his head at what Marcus shared with him. Marcus smiled and nodded his head, leaning closer so none would hear.

" 'Tis your time to step into your rightful place, my friend. The gods have declared my time is done."

Corann struggled to speak, but his body had been so damaged that he could not. Marcus put his hand on Corann's forehead and sent a burst of healing sleep into him.

"Good-bye, my old friend," Marcus whispered as he left the tent and saw to the other necessary tasks he must complete in time.

After speaking to Brisbois, Aislinn's guard and the only other human who had survived within the circle during the ritual, Marcus understood his place and praised his gods for such an honor.

CHAPTER 21

Hugh watched as the priest conversed with his bishop. So far, over the last two days, the bishop of Orkney, the pope of Rome and even the king of Norway had visited the priest as he hung chained to the wall. The bishop was giving the priest a special dispensation to follow Hugh's orders, as a secret mission against the true evil—the Warriors of Destiny.

The pope had offered the priest a plenary indulgence of three years to take up the robe of martyr against the evil ones who sought to destroy the Church. The king had convinced Ander that the real leader in this endeavor against evil was Lord Hugh, and a reward of gold would be his if he joined Hugh. When the priest had hesitated at a worldly reward, the king had instead offered him a choice of serving God in any part of his kingdom.

The fact that the bishop was Eudes, his commander and half brother, did not matter. That the pope was a soldier who served as guard or that the king was actually Svein's housekeeper who now did anything Hugh bid her do mattered not. In the mind and thoughts of Father Ander, the bishop, pope and king had come calling.

The sacrifices he'd witnessed and the burnings of his own skin were not worship to a false god, but were the results of the fiery purification by the archangel Michael with his flaming sword, the pope told him.

That the priest could fight his efforts did surprise Hugh. He'd seemed weak-willed at first. The fact that he yet lived also, for Hugh had been continuously invading the man's mind and forcing his beliefs into him. Soon, very soon, Father Ander Erlandson would be ready to fight the evil warriors, including his friends Soren and Ran.

Over the hours of relentless indoctrination and on top of the pain and deprivation, the priest broke and then was rebuilt by Hugh. By the time he was taken to the circle, Ander would do whatever Hugh told him to do and believe whatever Hugh told him to believe.

Eudes stepped out of the chamber and nodded to him. He had, as bishop, delivered God's call to Ander and the word of God said that the stormblood and waterblood were trying to open a doorway for evil to enter the world. And he must do or say whatever was necessary to thwart Soren.

"He has taken up the call of his God, my lord," Eudes said. Eudes had never refused an order or failed him in this work. Oh, he had killed the priest they'd captured, but his work with Ander had made up for that.

"Very well," Hugh said. "Take him out and clean him up. Feed him and have that woman see to his injuries. He has only today and part of this night before he must perform the ritual."

"And the stormblood? What will he say when he sees him?"

Hugh shrugged. "He knows he was a prisoner. At least he is better off than the other one."

Svein Ragnarson could be a problem. Hugh had promised him to Soren alive, and though he had no intention of letting him live, the man had to at least appear to have a chance at survival.

"See if the woman can do anything for him. When the waterblood arrives, tell me."

Hugh left the chamber and went outside. Within a few hours, his men would be positioned at the entrances to the spit of land where the major stone henges sat between the two lakes. No one would get in or out of it without Hugh knowing about them. He'd also prepared his ships. That did not mean he thought he would fail, but he was pragmatic and liked to have alternatives when dealing with such unpredictable creatures.

His biggest advantage was that they still thought like the humans they once were. They thought they were somehow limited. So, he planned to remind them of their humanity. Until or if they moved beyond that Hugh knew he would succeed.

Though Soren had promised cooperation, he would reveal neither the specific location of the circle nor the words needed to open it. Hugh did not blame the young man, for keeping that knowledge to himself gave him some leverage. And kept both of them alive for now.

Now they waited for the night and the rising of the moon to begin. He bristled with anticipation of seeing the stormblood and waterblood reveal the circle, long buried and hidden away.

And for the release of his goddess.

Ran knew she must leave soon. The plan Soren explained would have her arrive at sunset at her father's house. She sought out Aislinn to speak to her about the ritual and found her in the tent of the healers, packing up supplies and preparing to leave.

"Aislinn, may I have a moment to speak to you? I have questions about . . ." The young woman turned and nodded.

"Come outside so we will not disturb the last few moments of rest they will get." The burly, silent guard accompanied them.

"Have you seen Marcus?" Aislinn asked once they were outside the tent. "I have been looking for him since sunrise and cannot find him."

"Did he leave with William and Brienne?" Those two would be close by the area when she and Soren uncovered the circle and having the older priest with them made sense. "I will tell him you seek him if I see him."

Aislinn nodded to the guard who moved a few paces away, though his gaze never strayed from the priestess or anyone who approached her. Then the young woman studied her with an unsettling intensity.

"You have bonded," she whispered. "The gods be praised!"

"Bonded?"

"You have mated and merged your beings, your powers. It will strengthen each of you and your child."

The world tilted under her feet and only the quick

action of Aislinn's guard kept her from falling. "My child?"

"When you are blessed with one, your powers will be combined in that child," she explained. "We did not know if, like the ancient ones, those of the bloodlines would mate with priests or priestesses, or if they'd mate with each other. To carry on the powers to the next ones."

Thinking on the fertility ceremony she'd seen, Ran did not want to consider how the gods mated with humans. Or the price of those joinings.

"So many of our practices have been lost to us," Aislinn said. "We are learning even as you and the others do. With William and Brienne, his powers rose when she was endangered. Hers rose upon meeting him. But we did not know if each pair will be connected in that way."

"Why do you not know more? Are there no records?" Ran knew that the Church had records and written texts from centuries ago. As did the kingdoms and other governments.

"Ours was a tradition passed down through stories and prayers. Truly, seeing what Soren's grandfather created was the first time we have seen all of it in one place. Marcus believes we should begin the practice of recording our ceremonies and prayers on parchments or tablets." Aislinn looked around the camp once more.

"I am certain he is simply busy with arrangements," Ran said. "I know you have many tasks, so I won't keep you. I just wanted to know if there is anything I should know about the ceremony. I worry about Ander being able to chant the prayers."

"He has been in the hands of the evil one for days. I

pray that he is strong enough to withstand what is done to him."

"And if he cannot finish it? Marcus said that beginning and not ending the chant will bring about the destruction of the circle?" Ran asked, knowing that was what Marcus had said. "So, I thought that you could teach it to me. If Soren's attention is on Lord Hugh, I can instruct Ander. I think it would be better. . . ."

"None of the rituals are the same. Oh, we begin in the same way, calling on the Old Ones to protect us from evil, but then each circle has its own chant."

"How do you know which one it is?"

"I heard it when I entered, when Brienne and William joined us inside the circle. This time, they were revealed to Einar, who was supposed to teach them to us when the time came. At least he taught them to Soren, who can pass them to Ander."

Ran had a bad feeling then.

"So there is nothing I can do to be ready?"

Aislinn reached out, her green eyes glowing and the color of moonlight blazing around her, and touched Ran's arm where the mark lay.

"You are waterblood. You are ready. You are bonded to the stormblood now. Act as one. Rely on no one but each other. Accept his strength, forgive his weakness." Aislinn squeezed her arm. "Be one with him."

Her blood surged at the prayer of this powerful priestess of the Old Ones. The sea was in her and she was with the sea. She held the powers of water within her.

"Your eyes," Aislinn said. "They are the sea! The goddess dwells within you!" The priestess released her and knelt before Ran. Bowing her head to the ground, she whispered something. Raising her head, she smiled and nodded at Ran.

Shocked by the priestess's actions, Ran made her way out of the camp and joined with the sea. It was different now. She did not look out at the sea; she looked inward at it. She was the water. She flowed. She sustained.

The merging with Soren had caused some change in her power and in herself. She was much stronger with him. Her trust was the price of this change and her pride the cost.

Flowing around the island, she did not go to Orphir, but to the lake. Leaving behind the fear from her last encounter, she moved through the bay, past Hamnavoe and through the thin connecting channel. In the lake, she slid along the bottom, looking for the circle.

It was there!

Under a thick layer of silt and debris from thousands of years of waiting, the circle was there!

Some stones stood while others had fallen. Eight stones in the middle. More in a wider circle around them. An altar stone to one side of the center of it all. Bigger than Stenness. Wider than Brodgar. A huge complex for worship and then a gateway to another place.

As she moved over it, she felt the power simmering there. But the power stuttered as something beneath it pushed against it.

Sister, you will not succeed, she heard herself say.

I will be free, Chaela said from deep under the circle.

We put you there and you will remain, she told the goddess who'd been like a sister to her. Nantosuelta's heart and spirit hurt at the actions they'd been forced to take.

You think you are more powerful than me. You will pay

for your betrayal, Chaela said, screaming and pushing against the barrier that held her within the prison of the void. *I will be freed.*

No matter the cost, you will not, she promised the evil one her sister had become.

Ran streamed back to sea and around to Orphir. Rising from the sea, she walked across the beach and confronted Chaela's minion, who watched her with widened eyes. Oh, aye, let him worry.

"Take me to Svein Ragnarson," she ordered. Changing to her human form, she repeated her demand. "Take me to my father." Her voice sounded different to her and echoed in a strange fashion.

He stumbled back, motioning for her to follow, and she walked into the house that used to be hers. Those who had served Svein Ragnarson before now stood broken and wretched along the corridors of the house. They shuffled aside as Hugh de Gifford approached. All but one woman.

"Dalla," she said. No longer proud or pretentious, the woman could not even raise her gaze to Ran's.

"Is that her name?" Hugh asked. There was no hint of sarcasm in his voice now.

"What have you done to her? To them?" she asked. They turned down a corridor that led to the servants' rooms.

"They have been made to serve me," Hugh said. "She thought her place as Svein's favorite would save her somehow. She offered his secrets and his wealth to bargain with me." They stopped before the smallest chamber in the house and Hugh lifted the latch. "They all learned."

Ran stumbled and gasped when she saw her father. All sense of power seeped away in the face of his condition. For a moment, she was simply the daughter of a dying man. A dying man with his soul lost.

"Father?" she said, kneeling at the side of the small cot. "Father?" She took his hand and found it cold. "Papa, can you hear me?"

Ran could hear Hugh behind her. Turning, she found him smirking. He had done this. He had taken her father, her people, even her house and destroyed all that was good. With no more thought than that, she created a wall of water that knocked him down and pushed him from the room. Ran dropped the bar on the door. Hugh could return and get in if he wanted to but she did not want him there now. Face him, she must, but it would be later.

She leaned in closer and examined her father. His breaths were barely raising his chest, and his skin was gray. She lifted the bed linens and pulled up his sleeve. Burns. Burns. Bruises on his stomach when she looked there. More burns and bruising on his legs.

He did not move with one exception—his lips tried to speak. From the bruising on his neck and throat, she doubted he could get a word out at all. Leaning closer, she tried to hear, but they were simply breaths without sound.

Ran placed her hand on his face and moved into him, her water joining with his. As it coursed through his body, she saw the injuries that were not visible outside. But when she came to his head and his mind, she pulled herself back.

His mind was gone. What made him Svein Ragnarson was gone.

Knowing the only thing she could do was keep him at ease until he passed, Ran entered his flesh again and sent more of her healing water into him. Circling through him, pushing herself into his muscles and bones, she did what she could. But even with the goddess's power, she could not sustain his life.

She formed at his side, pulling back into her human body, and watched as he sank into a deeper sleep. His pallor was not as gray as before.

It would be harder now, knowing the truth of his impending death. Her role in this tragic play was that of hopeful daughter. She must convince Hugh that her father was the price of her cooperation.

Give him words as smooth as the calm sea, the goddess said.

Ran stood and lifted the bar on the door, opening it to find Hugh waiting there. He entered and stood next to her father.

"He is the price of my help," she said, pointing at her father. "He is the only reason I will help you and Soren. When the goddess is released, I want him made whole and returned to me. Along with all you've taken."

"There will be many changes when the goddess returns, Waterblood," Hugh said. Not all of them good, she knew, even without his saying so.

"I want your word, your bond, on this," she said, holding out her arm.

His gaze narrowed as he took her hand in his. She shuddered when he sent his fire into her, but let the water flow through and against it. The silent battle continued as his fire fought with her water. The last time they'd touched, he'd won. This time . . .

He released her first. With a wary look, he nodded and stepped away. "And what about Soren?" he asked.

"I care not," she said. *Smoothly,* the goddess urged. "He betrayed me and destroyed my family. I want my father's life and nothing else."

The fireblood stepped closer and smiled. He was a handsome man and now filled with a vitality she'd not noticed before. He exuded a sensuality as he approached her. Arousal. He smelled of arousal.

"You care not about him, yet you have taken him back as your lover. You let him in your body. You pleasured him."

"I have needs," she said.

The heat in his breath against her neck had nothing to do with the fire that lived in his blood. He wanted her.

"I could see to them," he said as he slid his finger along her neck. "We could see to them."

Smoothly, daughter, the goddess urged.

"As you have said"—Ran turned to face him, moving away from his touch—"once the goddess is free, many things will be possible." Bile rose in her mouth as she said such a blasphemy, but she kept her expression one of interest. "It all depends on my father's life."

"And one other thing, my dear Waterblood," Hugh said as he walked to the door. "If you try to deceive me or not carry out our agreement, I will make certain that Soren and the others learn your secret."

Alarmed at such a threat, she looked at him.

"My secret?" she asked. The goddess whispered through her blood, calming her.

"That you killed that innocent man. That you sucked him dry of his life. Drop by drop."

Guilt filled her. She had mindlessly killed a man who had the bad luck to be standing near her. "I did not do it apurpose," she said.

Hugh walked back to her, moving in as closely as he had been before. His breath on her skin made her shiver.

"Ah, true," Hugh whispered against her neck, his body close enough for her to feel his aroused flesh against her hip. "But before you let your very human guilt fill your heart and soul, I felt it."

"Felt it?" she asked, not daring to move.

"I felt your thrill and wonderment at your power to do so. I felt it. Your desire for more power . . ." He pressed against her, harder. "We will seek many pleasures of many kinds when the goddess has risen."

Fighting off panic and guilt, she sought the power of her blood. Her heart raced, making it difficult to ease her breathing. He would read it as . . .

"Just so," he said, smiling. He touched his mouth to her neck and she felt the tip of his tongue on her skin. Her body shuddered and he stepped back. "Just so. You do as you've agreed and this ends well for both of us. Chaela will reward us for our part in freeing her. Your father will live. And we will have all the time we need to explore the extent and depth of our powers and pleasures."

She could not speak after such disgusting words, so she simply nodded. His smile must be like the one who greeted that first woman and tempted her to evil, too.

"We begin at moonrise."

And he was gone.

Ran barely made it to the bowl sitting in the corner before she began retching.

From fear. From guilt. From knowing the truth. From fearing that others would know it. Her stomach emptied itself until there was no more. On her knees, she prayed for forgiveness to any god who would hear her plea.

For as much as she wanted to deny it, using her power was pleasurable. Even when she took that man's water, she enjoyed how her power felt pulsing through him and pulling every bit from him. She was the water and reclaiming it to herself was gratifying in a physical way.

She vomited again, giving up nothing but bile now.

Pushing herself to her feet, she looked at her father and knew the truth. She must—they must—prevail. She'd felt the enticement and pull of evil and it was too strong to resist forever.

Sending more of herself into her father with a touch, Ran went to find Soren.

CHAPTER 22

Ander Erlandson was a humble cleric and a competent scholar in the service of his God. Now though, as Marcus peered into the window of the small chamber from outside, Ander lay bloodied and beaten on a clean bed. The woman servant had tended to his injuries and he lay unmoving.

Marcus knew the priest survived only because Lord Hugh needed him. But as he waited for the opportunity to enter the house, Marcus could feel the terrible results of the torture wrought on this innocent soul. Waiting for the house to clear of most of the guards, Marcus offered up prayers for his friends and their success . . . without him.

When the chance came, he took it, moving quickly and quietly inside and down the corridor that led to the small chamber. Marcus lifted the latch as carefully as possible and inched the door open. Ander sat on the edge of a small cot, whispering to himself. Words about saints and purification and evil echoed around him.

As Marcus crept into the chamber, Ander let out a

sigh of desolation and exhaustion. Then he laid back and stretched out on the bed.

"Father?"

Only more whispered prayers answered him.

"Ander Erlandson," he whispered. He slipped inside and closed the door behind him. "Father?"

Marcus moved quietly across the room, snuffed the candle on the table and walked to the bedside. The bed crunched from his added weight on the straw mattress. Then he laid his hand on Ander's forehead.

"You must open your eyes, good Father," Marcus said. Then he touched his fingers to the priest's burned mouth.

"You have been ill-used for your beliefs, Ander," Marcus continued. "Neither your god nor mine would require such things."

"Go from me, Satan!" Ander yelled, trying to push Marcus away. Waves of pain and confusion emanated from within the priest's soul and mind. He must offer what comfort he could.

"Hush now," he said, covering Ander's mouth with a gentle touch. "Rest now, Ander. Gain back your strength."

Ander fought the spell Marcus was weaving around him, trying to make him fall into sleep's grasp. This priest's purity of spirit gave his mind a strength Marcus hoped would protect him in the coming hours. Marcus kept his hand on the poor priest's head, waiting for him to sleep. Then, as he had with Corann, Marcus entered the priest's mind and soul to try to correct the damage the evil one's minion had created.

Though Ander had succumbed to Lord Hugh's torment, his spirit was strong. All Marcus could do was reinforce that strength and remove the constraints that Hugh had placed to make the man do his bidding. Lord Hugh's power was great, but Marcus knew his was stronger, especially in an already good soul.

He remained there, pouring the last bits of his priestly power into this good soul, begging his own gods and Ander's to show mercy to him and to strengthen him to fight against the evil that would use his goodness against him.

Only when the sound came of people approaching down the corridor did Marcus release the priest. He stood, certain he did not wish to meet his end on his knees.

Soren could feel Ran's distress and went to Orphir to find her. She stood motionless at the water's edge and so he took her into himself and merged with her. The thick cloud filled with wind and water floated out over the water.

Hold me, she said.

I am here.

They just remained there together in one form until they heard de Gifford's voice and felt his approach. Separating, they took human form on the beach before him.

"Is that how you will uncover it?" de Gifford asked, smiling, clearly excited by the coming events.

"I believe so," Soren said. Ran nodded. Something had disturbed her deeply. "As storm and water, we can push away the water and open the site."

"There are two rings of stones under the water," Ran said. "I saw them earlier today."

A chill went through the air and a keening sound echoed across the waters as the moon rose over the eastern horizon and the sun dropped below it in the west. He looked at de Gifford and then at Ran and nodded.

" 'Tis time." His own voice echoed across the beach and he looked at Ran. Her eyes glowed brilliant turquoise now as she reached for his hand.

"We will meet at Stenness," Hugh said.

"My father?" Ran asked, turning her gaze on de Gifford.

"I will take him and the priest there," Hugh said. "They have actually been sent on ahead of us." De Gifford motioned to his men to move out. "Wait until I arrive and then uncover the circle. Once you have done that, I will bring the priest to you and you begin the ceremony."

Soren nodded as did Ran.

"I will kill him if I think you are betraying me," de Gifford warned. "And then I will kill the priest."

"I will see him alive before I open the circle to you," Ran said quietly. "And I will see him alive before I carry out the ritual. If he dies—" Her words drifted off.

"Since we have all entered this bargain willingly, let us be done with the threats. We all have great things to gain in this endeavor," Soren said in a voice that sounded very different to him.

De Gifford left them, traveling to Stenness in his own manner. Soren took Ran's hand in his.

My love, it has been too long since I held you.

The words were not his, but he said them in his thoughts to her. She smiled back at him, walking into his embrace. Soren felt as though it was the first time he'd held her.

Taranis, my love. I have longed for you over these centuries, she said.

Nantosuelta, he said. *Come, let us carry out the ceremony.*

The voice in which he spoke was both foreign and familiar to him, for it was part of him and part of the god who now lived within him.

Merging your souls released us into you, Taranis said.

Now we are you, his goddess wife said.

In a moment, they were at the place between the lakes.

"There," Ran said, pointing to the area between Brodgar's Ring and the burial cairn on the opposite shore. "The circle lies there."

They turned and watched Hugh enter. He did indeed move between torches, ones his men must have placed in preparation. On the shore there, a wagon holding Ander and her father sat waiting. When Hugh stood before them, he nodded at his men. Ander was helped from the cart and walked toward them. Svein was carried over and laid before them.

Soren led Ran to the edge of the lake, across the path from the stones, and held out his hand to her. Embracing her, he lifted up into the sky and moved out over the lake to the place she'd indicated. From here, even in the gloaming, he could see something under the water.

"Give me your strength, Soren," Ran and the goddess said.

He began the merging, spinning faster and faster, letting the winds free to form a huge storm over the lake. She added her water to it and they grew. Lightning shot into the sky and into the lake.

Waters, move! The goddess called out from the storm.

Soren guided the heavy spinning clouds down to the lake, adding his winds to the force pushing the waters away from the circle. He expanded, wider and wider, stronger and stronger, until they became a cyclone over the circle. When the water cleared away, he pushed deeper and harder to clear the accumulations of silt and debris from within the rings. Finally, the stone-inlaid floor was visible and he knew he'd reached the bottom of the structure.

Now, stand the stones! Nantosuelta called out.

He drew his winds tighter around them and strengthened them. When they were so strong they could not be resisted, they moved around the ring, pushing the stones upright and into their places. Before dissipating, Soren pulled Ran to him inside the winds.

"No matter what happens, Ran. Know that I love you," he whispered to her.

"And I you," Ran whispered back, kissing him as though it was their last time.

Though they'd never spoken it, they both knew that they would destroy the circle and themselves before opening it for evil to enter.

No matter the cost, she and the goddess whispered.

Soren let the winds go and brought them down to the beginning of the path leading out into the lake, where the twin stones stood marking it. All of it had been right there—marked by the upright stone and its twin that pointed right out to it.

Ran glanced over and commanded the waters to

stay away. Then they waited for Hugh to bring Ander to them. He must enter the circle first to begin the ceremony.

As he watched his friend approach, he knew something was very wrong. Ander did not feel right to him. Confusion poured out of him and his gaze darted quickly from one to the other, to Hugh, to the rings, to Svein.

"Do we begin?" he asked in a voice that did not sound like his own. It was familiar, but Soren could not identify it.

"Aye, Ander," Soren said, holding out his arm. "Let me guide you." But Lord Hugh stepped forward first, placing his arm on Ander's shoulder.

"Are you ready, Father?" he asked the priest. "Are you strong enough to carry out the task?"

The words had a strange sound to them and Soren realized he was using his power to control people by pushing his thoughts into their minds. Taking over their wills.

"Aye," Ander said, now in his own voice.

"Very well," de Gifford said, releasing him. "Seek out the inner stones and the altar and begin the ritual."

Soren watched his friend walk along the path slowly, turning this way and that, staring into the circle and then to the sky . . . or the heavens, mayhap. When he reached the first of the rings, he touched the nearest stone before entering.

Soren took Ran's hand and they walked side by side down the path leading into the lake. Glancing back, he saw that de Gifford now held Svein before him, a dagger at his throat.

"Ran Waterblood!" he called out.

Though Soren knew the threat that was coming, he had to look back with her.

"This will be your father's fate if you think to betray me." Two of the soldiers near the wagon lifted out a blanket-wrapped form and tossed it free.

Marcus's dead body lay at the foot of the twin stones.

When Ran screamed and tried to run to her father, de Gifford met his gaze and nodded. Soren nodded and pulled her once more toward the ring in the lake. Suddenly another scream filled the air. As they watched, the torches flared around the area until Brienne materialized before her father.

"What have you done?" she screamed, taking her human form and running to Marcus's body.

"He tried to meddle in my plans," Hugh said. "He knew the price."

When Brienne turned to fire and began to attack Hugh, her father simply moved Svein before him and smiled. Unable and unwilling to kill an innocent, Brienne stood waiting—most likely for her chance to save Svein or stop her father.

Hugh's men began pointing in the distance and shouting.

He'd seen the warblood rise to take his form in practice, but nothing he'd seen prepared Soren to see this. He understood why Hugh's soldiers began fleeing.

Almost as tall as the stones of Stenness at his back, the warblood stood now as a blue-skinned berserker of legend. His eyes glowed red as he moved with a lethal grace across the path to the twin stones. The ground shook with each step he took. Soren blinked several times, still not believing the sight of him. One of his massive arms was now a sword that no man could carry and the other was a war hammer worthy of Thor Odinson himself. The scream the warblood released made even his own blood curdle at the sound.

"Harm her and I will destroy you, Fireblood!"

"We seem to be at a stalemate for now," de Gifford answered. "But when the gate is opened, you will pay for your choosing to resist me."

"Soren! Ran! Do not help him!" Brienne screamed out.

"We have a bargain, Stormblood. Waterblood, you sealed ours with your water," de Gifford called out. "Go now! Chaela awaits."

"Come," Soren said to Ran. "I think he has Ander under his control," he warned.

"What will we do?" she asked. "What song will you teach him now?"

One to open, one to close, his grandfather had taught him. But there had been that third one, one his aunt said called down the protection of the gods against evil. He told Ran of the three as they walked to the altar stone at the northern edge of the center where Ander stood.

With each step toward the circle, a noise began at its center and spread outward. Almost a chiming of bells but something different. When they entered together, a wall of light surrounded the structure, cutting them off to everyone outside. Though he could see through it, the only thing he could hear was that sound.

And then a second terrible noise joined the first.

Like the scream of a wild wounded creature this one rose into the air. As they watched, the stone floor disappeared and they could see into the void.

Streams of fire collided with the barrier and they could feel the heat of them. Then sharp talons, like an eagle's, scratched at the barrier, trying to break it open.

"Ignore that!" Soren yelled, pulling Ran to the altar.

"Is that Chaela?" she asked. "What is she?"

"Something unimaginable," Ander said. "Evil incarnate."

"We must stop her, Ander," Soren said, touching his friend's arm. "We cannot let her rise to power once more."

"Stop the evil," Ander said.

"Ander? Can you do this? Can you help us close the circle?" Ran asked. Another scream emanated from the void at her question.

Soren began the third song then, humming the melody of the song to protect them from evil. He could see his grandfather in his mind, sitting next to him, singing the words. He let his voice grow stronger and stronger until it filled the entire ring. When he looked over at Ran, she nodded in encouragement, holding his hand.

It was quite a shock when Ander joined in, singing what sounded like Latin to the same tune he sang the words of Old Einar's song. Ander's higher voice complemented Soren's deeper one. The fact that the songs had the same tune could not be a coincidence. They finished the song and Ran nodded.

"I asked God to protect me from evil, now and at the hour of my death," Ander whispered, wincing in pain as he spoke the last few words. Clutching his head, he shook and struggled against something inside.

"Must stop evil," he screamed. He fell to the ground and rolled there.

Soren could not think of what to do. The ceremony had begun with that song, that prayer. To leave or try to leave now, even to help Ander, would destroy all of them and the circle. Though he and Ran were prepared to give their lives to end this, their deaths would not prevent Chaela from entering at one of the two other circles.

As Marcus had said, it would leave them without two of the bloodlines in the coming battles.

As Marcus said . . .

"Ander, did Marcus visit you? Have you seen Marcus?" He took hold and shook his friend, trying to get through the pain.

"The priest? Marcus?" Ander asked. "So many came. The bishop. The pope. The king," Ander said, still clutching his head. "The priest came—I thought he was a soldier until he prayed me to sleep."

Could it be possible?

Aislinn and Marcus had told him of the bond forged between the priests. It was a way to share thoughts and prayers amongst their community. Had Marcus tried to bond with Ander and been caught by Hugh?

"How did he pray you to sleep, Ander?" Soren knelt next to him. "Did he touch you?"

Ander screamed out again and then fainted, unable to fight it any longer. Soren had no idea if there was an allotted time to complete the ritual here. They could not leave now, he knew that, but must they complete it soon?

CHAPTER 23

Ran reached out to Ander much as she had to her father. She let go of the fear that threatened to over power her and let her water go into him.

When she reached his mind, she stopped, over whelmed by the cacophony of voices there. No wonder Ander was in pain. She sorted through the real and the imaginary ones, washing away those that harmed this man of God and leaving the truth. His memories of his friends, his belief in his God, his knowledge of right and wrong, truth and lies and good and evil . . .

And the prayers and memories and knowledge that Marcus left for him. Ran smiled at that. Marcus did not die in vain. His death was not an empty one. Pulling back from Ander, she looked over at Soren.

"Is that what you did for me on the beach?" he asked.

She nodded. "Your injuries were slight compared to what de Gifford did to Ander and to my father," she admitted. "I know not if it will help him. I could not help my . . ." Tears filled her eyes then and he pulled

her into his arms and held her. She knew her father was
dead even now.

"I am sorry, my love," he whispered to her. "I wish
we could have saved Svein. I think he knew. I know
Marcus understood what he was doing as well."

"Marcus did. He was following his gods' path."

The winds swirled above them, the lake churned
outside the perimeter of the ring and the chiming
sounds echoed as he kissed her. She clutched him to
her and took the love he offered. If they had to perish,
at least he would be with her, giving her the strength to
face it.

Accept his strength, Aislinn had said. *Forgive his weakness. Be one with him.*

How could she die without forgiving him?

She changed then, letting go her form. He accepted
her into his body and then changed so that they became
one. Existing in that form, she could hear his thoughts
and he could hear hers.

*I forgive you, Soren. I cannot face this without you know-
ing that I have.*

You do not know the truth of it. Look within. 'Tis here, he
said, opening his mind and heart and letting her seek
the truth.

She moved through his memories, going back and
back until she was in his life two years ago. Watching
his feelings and thoughts as his—their—lives were destroyed . . .

By her father.

Her father had been behind it all. Soren had been
faithful to her. Aslaug had not carried Soren's child.
Soren's guilt over her suicide. Her brother could never

know for it would tear his heart out. Svein Ragnarson was the one responsible. His greed and hunger for power drove him to it.

Why did you never tell me?

You did not want to hear it at first, he admitted in a sad tone. *Then you were gone and I had no hope of seeing you again.*

Why did you not tell me now? Why did you try to save him from Hugh, knowing what he did to you? To us? she asked.

He did not say the words; he did not have to, for she could feel everything in his heart. For her. To protect her. So she would not hate her father. To give her the life she deserved. And so many other stupid reasons that only Soren Thorson would believe. But at the core of all of them was his unwavering love for her.

"Pray for us sinners, now and at the hour of our death. Amen."

Ran and Soren separated and looked down to see Ander awake on the ground. They both recognized the prayer, a Christian one they'd been raised on.

"Ander?" Soren asked. "Are you well?"

"I know not. Where are we?" Ander asked, as Soren reached down and helped him up to sit. "What is this place?"

A terrible roar came from the center, reminding them of their task. They helped him to stand and the priest looked around in wonder.

"This is the circle, the gateway," Ran explained.

"I thought I had died. The pain in my head, the vision of angels above me. The chiming."

"Angels?" Ran asked.

"Two beings of light floating above me. Angels?" Ander asked.

Soren laughed and looked away. Ran shook her head. Whatever he might have thought he saw, it was not angels.

"Lord Hugh convinced me you were the evil ones, trying to let *that*"—he nodded at the being trying to escape—"out. But Marcus told me the truth. Where is he? I must thank him."

"Marcus is dead, Ander. Hugh had him killed when he was found with you."

Ander mumbled a prayer under his breath—it came so by rote that it made Ran smile.

"Eternal rest grant unto them, O Lord, and may the perpetual light shine upon them. May they rest in peace. Amen."

"Amen," they said.

If Ander could pray a Christian prayer for a man who worshipped other gods, how could she argue? Did it matter to the gods who created this circle if a prayer of a different god was offered? She thought not.

"So what must I do? What must we do?" Ander asked them.

"Aislinn and Marcus told me that you must say the prayers while we shed our blood together on the altar. Then we must find the stone carrying our mark and place the blood on it."

"And then?" he asked.

"Then the gods who built this place will seal it once more and she cannot get back into the world."

"You will teach me the prayer? 'Tis a song?"

"Aye," Soren said.

They helped him to walk to the altar, giving a wide pass around the opening to the barrier. Once there, Soren drew out his dagger and handed it to Ander. "Begin this way . . ."

Soren sang the first line of the song and Ander repeated it. Ran held her breath or sang along under it, alternating back and forth and hardly able to breathe at all in the tenseness that surrounded them.

By the end of the second line, the stones began to vibrate. At the third, the chiming reached an earsplitting level. Ran prepared herself for the final line. Soren sang it and Ander hesitated for a moment, not repeating the last part of it.

No one moved as Ander fought some battle within himself. He managed to keep from saying another word as some fragment of Hugh's will struggled to overwhelm the priest's own. The stones clamored and the goddess shrieked as though close to gaining her freedom. The light surrounding the rings shot off bursts into the night sky.

The wrong word and they would be destroyed.

Was that Hugh's plan after all? If he could not get them to open the circle, he would destroy it?

Nay! It would happen like this. Ran would not let Soren and Ander die.

Touching the priest and Soren, she nodded and Soren followed her lead, setting the winds to spin around the three of them, blocking out everything else. Then, she accepted Soren's strength and passed it to his broken friend.

Ander gasped but did not speak at first. Then his smile spoke of success. As he gave voice to the last part, they joined hands and he cut with the dagger over the altar. Her turquoise blood and Soren's silver mixed with the wine red of Ander's. The pool of it glowed with power. Their marks all lit as though afire.

"Put the blood on your mark and find the place on the stone that is yours," Soren said. "I will help Ander."

Soren half carried, half dragged Ander around the circle until he found the one for the priest. Leaning him there, he helped him raise his arm to the mark. Ander hissed as he touched the blood there.

The screaming and torment became louder and louder in the center as Chaela realized she would fail. Ran rushed to the stone marked with the waves and held her arm up to it. She watched as Soren found the one marked for the stormblood and, with a nod to her and then Ander, he lifted his arm and touched the blood to the mark.

The stones groaned, bending and twisting as stone could not. They expanded before their eyes, stretching higher and higher into the sky above them. The chiming within them grew louder and louder until Ran wanted to scream against it. Her arm, her mark, her blood were still sealed to the stone behind her.

Now, above them, were six creatures or beings, all glowing in the colors of their bloodlines, the same as in her vision. The goddess Nantosuelta smiled at her as Taranis blessed Soren. Then, impossibly, the stones reached over the circle, meeting in the middle and melded over the void. With a crash, the altar stone cracked, spilling their blood onto the floor. It trickled across, following the spaces between the stones until it reached the barrier.

Then the light was in the circle, shining out around

them, sealing the barrier so no being could escape. The shrieking grew softer and softer until it faded out of existence.

And all was silent.

In an instant, the stones were as they had been when first placed there. The light and sounds were gone and the three of them stood in the middle of it all on the stone-laid floor. Ran looked around and saw William and Brienne standing near the path.

Soren met her gaze and nodded at the stone behind her. She turned to find the goddess there. Glancing back at him, Ran saw a man behind Soren. *Taranis*, the goddess whispered. As the goddess entered her, the god entered Soren once more.

"De Gifford is a coward," Ander said when Brienne and William reached the ring.

But there would be time to speak of such things and to deal with her grief when the goddess left her. Now, Ran understood what last service they asked from their bloodline. She met Soren in the middle of the circle and let the goddess forth.

Taranis, my love, the goddess said, taking him in her arms and kissing him. She opened her mouth to him as she would open her body for him.

The winds rose around them, and the fireblood understood. She led the warblood and priest from there, leaving the henge to them.

Nantosuelta, must we part? Taranis asked her. *I cannot bear the separation.*

Love me now, husband. Love me enough to last until we are returned to each other, she urged.

He rose like the winds and took her, joining their

bodies and their hearts a final time. He thrust into her and she took him in, accepting his force, his strength and his desire. He filled her with love and power and life itself.

They melted together and cried out their pleasure into the winds and the sky and the sea. It echoed across time and across space. It echoed . . .

Then Ran and Soren were alone, lying together, still joined, in the middle of the stones. The goddess whispered to her, and then walked away. She turned to see the goddess and the god fade into the stones in the ring.

They lay there in the silence now, replete and satisfied and safe. Soren rolled to his side and held her close.

"What did she say?" Soren asked, kissing her gently.

"That I will bear you a son," Ran said. "A son who will inherit great power." Ran felt life stir within her.

"Do you?" he asked, sliding his hand over where hers now rested. She nodded.

"Soren! Ran!" Ander's much stronger voice carried across the stone ring to them.

"At least they left our garments," Ran said, pointing to the pile of clothing next to them.

When they were garbed, they left the ring and walked up the path out of the lake. Ran found her father's body, killed by Hugh's hand and left there next to the lake. Soren remained with her as she sat, grieving for the loss of the man who'd given her life.

More of the followers and priests had arrived, but the cry that pierced the air told her that Aislinn had found Marcus. Even with her loss still fresh, Ran's heart broke more when she saw the young woman grieving at Marcus's side, holding his hand and praying.

Each priest and priestess came up and knelt for a time beside him, offering prayers, but Aislinn never moved away.

"He was like a father to her," William explained. "He raised and taught and loved her since she was brought to him as a child."

When the final person to pray at his body knelt, Ran began crying too. Father Ander, in his priestly garb, with his prayer beads in hand, remained there, holding Aislinn's other hand and praising Marcus for his sacrifice. Finally they wrapped his body in a clean cloth and blessed it.

Ander went and offered prayers at her father's body and then came to where Ran and Soren now stood with William and Brienne.

"'Tis their custom to burn their bodies after death," Ander said. "Aislinn told me it purifies their soul."

"I think we should do it in the stone circle there," Soren said.

"Our circle disappeared after we sealed it," Brienne said. "If this is still here, it is for a reason."

Aislinn walked up to them and Ran held her close. Both of them had lost fathers in this battle against evil. "Ander suggested we place Marcus in the circle, Aislinn," Ran said. "What think you of that?"

"He said he wanted us to learn more about our earlier practices. He did not have to be the first to teach us," the woman said sadly. "But he will be honored by such a thing, too."

CHAPTER 24

They built the funeral pyre not in the center of the circle, but in front of the stone marked with the sign of the priest. Ander, in a touching gesture, escorted Aislinn, who led the procession of priests carrying Marcus's body down the path to the henge. William and Brienne and Soren and Ran followed next. Then the rest of those in their company. For once, the Norman guard was not at Aislinn's side, but offered begrudgingly accepted help to another of the injured priests.

Of all those mourning, William's man Roger seemed the most devastated by Marcus's death. Though Aislinn openly grieved, Roger did so in silence, holding the mark on his arm that Soren learned Marcus had made to link them all.

When they entered the outer ring, they turned and walked around the perimeter seven times. Then entering the inner circle, they walked in the other direction seven more times. Reaching the pyre, they placed his body on top of the wooden slats and branches.

Aislinn offered a final prayer aloud and then the

priests surrounded the pyre and prayed in silence for a short time. As the sun rose to begin a new day, Ander lit the fire under the body and stepped back. Kneeling next to Aislinn, Soren's friend offered prayers in the Latin rite for the dead.

They would remain for a time and then leave, also in procession; any remains of the body would be left to excarnate on the pyre.

Just as Aislinn began to rise to signal their departure, Ander grabbed her hand and held her there. Aislinn stared at Soren's friend and shook her head. Soren took several paces toward them when she waved him off.

Ander spoke out in a loud voice then and it carried out over the circle.

"When the threat is revealed and the sleepers awaken, a Warrior seeks the truth while the Fire burns away the deception. Begin in the East then North, then South then West, find the true gate amongst the rest."

"The prophecy!" William said.

Then Aislinn spoke: "While those of the blood advance and the lost lose their way, Water and Storm protect the hidden. The hidden reveals its secrets only to those who struggle with their faith."

Soren noticed everyone waiting for the next part. The prophecy was supposed to be revealed when the gateway was closed, but Ander did not know how to find it. But when Ander spoke again, saying words they had not heard, Soren realized that it mattered not, for the prophecy had found him.

"The faithful are lost and the lost have faith. The Bringer of Life cares for the Caretaker, and the one who loses all will gain the most."

In one motion, Aislinn and Ander faced south and each pointed in unison toward the west of England.

Now they knew where the next circle would be found. Soren had heard that there was a great stone henge and many other standing stones in the western countryside on the ancient plain of Sarum. But where would they find the hidden one?

William and the other leaders decided that they needed to rest and organize for a journey that far. He sent word to those in Hamnavoe to wait for their arrival three days hence, and the groups traveled down to Orphir, both to bury Ran's father and to reclaim their property.

The organized camp Soren had found was gone. The ships were gone. Hugh de Gifford was gone. The house was empty of people and supplies. And neither Ran nor Ander would remain inside it. Soren arranged a shelter for himself and Ran in one of the unused barns, and Ander found a place to sleep amongst the other priests.

As warrior and strategist, William scheduled guards and set up duties and tasks for all his men for the next days until they would leave to travel south. Messengers came and went. Supplies were purchased and sent to the ships in Hamnavoe harbor.

Soren decided not to seek out his grandfather's cottage before they left Orkney. Arrangements were made to find Ingeborg and explain the events to her. Something deep within told him that Hugh had sent someone there once he'd learned of Einar's powers and his knowledge.

"You are frowning," Ran said, stroking his back as

they discussed what she would tell her brother. They sat at a table brought out of the house, working on a letter. Ran had resisted entering the house since they'd returned.

"I was thinking," he said. He did not want to speak about Einar. "I think Erik should know the truth about Aslaug, but I think telling him the truth about the bairn would be cruel," he explained.

"Crueler than deceiving him?" Ran asked.

"I think we should wait and tell him to his face," Soren said, leaning back and pulling her to him. " 'Tis not something he should find out this way," he said, pointing to the parchment she'd begun writing on.

"Do you think we will live to tell him?" Ran asked.

Soren took her hand and kissed the palm of it. He leaned into her, enjoying the experience of having her close at hand and knowing she would be.

"I cannot say what the future will hold for us," he said. "But with the gift you carry, I pray—as does good Father Ander—for a swift end to the evil one and her henchman."

"Ah, you mention his name and he appears," Ran said, standing to greet Father Ander and the priest who Aislinn said would be consecrated as their high priest.

"Soren. Ran." Father Ander smiled and greeted them. "Corann has asked me to present him to you."

Soren stood and helped Corann to sit. His leg was splinted as was his arm. Bruises of purple and green lined the edges of his jaw and cheeks. "I have seen you before, Corann. Aislinn tells us you are to be high priest?"

"Not by my choice," Corann said. He was not an old

man, not as old as Marcus had been, but his voice was filled with a tone that spoke of experience and knowledge. "Marcus designated me when he learned of the gods' plans for his own end." Corann paused a moment, thinking, Soren knew, about that ending. "I will do my best to teach and care for our people."

"When will you gain your new position, Corann?" Ran asked as she sat back down. "Is there a ceremony?"

"There is always a ceremony or ritual to be held," he said with a laugh. "Those have held us together over the generations. They connect us to our past and will connect us to future generations to come." He finished with a strange stare at Ran.

"So is there something we can do for you? Is that why you wanted to meet us?" Soren asked. The odd expression remained as the priest watched Ran with a special curiosity.

"Nay! Nay," he said, shaking his head. Then Ander nodded at him and Corann continued. "Ander and I wanted to offer our services to you. To you and Ran," he said. "That is . . ." He paused and frowned at Ander. "I mean . . ."

Soren laughed then at the man's clear discomfort at whatever the topic was to be. "What services would they be?"

"Aislinn has explained to me, gods forgive me for not being there to witness it myself, that you and Ran actually had the god and goddess within you for a time."

Ran blushed at him, thinking of the same times when they had given their bodies over to the deities. "Aye. Several times," he said.

He did not need a deity inhabiting his body to merge with Ran. Indeed, his body gave him a clear sign that he would be willing even at that moment.

"So, we two wondered if you would want to have your union blessed before the community? Our community. All of us," Corann finally got the words out.

They'd been busy handling so many tasks dealing with endings and departures that Soren had not thought about that. Although he knew he would never give Ran up and that they had joined in a way unlike any he'd imagined possible, they had not spoken of marriage.

Not since the pledge they'd made between themselves had been broken two years past. She'd not said a word during this whole time, so he turned to her.

"Would you be my wife, Ran? I think we have waited long enough to claim each other in marriage." He held out his hand to her. He had no doubt of her decision, but he wanted to hear her say the words, now that all barriers between them were gone and the unhappy past could be just that.

"Aye, Soren Stormblood," Ran said, taking his hand. "I will wed you and take you as husband."

"Praise be!" Corann shouted. His voice carried and drew the attention of those working nearby.

"Praise God!" Ander added.

"When should we celebrate this wedding, Corann?" Ran asked.

"Well, we usually perform weddings under the new moon. 'Tis so full of promise, you see. However, considering . . ." He glanced at Soren and then gave that odd expression to Ran. "Well, considering, that you are . . . you are . . ."

Once again the man could not say the words intended. Soren now understood the peculiar looks—somehow Corann knew about the baby Ran carried. The news about which neither of them wanted to share yet.

"Impatient, Corann? We are impatient to marry," he said with a laugh. Ran understood. "When do you suggest an impatient man and woman marry?"

"We think on the morrow since we leave the day after that. It will give our people something to feel joyful about."

Corann rose and limped away, talking to Ander as though an old friend, calling back instructions as he went.

"If we had done this two years past, there would be banns to be called and a bishop presiding," Ran said, moving over to sit on his lap.

"Now we have a pagan priest and a fallen Catholic one presiding with no banns being called," Soren said. "In some moments, I cannot fathom what has happened to us in these last weeks. I thought I had lost you two years ago. I thought I would lose you several times since this all began."

"And now, you know you will never lose me," Ran said. Leaning down closer, she kissed him.

"Promise me I will never lose you," he insisted. "Promise me." He slid his hand into her hair and held her mouth on his, kissing her several times before he released her.

"That is what will happen at our wedding, husband-to-be of mine. Promises made. Promises blessed. I think I should speak to Brienne and Aislinn about this." She laughed and kissed him quickly once more. She stood to leave him, but turned back to him at the last moment.

Her eyes glowed and the turquoise aura she carried grew brighter. She spoke with the voice of the sea and it sent shivers through his entire being.

"Sea and sky, never to be parted, never not touching. You have always been and shall always be part of me, Soren Stormblood."

He met her gaze and spoke in a voice as deep as the rumbling thunder in a storm.

"Sea and sky, never to be parted, never not touching or being touched. You will always be part of me as I am part of you, Ran Waterblood."

The words came from his soul in response to hers and Soren discovered the next evening that they made the perfect wedding vows.

CHAPTER 25

Aislinn thought it was appropriate for them to exchange their vows in the same sacred place where they had defeated evil. But rather than inside the ring, they chose to speak their words at the entrance to it, on the shore of the lake.

Corann and Ander led them to that place and faced them and the community, who stood at their backs. Although she was filled with grief at the loss of Marcus, Aislinn did feel joy for these two souls who would pledge their hearts and bodies and love to each other.

She watched as Soren and Ran faced each other and joined their hands in between. The priest of the one god began, saying words in Latin and offering prayers she'd never heard. After he finished, he motioned to Corann. Ander was not familiar with their customs, for they believed the man and woman should offer themselves and the priest simply watched. So Corann did just that, less than how Marcus liked to bless marriages, but each high priest would have his own ways.

"Soren Thorson, we are sea and sky, never to be

parted, never not touching. You have always been and shall always be part of me and I take you as my husband," Ran said first. From Soren's expression, he'd heard these words before. She nodded at him and then at the priests.

"Ran Sveinsdottir, you are sea to my sky, never to be parted, never not touching or being touched. You will always be part of me as I am part of you, even as you carry a part of me within you now," Soren said, revealing their secret to one and all. "And I take you as my wife before this community."

Aislinn watched as a blush filled Ran's cheeks, and then they kissed. Cheers and good wishes were shouted out before Corann raised his hand over them.

"It is right. It is blessed. It has been foretold. The waterblood and stormblood are blessed by the gods. Their union is a holy one. Praise be!" Corann shouted out.

Tears streamed down her cheeks now, listening to the words and knowing that Ran and Soren were two halves of one whole heart and soul. She wiped them away with the back of her hand as she went to offer them her good wishes. And then changed her mind.

Remaining in the shadows, Aislinn let the others celebrate without her sadness interfering. Staring off at the stone ring she did not hear the woman's approach.

"Tears of happiness for the waterblood and stormblood, priestess?" the woman asked. She did not know this woman and yet did not feel fear. A hazy red shadow outlined her, but that was likely caused by the light of the many fires along the water's edge.

"Aye," she said nodding. "I am happy for them."

"And you, young one? Do you have someone you wish as your own?" The woman moved closer to her and whispered, "Have you dreamed of him yet?"

"Nay," she said. "There is no one. I have too many tasks to complete for the gods before I think about marriage."

"You are blessed, Aislinn of Cork. Yours is a special destiny. A difficult one. But you should pray to see him. The gods will be gracious to one who is in their favor."

Something fell at her feet and she bent to retrieve it. A small carved horse lay there, one such as a child would play with. The woman must have dropped it. Turning to find her, Aislinn found the area around her empty. Brisbois stood his usual distance from her.

"Brisbois, where did that woman go?" she asked. He must have seen her. Their paths should have crossed.

"There was no woman, priestess. Only you." He crossed his arms over his massive chest, signaling that he was done talking.

"You must have seen her—she dropped this toy. I would like to return it to her." Brisbois simply let out an aggrieved breath and shrugged.

Only as she returned to her tent did she realize what the woman had called her.

Aislinn of Cork.

No one save Marcus knew of her birthplace. No one save Marcus knew her origins. No one could. It was too dangerous, he'd always told her.

She must have misunderstood the woman. According to Brisbois there was not even one. Mayhap her grief and exhaustion caused her to mistake the words? She prepared for sleep, but held on to the carved piece of wood.

And that night, for the first time, she dreamt of a man. A handsome young man of black hair and blue eyes who seemed to know her when he saw her. A man who was special, surrounded with a red aura as the other bloodlines were with the color of their gods. A man who called her by name before he disappeared.

He called her Aislinn of Cork.

Soren stole Ran away, taking her up the road to Brodgar's Ring. He'd checked and made certain that the shelter he'd set up there for them that first night was still in good condition. It would be far enough away from the others for the privacy deserved on a wedding night.

They would depart in the morning on ships on a journey that would take them away from the only home he'd ever known to a destination filled with danger. They would depart with the dozens and dozens of others on their shared quest and would, according to William and the others, meet more in the next place.

So, this night would be his last alone with her. As they reached the place and he slowed the horse, she leaned over and looked around him. Seeing the hut, she laughed.

"We have been here before," she said, as he helped her down from the horse. "But it looks much more comfortable than I remember." She walked up and he knew the moment she saw his preparations. Several thick blankets. A basket with food and ale. More blankets. "You did this?"

"Aye. I thought this would be the perfect place to consummate our wedding vows."

She smiled and nodded. "I wanted you that night," she admitted. "I was furious at you and angry that I could still want you."

"But you did not recognize this place that night, did you? Do you now?" he asked, walking up behind her and standing close. He thought that might spark her memory.

When she shook her head, he reached out and took her hands in his. Leaning forward, he placed them on the frame of the hut above her head. Then, he crouched down behind her and slid his hands up under her gown, following her long legs up and up. Her body reacted, pressing back against him. When he'd gathered her skirts in his hand, he tossed them up on her back, out of his way.

"Not yet?" he asked, sliding his hand between her legs.

"Nay," she said on a gasp.

Her body arched, bringing the full flesh of her arse against his cock. He loosened the ties on his breeches and let them fall. Pressing his other hand on her lower back to open her for him, he slid his prick into her.

"Yet?" he asked, sliding his length slowly and completely into her flesh.

"Nay." The word came out on her breath as he moved more forcefully against her. Holding her hips, he plunged in and drew back several times, feeling the muscles inside her grasp his cock, trying to milk it dry already.

"Not until you remember," he warned. He slid one

hand around and palmed her belly and mons. She moaned then. One finger then two moved deeper into her cleft and teased her there. One slight touch in that sensitive spot and she clenched her flesh together.

"I cannot believe you do not remember this place," he said, stopping all movement. "I thought women were the maudlin ones."

"Mayhap I remember and just want you to tease me this way?" she asked, pressing her arse against him, pushing him in deeper.

"Liar," he whispered against her hair as he leaned over her. "You know I will draw this out for you. You know I would do anything you asked of me."

"Tell me," she said, breathily. "And move as you do."

He laughed. He loved those kinds of demands. He moved. He moved faster and deeper, his fingers stroking the folds harder and faster, too. He knew she was close. He knew her body well. He knew every dimple and fold. He knew the places to drive her to madness and the ones that would ease them to it.

"This is where we . . ."

He'd waited too long. One more stroke against the sensitive bud between her legs and she came undone around him. Shuddering, her body sent wave after wave of spasms around his flesh, drawing him ever closer to release. But, he had more planned for her this night, so with another thrust of his hips against her, he sent her screaming toward satisfaction.

He held her tightly against his body as she did, giving her the security she needed to let go. When her body calmed, she let her arms go, and then slid to her knees, him still seated inside her.

"We stood in this direction so we would see anyone approaching," she said. "But you complained that I made too much noise and would expose us anyway."

"It was my first time with a woman; how was I to know that loud was a good thing?" he said.

"A young man filled with desire but no knowledge can be a dangerous thing," she said.

"A young man filled with need but an earnest desire to please a young woman filled with lust can be a very good thing," he corrected.

He was still hard within her. He waited for her to tell him she was ready. When she wiggled against him, he knew.

"And an experienced married man with a willing wife can be a wonderful thing," she said.

Soren took the rest of the night to show her how much better a married man could be.

By the time the sun rose the next morning, they had dressed, gathered up the blankets and were about to return to the camp. That was when the rumbling began over the hill. Soren ran toward it, warning her away in case they were in danger. The daft woman, of course, ran along with him to the top of the hill.

With Brodgar at their back and the Loch of Stenness before them, the newly revealed stone circle filled their sight. The rumbling grew deeper and louder and the ground around them shook and shuddered. He grabbed her hand and held her close as the water began to swirl around the henge.

The water swirled and winds ripped around it, knocking stones over, this way and that, until the circle began to both slide and sink back beneath the surface.

In a few minutes' time, the entire structure was gone, now lying deep enough to be completely hidden from view.

A few more minutes and the waters calmed. They rushed back to the stones at Stenness and the path that had led to the circle just a short time before. William, Brienne, Aislinn and others reached it at the same time.

"Did you two do that?" William asked. "Return the circle to its hiding place?"

Ran looked at him and shook her head. Soren did too.

"The gods have reclaimed it," Aislinn said. "Hiding it away now that it is sealed." She looked at each one. "Praise be."

"May it never rise again," Brienne said softly. They all understood her prayer.

"Amen," Ander added, as he arrived.

Within a few hours, they had boarded the waiting ships to journey to the south of England.

EPILOGUE

Two days later
North Sea, east of Orkney

From the moment he'd sent the priest into the circle, Hugh had had a very bad feeling about how the ceremony would turn out. His power to control another's thoughts had always worked before, but the others had already been controlled by fear of him. Ander Erlandson had no fear to use against him.

Then, when it seemed that hours had passed with no changes or signs, he suspected the worst. And when the stones began to chime and stretch, he knew the one thing he could not afford to have happen had just occurred.

He used a moment when his daughter and the warblood were distracted by the sights and sounds within the circle to kill Svein and toss his body on the dead priest's. By the time they noticed, he had already escaped to the waiting horses over the hill. Eudes had everything prepared for their departure and it took little time to accomplish.

And now they were trapped by an angry sea, off course and out of control. As they drifted farther and farther east, Hugh could only hope that his last remaining spy could give him the words of the prophecy. For now, he held on as huge waves thrashed the ships and the sailors lost hope of survival.

Hugh knew the Warriors must feel very satisfied. They had managed in two different ways to seal two different circles. Oh, he had taken their high priest, but another had been put in his place already.

Well, they had better not feel too comfortable believing that they would win again. For he knew one truth about himself—he was a dangerous man to have as an enemy. Now more so since he had failed his goddess twice. Desperate men lost all care for limitations.

Worse, he knew it would not be the pleasure he always anticipated the next time he communed with her. The pain and agony usually reserved for sacrifices or enemies would be his. She would hold back nothing to show her displeasure. He would not come out of this unscathed, he knew that. And he feared the cost of this second failure. Would he even survive the punishment she would mete out?

He shivered then, not with the usual arousal that anticipation of touching her fire brought him. Nay, this was cold, steely fear in his gut.

Everything he had planned, everything his father and generations before him had worked toward was in jeopardy because he had underestimated the power of a pure heart. As the possible punishments he would suffer filled his mind, Hugh knew one thing—he would not fail her again.

If she let him live . . .

Author's Note

Orkney lies just to the north of Scotland and has been inhabited for thousands of years by a succession of peoples and more recently by Picts, then the Norse and then the Scots. It is made up of seventy islands, though people live on only twenty or so.

It is a magical place and its landscape is covered with reminders of all those who had come before—stone circles, burial mounds, stone cairns and buried villages.

I've had the opportunity to visit there twice and even did a full-day archeological tour on my last trip in 2009. I spent the day walking, climbing and crawling my way around stone circles, into burial mounds and cairns, through ruins and even across the causeway that connects the Brough of Birsay to the Mainland. Because it's a tidal island, there are only a few hours each day when that's possible!

So, when this series began forming, I knew that Orkney *must* be the setting for one of the stories. Little did I know that the places I chose for some of my scenes—including the huge stone circle they discover under the lake—would actually be discovered!

The first little serendipitous moment came after I'd written the scenes involving the under-chamber beneath the Broch of Gurness. Apparently there really are not under-chambers in these round stone towers, but I needed one for my story so I created it . . . or so I thought! While proofing my scenes, I found a Web site about the Broch that revealed experts had just discovered a buried stone stairway leading down to an underground chamber . . . beneath the Broch!

Then, in planning the location of the gateway circle, I needed it to be near some of the other more famous circles on the Mainland of Orkney—Brodgar, Stenness—but not one of them. In looking at both current and historical maps, I knew I wanted it set in the middle of what is now known to be the center of Neolithic Orkney. With the recent and ongoing excavations at the Ness of Brodgar, I knew "my circle" was nearby. With two huge lakes surrounding the sites, I decided to strategically place mine IN THE LAKE and have the hero and heroine use their powers to uncover it.

Guess what! In researching the area and the water levels thousands of years ago, I found an article about the changing levels in Orkney and a new geological study/sonar mapping they've just finished in that area . . . and they've found something that looks like a large stone circle, bigger than Brodgar, IN THAT LAKE! I got chills when I read it, realizing that what I call my "story's magic moments" had happened again.

As a writer, it is such a thrill when those kinds of moments happen. It's like the story in my mind is tying itself to something bigger and telling me things I did not know. It gives me shivers when it happens, and the whole Novels of the Stone Circles series has done that time and time again!

If you would like more information on today's Orkney, I would suggest visiting the official tourism site:
www.visitscotland.com/destinations-maps/orkney/

For lots of historical information and info on the cur-
rent/ongoing archeological excavations, these sites are
great: www.orkneyjar.com/index.html and http://ngm
.nationalgeographic.com/2014/08/neolithic-orkney/
smith-text.

This page had a great map of the area where
"my circle" is: http://www.orkneyjar.com/ archaeology/
nessofbrodgar/

The Warriors of Destiny will next move south to
England in their battle against evil, and I've already
experienced a couple of "magic moments" about that
area. Stonehenge and the area around it are revealing
more and more secrets, and the story in my mind has
already tapped into some of those! Did you know that
more than fifteen stone and wood henges have been
discovered all around Stonehenge? And that . . .

I think I'll wait and share those tidbits in the next
story!

Terri

Read on for a sneak peek at the next
Novel of the Stone Circles,

BLAZING EARTH

Coming out in April 2016 from Signet Eclipse.

lethea looked up from her mending at the soft
knock on her door. A more insistent one would
have meant one of the villagers needed her attention.
This kind signaled only one thing to her—the arrival of
Tolan. She placed the torn tunic back into the basket
sitting by the small hearth and went to see.

After lifting the latch, she eased the wooden door
open a scant inch and glanced outside. In the dark of
the night, he stood there outlined by the full moon's
light, taller than most men in the village. She recognized his form at once.

He nodded and, in that deep tone of voice that never
failed to send whispers of heat through her, Tolan greeted
her. "Elethea, how do you fare?"

She wanted to laugh. His words were so commonplace, as though his arrival at her cottage in the hour
when most of the village slept followed the way things
were in Durlington. Elethea did not doubt for a moment that many knew of their assignations. Still. . . .

"I am well, Tolan." She stepped back and opened th door wider. "And how was your journey?" He'd been away seeing to their lord's concerns for almost a fort night.

He'd accepted the invitation as he always did—in calm, even manner. She doubted that anyone who'e met him, save for possibly his dead wife, had ever seer the passion that lived within his composed exterior. Bu Elethea had glimpsed it once in the fields, observin him as he'd tended to his lands, and then every tim he'd joined her in her bed.

Before closing the door, she took the small lanter from the rock that sat beside it and brought light inside It had been her signal to others that she was still awak and could help them. With Tolan's arrival though, sh wished no interruptions.

He stood in the middle of the room, his head near touching the roof above. And he watched her with dark intensity that her body understood. "I am well. He loosened his cloak and tossed it over a bench again the wall.

"But I have missed you, Thea." He crossed the di tance between them in two strides and pulled her int his arms. "I have missed you greatly."

His mouth captured hers, and she gave herself ove to him, waiting for the passion within him to over whelm the calm control he exuded. Two weeks withou him had left her restless and needing his touch. Neec ing the taste of him. Needing the strength and passio he would show her.

He took her breath away even as he'd kissed her tha first time. By the second and third and fourth kisse

he lost the ability to stand. Tolan slid his arms around
her, holding her up and drawing her close.

"I think you have missed me, too," he whispered.

He kissed down her throat and used his teeth on that
sensitive spot just near her shoulder. She arched against
him, aroused by everything he did. His answer was to
slide his hand down, caressing the fullness of her breast,
and then over her stomach until he reached . . .

The sigh escaped as he grazed his hand over the junc-
tion of her thighs. Another as he rubbed harder there,
the friction and pressure of his touch even through
her garments caused her body to heat and weep its
own moisture. She ached now, worse than the moment
before, and she pressed against his hand, begging for
more.

"End this, Tolan," she whimpered out as his fingers
slid between her legs, all the while continuing to caress
and press the place where she wanted . . . him.

"Ah," he whispered after he'd claimed her mouth another time, "I think you have missed me greatly, Thea."

Elethea held her breath and his gaze as his hand slid
down her gown and gathered it up. His fingers on her
skin made her shiver, her body tensing in anticipation.
Then, he moved slowly up her thigh and she panted
with each inch closer. When his fingers slipped into the
sensitive heated folds there, her head fell back and she
gasped at the pleasure of it.

His mouth on her neck made her shiver again, and
he reached up to untie her own laces, wanting his
tongue on her breasts. He chuckled, understanding the
madness he was causing, and when she'd somehow
managed to loosen the edge of her gown and tug it

down, his mouth was there, tasting and nipping along her skin.

He ceased neither his mouth nor his hand, pushing her body toward the edge of control. Somehow they'd moved a few paces, and now she felt the wall behind her, giving her support as he relentlessly pleasured her. He lifted his mouth from her and caught her gaze. She knew what he would do now. He liked to watch her face as she reached completion.

Her body wound tighter and tighter until she could not breathe or speak. He forced moan after moan from her until the tightness exploded within her and she arched against his hand over and over. Tolan's fingers teased that small bud within the folds until she could do nothing but feel wave after wave of pleasure coursing through her body as her release occurred.

Tolan watched the way her eyes glazed over in passion as he stroked her deep and fast. Her body reacted in ways she probably did not even know, but he could see them and feel them and even smell them. His hand between her legs grew wet with her arousal and the bud beneath his finger stiffened, much like his own cock did.

Her mouth grew rounder, and she licked her lips as her body kept pace with his hand. When he brought her to release, her gasps grew stronger and louder until she screamed out in the quietness of her cottage.

His body throbbed and ached for its own release but this time was for her. It had been too long. Too many nights without being inside of her body and finding that moment of joining and complete pleasure. He held her there, pressed against the wall, his hand slid ing in gentle caresses as her body eased down from the height of passion. When she sighed, he smiled and kissed her one more time.

"I have a perfectly comfortable bed right over there," she said, nodding behind him.

"Aye, you do." He nodded as he spoke. "But I could not wait."

Tolan removed his hand and let her gown fall. She did not cover her breasts, and he wanted to lean over and suckle the rose-colored nipples. He would. And she would scream again for him many more times before dawn's light brightened the sky and woke the village. Thea trembled when he stepped back and she reached out to grab hold of his arms. She let out a soft laugh as he guided her to a stool.

Something deep within him felt satisfied that he could cause such a reaction in her with only his touch. His cock, still hard and erect, reminded him that there were other ways to seek release.

"Can you stay, or must you return to your house?" she asked, reaching up for her laces.

He stayed her hands with his, sliding his finger along the edge of the opened gown and shift. She shivered as he touched her nipples. His flesh throbbed with need. Tolan crouched before her and pulled the garments out of his way. Her breasts pressed against his fingers, and he teased them.

He watched as a lovely blush rose up into the skin of her breasts and then into her neck and cheeks. But this was not embarrassment. It was arousal. Tolan leaned in and tasted first one and then the other, licking around the edge of each nipple before pulling it into his mouth and sucking it. Her reaction was immediate; she arched against him and grabbed his hair. When he lifted his mouth from her skin, she pulled him back. Laughing, he looked up into her dark brown eyes and smiled.

"I am staying the night, Thea." He slid his arms around her and lifted her from the stool. "Let us put that perfectly comfortable bed to use," he urged.

It took little effort and time to reach the bed, and soon their garments were removed, and they drove each other mad with desire, delaying their releases until they could not resist.

Tolan had missed everything about her while away from Durlington on the lord's business. Not just this, but also the way she smiled when she greeted him. Especially when she came upon him unexpectedly and her eyes lit at the sight of him. He loved the way she saw to the needs of the injured and sick of their village, her touch gentle and her care thorough and compassionate. She was as successful a healer as he was a farmer.

Once the fires of passion were tended, and as the light of the morning sun began to creep into the lower edge of the sky, Tolan knew that this was the woman he wanted in his life. The woman he wanted as his wife, to be at his side and in his house and bed . . . and most important, in his heart.

The miles that he'd crossed and the days away from her had made that clear to him. He'd remained unmarried since Corliss's death a few years ago, and he'd raised their son on his own. Now, though, now he was ready to marry, and he prayed Thea would say aye.

She roused in his embrace, sliding her leg over his

and smiling a soft, satisfied grin. He held her close and tried to think of the perfect words to say to her. Her gaze narrowed onto his, and she spoke first.

"What is it, Tolan?" She reached up and caressed his brow and cheeks with her fingers. "Is something wrong?"

"Nay, Thea. All is well." Tolan eased back just a bit, still keeping her near, but with enough room to speak. "I have a matter to discuss with you. That is all."

"This sounds serious." Thea pushed up to sit, her long brown hair flowing over her shoulders and pooling onto her lap. It hid nothing of her charms from his sight.

"It is serious. It is a matter of marriage."

At the hint of a frown, quickly hidden, Tolan suspected that the topic did not please her, and her answer would not please him.

About the Author

Terri Brisbin is the *USA Today* bestselling author of the
Novels of the Stone Circles series, featuring *Raging Sea*
and *Rising Fire*. A three-time RWA RITA® finalist, Terri
has sold more than 1.7 million copies of her historical
and paranormal romance novels, novellas, and short
stories in more than twenty languages in twenty-five
countries around the world since 1998. She lives in
New Jersey with her husband. She has three sons and
two daughters-in-law and is a dental hygienist.

CONNECT ONLINE

terribrisbin.com
facebook.com/terribrisbin
facebook.com/pages/terribrisbinauthor